Karen Whiddon started weaving fanciful tales for her younger brothers at the age of eleven. Amid the gorgeous Catskill Mountains, then the majestic Rocky Mountains, she fueled her imagination with the natural beauty surrounding her. Karen now lives in north Texas, writes full-time and volunteers for a boxer dog rescue. She shares her life with her hero of a husband and four to five dogs, depending on if she is fostering. You can email Karen at kwhiddon1@aol.com. Fans can also check out her website, www.karenwhiddon.com.

Also by Karen Whiddon

The Texas Shifter's Mate
Finding the Texas Wolf Whisperer
The Wolf Princess
The Wolf Prince
Lone Wolf
The Lost Wolf's Destiny
The Wolf Siren
Shades of the Wolf
Billionaire Wolf
A Hunter Under the Mistletoe (with Addison Fox)

Discover more at millsandboon.co.uk

FINDING THE TEXAS WOLF

KAREN WHIDDON

MILLS & BOON

First Published in Great Britain 2018
by Mills & Boon, an imprint of HarperCollins*Publishers*
1 London Bridge Street, London, SE1 9GF

Finding the Texas Wolf © 2018 Karen Whiddon

ISBN: 978-0-263-26682-5

49-0618

MIX
Paper from
responsible sources

FSC
www.fsc.org

FSC™ C007454

This book is produced from independently certified FSC™ paper to ensure responsible forest management.

For more information visit: www.harpercollins.co.uk/green

Printed and bound in Spain
by CPI, Barcelona

To all my "family" not related by blood ties. You know who you are, always offering help or a smile or a shoulder to cry on. Many of you are my friends, but oh so much more than that. I appreciate you, I love you and I'm grateful you're in my life.

Chapter 1

The heavy oak door, scarred and weathered, looked like something out of a medieval castle. Above, a simple sign. No words, just a rusted iron bar from which hung two chain links, each half of what had once been whole. There were no lanterns, not even a streetlight to illuminate the shadows. The entrance sat near the end of a dead-end alley, innocuous enough that no soul, human or otherwise, would give it a second glance. Unless, of course, one knew what lay inside.

Maddie Kinslow usually preferred to take her time. Her slow and steady approach, sometimes viewed by others as reticence, enabled her to take full notice of her surroundings. When in her human form, her eyes were her primary tool, and when she shape-shifted into her wolf form, her nose took precedence over her other senses.

Tonight, with the moon a perfect sliver in the cloudless sky, she walked a little faster than normal, intent on reaching the dead-end alley that led to Broken Chains, the Galveston bar where only others of similar ilk were welcome. She, along with two of her best friends, had recently formed The Shadow Agency, a private investigative firm catering exclusively to Shape-shifters, Vampires and Merfolk. They'd recently successfully closed their first case and she'd gotten a lead that someone might be in the bar tonight who wanted to set up a meeting about becoming their second client.

Since Maddie lived and breathed her goal of making The Shadow Agency a success, her eagerness to meet with this individual had her practically running.

Until she stumbled over the bloody and beaten man halfway up the alley.

She tripped, caught completely by surprise, screamed once and fell. Right on top of the unfortunate human, who let out a guttural groan.

Naturally, she scrambled up, away from him. "What happened to you?" she asked, not even sure he could answer her. He appeared to have been on the losing side of a run-in with a semi truck. Digging her phone from her pocket, she realized she couldn't call 911. Not from here, so close to the unmarked door. By spell or by due vigilance, it would never open, not for humans and not without potential death. To be safe and prevent any unnecessary curiosity, she needed to get this poor man out of the alley.

"I was beat up," he said, his voice clear, despite the fact that his lip had been split. "Two big guys."

"Were you robbed?"

"No."

She watched in disbelief as he managed to heave himself off the ground to his feet. With one eye swollen shut, he squinted at her with the other.

"They went in there," he said, pointing at Broken Chains' unmarked door.

Heart pounding, she shook her head. "In where? There's nothing around here but some old abandoned warehouses."

"Lady, come on." He swayed slightly as he took a step toward her. "You know exactly what I'm talking about. I've been watching this place. I've seen you here before. What I want to know is what's going on behind that door? People come and go all night. I don't know what they do to get inside, but they do. I've tried, but no one will let me in."

He had no idea what kind of danger he'd placed himself in. A human, trying to gain entrance to Broken Chains? Now she understood. A couple of the bouncers must have taken exception to him pestering them. In light of that, he was lucky he'd only been beaten rather than killed.

"You need to go somewhere else." She didn't even bother to try to hide the urgency in her voice. "It's not safe here for you. Go away and forget you ever saw this door."

Judging from the way he perked up, her heartfelt warning only made him more determined to stay. She eyed him—as far as human males went, he looked tough, with his broad shoulders and muscular build. But even the most fit human had no hope of fighting back against a Shape-shifter or Vamp. Both had power reserves of at least ten times those of any human.

Which explained why this guy's swollen face made his features unrecognizable.

"I'm not going anywhere." He crossed his arms, exposing purpling bruises and several small cuts that still oozed blood. In addition to the split lip and black eye, and judging from the multiple bruises and swelling, he'd been pummeled. Again, lucky to be alive, even if he didn't get that. "My name is Jake Cassel. I'm an investigative reporter."

"You can barely stand," she pointed out. "I'd think you'd want to get yourself some medical assistance."

"Good idea. I'll dial 911 and when the paramedics arrive, I'll ask for them to also send cops. I'm sure they can find out what's behind that door."

Exactly the situation she hoped to avoid.

"It's not safe for you here," she reiterated. "How about I walk you to my car and drive you to the ER?"

Her offer appeared to confuse him. "What? Why? You don't know me. What if I turn out to be a predator? You'll be alone with me."

Of course she had no answer for that. She wasn't about to tell him that as a full-blooded Shifter she knew she'd be safe. "I'll be fine," she finally replied. "I might even be willing to tell you what I know of that door."

That finally got his attention. "Seriously?"

"You sound skeptical. I don't blame you." Somehow, she managed to keep herself from glancing at the still-closed door. "But I should also let you know that I expect those guys to come back at any moment." And she did. "If they attack you again, which they will if they find you still here, they'll kill you this time."

While she had no idea if he believed her or not, he shuffled forward. "Give me your word," he demanded. "Give me your word that you'll tell me the truth about that door."

"I'm Maddie Kinslow. You have my word." And she would tell him. Because one thing she'd learned was to be very specific when relaying what one wanted. This human had asked for information about one item only—the door. She knew where it had come from, when it was installed, what kind of wood it had been made of and how often it was painted.

And a careful reciting of those facts was exactly what he'd get.

Driving as fast as she could without breaking the speed limit, Maddie soon pulled up in front of the ER at UTMB Health John Sealy Hospital. Despite his best efforts to remain alert, her passenger lost consciousness before they arrived. Well aware of how these human hospitals worked, she hoped Jake Cassel had his ID and an insurance card on him.

After leaving him in the car, she rushed inside and up to the triage window. "I found a man beaten on the sidewalk," she said. "He wouldn't let me call for an ambulance, but he allowed me to drive him here. He's outside in my car, now unconscious. I need help getting him inside."

If she expected a medical team to jump into action like they did on TV, she was wrong. The nurse simply nodded and told her she'd send someone out with a wheelchair in just a moment.

Eventually, after what felt like an eternity but was in fact four minutes, an orderly appeared with a wheelchair. She led the way out the double doors to where she'd left her car parked, with the injured human in the front seat.

But the front seat was empty.

Cursing under her breath, she spun around. "He couldn't have gone far," she promised. "He was pretty beat up. And he lost consciousness on the way here."

The orderly squinted at her. "Okay," he said. "Come and get me when you find him." And he turned to head back into the hospital.

He had a point. There really wasn't anywhere to hide. The helipad sat behind a metal rail, and the tall palm trees dotting the landscape didn't provide much in the way of shelter.

"Wait," she ordered, stopping the orderly in his tracks. "The man can barely walk. I was inside for under five minutes. He really can't have gone far."

"Is that him?" He pointed to the covered bus stop near the road.

A lone figure sat on the bench. A quick calculation revealed that maybe, just maybe, Jake Cassel could have made it to there.

"I think so," she said, letting her excitement show in her voice. "He's wearing the same color shirt. Come on, help me go get him."

"I'm sorry, I can't." The orderly appeared apologetic. "I'm not allowed to leave the ER grounds."

Of course he wasn't. The way this day was going, she'd begun to wish she'd never set eyes on the beat-up human. "May I borrow the wheelchair?" she asked.

"I don't know." Clearly wavering, he looked uncomfortable. "I'll get in trouble if you steal it."

"I won't," she assured him. "I just need to retrieve that patient."

"I think you might be too late," he said, pointing. "The bus is coming. Your guy might not be able to walk too well, but he apparently doesn't want to go to the ER. I'm guessing he's getting on the bus."

Calculating, she knew even if she started running, she'd never make it in time. Instead, she watched as the bus pulled up and as Jake, doubled over in pain, managed to climb on board.

Cursing, she turned and sprinted back to her car instead. She knew the bus would continue down Avenue D to 22nd Street, where he'd have to get off and switch buses or ride back to the hospital. She planned to be there either way.

Because what he'd done didn't make sense. Jake Cassel had been severely beaten. He needed X-rays and possibly stitches, definitely pain meds. He wouldn't have fled unless he had something to hide.

And Maddie had never been able to resist uncovering the answer to a good puzzle. The trait was what made her such a doggedly good PI.

She managed to catch up to the bus after its first stop. She watched as the two elderly women who'd gotten off slowly crossed the street.

Next up would be the 9th Street stop. The bus slowed, but continued on. It made several more stops, but he didn't disembark. Finally, at 22nd Street, it turned into the new downtown terminal. Her heart sank. If he got off in a crowd, she'd never be able to tell if he got on a different bus. She could only hope his slow and painful movements would help her locate him.

As she drove past the terminal entrance, her luck held. There. Jake. Arms still wrapped around what had to be an aching middle, he shuffled down the sidewalk as the bus rumbled off.

Where could he be headed? If he'd driven to Broken Chains and parked, his car was in the opposite direction. It would have been much easier to reach from the hospital. Perhaps he had friends in this area or, even better, lived nearby himself.

Instead of immediately confronting him, she decided to follow him and see where he went. She hoped his destination would give her some answers.

She got caught at a streetlight. While she waited, she kept her eyes on him, aware that at his pace he wouldn't be able to get too far ahead of her. There were only two cars coming from the cross street. One continued past, but the second—an older model black Lincoln with dark, tinted windows—pulled up alongside him.

Jake lifted his hand in greeting and carefully got in.

The Lincoln took off, past City Hall, making a left on Avenue M. It disappeared in traffic before her light changed. Though she drove as fast as she could, by the time she got to heavily congested Seawall Boulevard, she had to concede that he'd lost her.

Worse, she realized she'd stood up Carmen. They'd agreed to meet at Broken Chains to discuss strategy for their next Shadow Agency case. Maybe she wasn't too late. She swung the car around and headed toward Harborside Drive. Most likely, Carmen was still there.

Earlier that night, when he'd been in the alleyway by the door that wouldn't open, Jake Cassel hadn't seen the two large men until he turned and saw them right behind him. Since the alley was a dead end, they must have come through that door. He cursed silently, moving aside to get out of their way.

But instead of pushing past him, they stopped. Too late, he saw the anger in their faces. Hostility radiated from the jerky way they moved to their clenched fists.

"I mean no harm," he began, about to offer them his wallet and his watch, whatever they wanted. But when one of them punched him, followed by the other, raining down blows so swiftly he barely saw them move, he realized this was not a mugging. No, this was a beating, and he'd be damn lucky to survive.

Though he could hold his own in a fair fight, not only was this two against one, but they were built like linebackers. So he curled himself into a defensive ball and tried not to make a sound, hoping eventually they'd leave him for dead and he wouldn't be.

The next thing he knew, the redheaded woman was tripping over him. She let out a little scream as she fell, the sound letting him know he'd somehow survived. He must have lost consciousness, because the last thing he remembered before that was the two men whaling on him. They'd even gotten in a couple of kicks, catching him right in the ribs.

He wasn't sure he could breathe, never mind stand, but somehow, he managed to push himself to his feet. This woman had been here before. He'd watched the alley for weeks, and she'd visited at least twice. Maybe three times. Since he could only watch the entrance to the alley, he assumed she'd gotten the door to open for her. Because she'd gone into the alley and hadn't come out for hours.

He'd observed all kinds of people heading into that dead-end alley. From suit-wearing business types, to hipsters, to the grunge-slash-metal crowd. They never came out immediately. Whatever they were doing in there, behind that mysterious door, had to be interesting.

The wondering consumed him. Every single journalistic instinct he possessed kicked into overdrive. Whatever went on behind that door had to be a story. A big story. Not just mildly interesting.

Because one night when he'd been staked out watching the alley, he'd seen a man emerge, unsteady on his feet, clearly inebriated. The guy had walked to where the alley met the street, looked left and right and, right there on Jake's cell phone video, began to shimmer. His form had wavered, too, changing from human to something definitely wolf-like, before going back to human once more. Then, the man shook his head, adjusted his clothing and walked away.

Not believing his own eyes, Jake had watched the video several times. He'd uploaded it to the cloud, knowing he couldn't take a chance of losing it, though he kept the copy on his phone.

This, if he could prove it, would be the story of the century. Because based on what he'd witnessed, he just might be able to prove to the world that werewolves truly existed.

If he could manage to live through this investigation, that is.

A groan slipped from his lips as he attempted to take a step after standing. She came to him then, using her slender shoulder to brace him, uncaring of the fact that his blood would stain her pretty dress. As she helped him move toward the street, she muttered under her breath.

"Did you just say *'Damn humans'*?" he asked, careful to hide his excitement.

"I don't know," she said, her voice cross. "If I can get you to the sidewalk, we can call for an ambulance."

"No ambulance," he insisted.

"We need to get you to the hospital. How else do you propose we do so?"

"My car is parked over there," he told her, pointing with an unsteady hand. "The keys are in my pocket." Somehow, he managed to dig them out. "Here. You can drive."

Though his pain level had been off the charts, Jake had known he'd have to ditch the redhead. Though he wasn't sure why exactly, he knew the reason would reveal itself soon enough. He'd learned to always trust his gut instincts. Always.

She'd been kind. Interested, even. And beautiful, the kind of beauty that once would have sent men off to war. While her beauty lured him, he didn't trust her. She knew things he didn't. Since she'd done everything in her power to hustle him away from the dead-end alley, she had no intention of sharing any of her knowledge with him.

He'd seen her go in the door. That damn door. What had started out as idle curiosity had become a full-blown obsession. So much so that he'd put his own life in danger.

The salt-scented, humid breeze made the cuts on his face sting. He thought he could make it back to his car, but he'd begun to second guess the instinct that had made him flee the hospital. While the woman—Maddie Kinslow—had put on an outward show of compassion, she was part of whatever secret lay behind that door. Call him overly paranoid, but he couldn't help but wonder if she'd been sent to finish the job the two thugs had started. He wasn't prepared to risk finding out.

Still, she'd been right about one thing. He needed medical attention. He suspected he had, at the very least, a couple of broken ribs. If not broken, then bruised.

An older black Lincoln pulled up alongside him. "Hey, man," a familiar voice said. "You need a ride?"

Wayne. One of the guys he played basketball with every Saturday. Jake had never been so glad to see someone in his life. "I do," he said, lifting his hand in greeting.

"Climb on in."

Jake did. When Wayne got a good look at his face, he whistled, low and furious. "What the hell happened to you?"

"I got jumped over by Harborside."

"By the cruise ship parking lots?" Wayne wanted to know.

"Yeah, sort of."

"What were you doing over there?"

Since his friend knew exactly what Jake did for a living, he told the truth. "Following a lead. I got a little too close for someone's comfort."

"Let's go to the hospital," Wayne suggested.

Since Jake felt dizzy, like he might pass out again, he agreed.

This time, he made it inside the ER under his own power. Though Wayne had offered to stay, Jake told him no.

Three and a half hours later, Jake learned his ribs were bruised, not broken. By some miracle, his most serious—and painful—injury was a dislocated shoulder. They gave him some muscle relaxers and a shot of something, and the doctor manually worked it back into place. When he did, it hurt like hell. Perspiring, trying not to swear, Jake managed to stay conscious.

When they were finally done and the doctor came to discharge him with a prescription for more pain pills and some antibiotics, he asked Jake if he had someone to drive him home.

"No. But my car is only a couple blocks away," Jake said, his tongue feeling thick in his mouth.

"You can't drive," the doc said firmly. "You need to call someone to come and pick you up. We gave you some strong narcotics. No driving for at least twenty-four hours."

"I'll find someone." He dug out his phone. Maybe he could talk Wayne into coming back and picking him up.

"No need," a cool, feminine voice said from the doorway. "I'll take you home."

The redhead. Maddie Kinslow.

"Perfect," the doctor said, smiling. "Take him straight home, make sure and fill these prescriptions, and force him to get plenty of rest."

"I sure will." Now she sounded positively cheerful. He turned to stare at her, wondering how she'd known to come back here looking for him.

"I'll send a nurse to wheel you out to the car," the doc continued. "Hospital regulations," he added when Jake began to protest.

Jack nodded. He waited until the doctor had left the room before confronting Maddie. "Are you stalking me?"

"No." She frowned, looking both hurt and angry. "I will say I was concerned, especially when you took off like you were afraid to go into the ER. Why was that? I wondered. Do you have a warrant out for your arrest?"

"No. And no. As you can see, I haven't been arrested. Where do you come up with this stuff?"

"I'm a PI," she retorted. "It's part of my line of work."

"A private investigator?" At first surprised, the more he considered, the better he felt. Ms. Maddie Kinslow might not realize it, but she'd just given him an idea.

She started to respond, and then closed her mouth. Lips a tight line, she looked away. Whatever she wasn't telling him, she clearly had no intention of saying anything else about her work. Which was okay with him. She'd said enough.

Luckily for her, a cheerful nurse arrived with a wheelchair. She ordered Maddie to get her car and pull up right outside the entrance. Once Maddie had left to do that, the nurse wheeled him out front to wait for her.

When Maddie had parked, the nurse helped Jack out of the wheelchair and into the passenger side. He was able to buckle the seat belt, wincing.

"Are you all good?" she asked, her candid gaze searching his face.

"Yep. Better than good," he replied. "I'm actually really glad to learn you're a private investigator. As it turns out, I want to hire you."

Judging by her sudden intake in breath, he'd shocked

her. "Um, my agency is specialized. We wouldn't be a good fit."

"Yes, we would," he insisted. "Plus, you're the only PI I know. I'll pay whatever your going rate is. And I promise, you'll find my job to be a simple one, easily completed."

She shifted into Drive and pulled away from the hospital.

"Well?" he pressed once she'd exited the parking lot. "What do you say?"

"I'm thinking. Give me a minute."

He gave her more than a minute. She followed his directions, pulling in to the driveway of his small home on San Jacinto. Once she'd put the car in Park, she turned in her seat to face him.

"What's the job?" she asked, her expression professional. "I really can't commit my resources until I know what is involved."

And here came the part she wouldn't like. He told her anyway. "I want to hire you to find out what's behind that door on the dead-end alleyway. The one where you found me all beat-up."

Chapter 2

Inside Broken Chains, Carmen Vargas sat back in her chair, took a sip of her drink and surveyed the smoky room. As always, every table had been taken, and those without a seat stood shoulder to shoulder. Carmen had arrived early and claimed her usual prime spot near the back, close enough to have a view of the dance floor, but not so close that the loudness of the band would make any attempt at conversation impossible.

Her friends Maddie Kinslow and Shayla Dover-Cantrell usually met her here, but Shayla had recently gotten married and was just getting back from her honeymoon. The three of them had formed a super-natural private investigative agency and had recently successfully closed their first case. Carmen imagined Maddie had already gotten busy hustling for a second. Still, she was very late. Not like her. Carmen figured she'd give her a little bit longer before calling her friend's cell phone.

"Have you got a minute?" The low growl of a masculine voice to her left had her betting he'd be a Shapeshifter. With a lazy movement, she swiveled her head to look. Damn. She, who never was shocked, sucked in her breath. Talk about hot. This guy had to be new. His aura revealed she was correct. Shape-shifter. And a damn good-looking specimen, too.

Exactly her type, if she'd had one. Tall, close-cropped dark hair, bright blue eyes, broad shoulders, narrow waist and muscular arms. He looked like a cop, or some other straight-laced profession. She'd learned from experience that those kinds of men were almost always the most fun in bed.

She let herself experience a delighted shiver before responding.

"Of course," she purred, indicating the chair next to her. "Have a seat."

He pulled out a chair and sat down, his bold stare frank and assessing. Confidence. She liked that in a man.

This evening had just gotten a thousand times more interesting. After so many centuries on the planet, Carmen rarely felt an overwhelming attraction like this.

"I work for the government," he said. No surprise there. "And I've been talking to the Pack Protectors. They let me know about your Shadow Agency, operating right here in Galveston."

A job. He wanted to discuss a job with her. Years of practice enabled her to hide her disappointment. She simply eyed him calmly while waiting for him to elaborate.

Instead, he glanced around. "Is there somewhere quieter we can talk? This is classified, so not information I'm comfortable shouting."

She took a moment to consider, enjoying the way his

gaze traveled over her. "Maybe later," she finally said. "I'm waiting for a friend and I don't want to lose our seat."

His gaze narrowed and his mouth tightened. "This is a matter of national security."

Though intrigued, she pretended not to hear him at first. Only when he leaned close, his mouth against her ear, and repeated himself, did she nod. "Perhaps you should make an appointment with our office. I'm certain you don't want to discuss such a weighty matter in a bar."

Instead of putting him in his place as she expected, a flash of annoyance sparked in his eyes. "This is urgent. I don't have time to make an appointment. If you don't want the job, just say so. I'm sure I can find someone else."

Rueful, she conceded. "Wait. I'm interested. If you could just give me a few minutes until my friend arrives, I'll find a quieter place where the two of us can talk."

"Five minutes," he said. "No longer."

Clearly, he was the kind of man used to giving orders. She found this incredibly arousing. Most men were too intimidated by her frank and blatant sensuality. They tended to fall all over themselves trying to please her.

"Five minutes," she agreed, smiling. Maddie had a tendency to run late, but never extremely so.

The allotted time passed. Still no Maddie. Handsome Guy eyed her and she knew he meant to leave.

"Come on," she said, getting to her feet. "They have private rooms in the back. Let me see if I can secure one and we'll go there and talk."

He followed as she strolled to the bar. One glance over her shoulder showed no less than six people had rushed the table the instant she'd left. They'd have to duke it out among themselves over who ended up with it. Or share.

As luck would have it, she was able to rent a small room for half an hour. She sent Maddie a quick text to let her know where to go once she arrived, and then led the way through the double doors to the private part of the bar. She'd heard stories about some of the goings-on in these private rooms.

Stopping at room number 7, she used her key to unlock the door. "Here we are," she said, entering. Handsome Secret Agent Man brushed past her and began looking around. As in, seriously searching for something. Fascinated, she watched, realizing he must be checking the room for recording devices.

When he finally finished, he turned to face her. "I'll need your cell phone," he said, holding out his hand.

"Thanks, but no thanks," she replied. "I'm not handing that over to a total stranger, just because he's cute."

Her choice of adjectives made him blink, but that was his only reaction. Disappointed, she pulled out a chair and sat. "You were about to tell me why you needed to hire me?"

"Not until I know for certain that you're not recording," he countered, stoned-faced. "At least put your phone on the table."

"Are you serious?" she asked, even though she knew he was. With a sigh, she retrieved her phone from the depths of her Prada bag and placed it on the table.

"May I?" he asked, as he reached for it.

"You can look at it," she replied. "But I want it back on the table once you're done." Though she had no idea what she'd do if he decided to drop it into his pocket. By virtue of being a Vampire, she had the elements of super-speed and strength on her side, but he was some kind of Shape-shifter, which made him a much more even match than, say, a human would have been.

Finally, he finished checking out her phone and placed it back on the table.

"My name is Rick Fallin," he said. "I'm a member of a covert intelligence agency within the FBI. Our country is being threatened by terrorists and we need the help of someone with your credentials."

"My credentials?"

"Yes. You are one of the top biowarfare scientists."

She nodded. "True. But you could have approached me at the lab. Why here? Why ask for help from The Shadow Agency?"

"Because we need you for one other reason. You're a Vampire. And as such, you'd be immune to a deadly, human-created virus."

"You're a Shape-shifter," she shot back. "And if you're full-blooded, you're also immune."

"We're not sure about that," he replied. "Let me explain. This is a completely new virus. We're not completely sure of the effects it will have on the paranormal population."

"Now I'm really intrigued," she drawled. "I can't wait to get a look at this thing."

Though several of his colleagues had warned him that he'd take an immediate dislike to the Vampire woman, Rick Fallin discovered they were all wrong. Instead of the usual revulsion his kind normally felt around those of her ilk, he got a jolt of attraction every time he looked at Carmen Vargas instead. Which he struggled mightily to do as seldom as possible, aware he needed to focus on the job and only the job. This was far too important to mess up.

"A terrorist group has developed a new disease," he

said, once he had her full attention. "Not a known group, either. They call themselves Sons of Darkness. This one appears to be newly formed. We're not even sure what kind of ideology they possess."

"Sons of Darkness," she mused, a flash of interest in her eyes. "Sounds like possible Satanists. Do you have proof of this disease?"

"Yes. I don't know if you heard about that junior senator who died so mysteriously a couple days ago?"

"I rarely watch the news anymore." She gave a delicate shrug. "Unless it pertains to my work or my friends, I'm content to keep my world knowledge as compact as possible."

Made sense. While he had no idea of her actual age, he'd always heard Vampires lived centuries. He imagined anyone would get a bit jaded after watching so many humans come and go.

"Let me fill you in then. Samuel Jansson was infected with this virus. We're not sure how or when, but most likely it was in a bar on the hill where he frequently stopped for a drink after work. He died a horrible death at home in his bed less than twelve hours later."

She whistled. "That's a fast-acting virus. But how do you know that's what killed him?"

"The terrorist group contacted us shortly before his body was discovered. But even then, we had the same doubts. We rushed an autopsy."

"And?"

"What killed him was a virus never before seen. We have no antidote."

Another flash of interest lit up her face. "What do they want in exchange? I'm assuming it must be something big, right?"

"Oh, it is. It is." He'd been instructed not to tell her if at all possible, to gain her assistance without doing so. Once he'd completed a full read-through of her dossier, he'd wondered what his boss had been thinking. A rational, intelligent, professional scientist like Carmen Vargas would want to know everything. If they needed the best, they'd have to give her 100 percent of the info.

"They want our country to go to war," he said slowly. "Unless we obliterate the entire country of West Latvia, they'll unleash this virus on our general population. It spreads through the air and kills fast."

"West Latvia?" She frowned. "Why?"

"They trade heavily with Russia. Whoever these terrorists are, they want something Russia gets instead. They haven't specified what exactly. We have people working on finding that out."

"You say this senator was found dead?" she asked. "What about the people who found his body? Have they been placed in isolation to avoid contamination?"

"Yes. The terrorists claim it's only active while the body is alive. We've got people working around the clock to verify this."

She nodded. "As you know, I'm a damn good scientist. I assume you want me to join one of your research teams?"

"Possibly. Though that's not the entire reason we need your Shadow Agency—and you. Many on my task force are full-blooded Shifters, too. As you know, only a silver bullet or fire can kill us. Normally."

Tucking away one wayward blond strand of hair behind her ear, she eyed him. "You aren't sure if this virus might be another thing that can take your kind out, are you?"

"Exactly."

"Since I'm already dead…" Her slow smile made his heart skip a beat.

To cover his unwanted reaction, he looked down, pretending to be lost in thought.

"Hey, it's okay." When she reached out and covered his hands with hers, he felt a jolt straight in his groin. His inner wolf, startled awake, sat up and took notice.

"I enjoy being useful," she continued. "What I need to do is get you a full printout of our rates. We charge by the hour, plus expenses. There's a flat fee—a retainer—that's payable up front and is nonrefundable."

Slowly he slid his hand out from under hers. "None of that matters. You're dealing with a well-funded covert government operation. If you agree to assist us, we can pay you this." Though doing so felt a bit melodramatic, he opened his briefcase to get a better look at the neat stacks of bills inside. "Twenty-five thousand dollars cash, up front. Another twenty-five once the mission is successfully completed."

If he expected her to gape, he was doomed to disappointment. She looked coolly from the money to him. "This is most unusual," she said. "I'll have to consult with my partners."

But he refused to accept this. "I happen to know your private investigative business is a start-up. You've only had one case, I believe. Cash flow has to be important. You can't afford to turn this down."

Stone-faced, she stared at him.

"And this is important," he continued. "It's not just a case. It's your chance to make a difference."

Watching her, he swore he saw that same flicker of interest in her eyes.

"Fine," she finally said. "I'm in. Representing The Shadow Agency." Her chin came up and she held his gaze. "But not just because of the money. I've always wanted to make a difference."

Admiration warred with attraction. He nodded, closing the one briefcase before pulling a manila folder from the other. "We've taken the liberty of having a contract drawn up in advance. I'll need your signature in three places."

Though she accepted the pen he offered her, instead of immediately signing on the dotted line, she began to read through the contract. "No," she said abruptly. "This part here is unacceptable." She stabbed her long, bloodred fingernails at the page. "I refuse to keep my partners in the dark about this job. We're in this together. Otherwise, you're not hiring The Shadow Agency. You're just hiring me."

Somehow, he sensed this minor issue would be the one thing that could make her walk away. As far as he knew, they didn't have a backup. "I agree," he conceded. "Strike through that part and initial it. I'll do the same."

Once she'd done as he'd suggested, she finished her read-through and then signed. Handing him back the papers, she held out one elegant, pale hand.

"I should have told you," Rick said, after neatly filing the contract in his briefcase. Then and only then did he slide the briefcase full of cash across the table toward her. "You and I will be partners for this case."

She stared. "I work better alone. Plus, I already have two partners."

"Not on this case, you don't. You might want to put that somewhere safe," he added, gesturing at the briefcase. "Once you've done that, you'll need to let your partners know that you have to disappear for a while."

"Disappear?" She didn't really protest. "They'll be used to it. It's kind of what we Vamps do."

He laughed, the full, rich sound filling the room.

"I just need to let Maddie know," she managed to say, sticking to the topic at hand. "She's the one I was supposed to meet here tonight. She's probably out there right now, anxious about where I am even though I texted her."

"Let's go find her, then. After that, you're coming with me."

"Okay. Enjoying this, are you?" she drawled. "You might be pretty, but this is serious business. I don't need a distraction, and believe me, I could see you becoming a big one."

To her annoyance, rather than fluster him, her remark made him laugh. "Nice try, Vargas. But it'll take more than that to make me go away. I'm going to be stuck to your side like glue, so get used to it."

"Fine, whatever." She gave in sullenly. "I was thinking I'd start in the lab first. I'm assuming you plan to provide me with tissue samples so I can begin to analyze the thing."

"That won't be necessary," he said. "We've already got teams of the best scientists working on that."

He'd managed to surprise her, and not in a good way. "I am one of the top biological specialists."

One corner of his mouth quirked up. "True, but there are others. We've got them in the lab working feverishly for answers."

He could see she didn't like that. "Then why do you need me? Honestly, if you want to develop an antidote, I'm of the best use to you in the lab."

"We need your help to neutralize the terror group. Time is of the essence. While the president has been fully briefed and continues to be, he's not sold on the idea of declaring war on West Latvia."

She nodded, watching him closely. "Have they given you a time frame?"

"Yes. Seven days. If war is not declared and troops deployed, they plan to infect Houston. If they release this virus into the general population, we'll lose a couple million people in one day. No, Carmen Vargas. We need you in the field. You and I are going to try to infiltrate the terrorists. Our job is to unmask them and take them down from the inside."

She nodded. "This job is sounding more interesting by the minute. How do you propose to do that?"

When he grinned, the flash of his white teeth made her fangs ache. "I have my ways. We've got people who've been working undercover. You and I are going to pose as people interested in joining the terrorist cell."

"I thought you didn't know who they were affiliated with."

"We don't. Not yet. They may be part of a larger group, or might have splintered off from one."

"With a name like Sons of Darkness, I wouldn't be surprised to find out it's a bunch of teenaged kids," she said. "Except for the virus."

"Except for the virus," he repeated. "I think we can pretty much rule out teens. Even if one of them turned out to be some sort of genius, I'd think they'd want cash rather than war declared on some small European nation sandwiched between Estonia and Lithuania."

"West Latvia," she mused. "I believe some of my ancestors came from that area, but I've never been there."

Though he nodded, his mind was elsewhere. When he looked up to find her watching him, he grimaced. "Sorry. I've been going over the plans. Are you ready to get started?"

She nodded. The rush of anticipation that filled her

was unlike anything she'd experienced in centuries. "I am. Tell me what you want me to do." She frowned. "But first I need to check on my friend."

If he hadn't known better, Rick would have thought Carmen was stalling. He stayed with her, right on her heels, as she proceeded to search the bar for her missing friend. They made two complete sweeps of the crowded place, upstairs and down, before she finally admitted defeat.

"This is so not like her," she said as they walked out the door. "She's really reliable. Always where she says she's going to be. I hope she's all right."

"Try calling her," he suggested.

"I have. Several times. Calls are going straight to voice mail. I left her a message—well, two now."

"That's worrisome."

"Maybe." She lifted one shoulder in an elegant shrug. "And maybe not. Maddie's always forgetting to charge her phone. It's entirely possible that it's dead and she has no idea."

He spoke without thinking. "She sounds like a scatter-brain."

"She's not." Rushing to defend her friend, Carmen sounded fierce. "We all have our own little character flaws. It's not such a big deal."

"Maybe not," he agreed, glancing at her sideways. "What's yours?"

His question appeared to puzzle her. "Mine?"

"Your little character flaw. I'll tell you mine if you'll tell me yours." He couldn't believe he was flirting with her, but then again, how could he not. They needed to get past this awkwardness with each other for the under-cover roles they were going to play.

"I don't have any flaws," she snapped. A second later,

she appeared to realize what she'd said. "I'm pretty damn near perfect," she elaborated, laughing. "As I'm sure you are, too."

As he gazed down into her smiling face, something shifted inside him. Damned if she wasn't alluring. He hadn't expected this sudden craving to hit him so strongly.

Outside in the alley, he led the way across the street to where he'd parked. "Do we need to move your car somewhere?"

This made her chuckle again. "No. I walked here."

Her statement almost gave him pause, considering that some of the neighborhoods nearby could be dangerous late at night. But then he remembered she was a Vampire. Anyone messing with her would get the shock of their life.

She settled into the passenger seat of his black Tahoe, even using the seat belt. He couldn't help but notice how her every movement contained a sensual sort of grace. "What now?" she asked. "Where do we go from here and what's the plan?"

Now was as good a time as any to tell her. At least they weren't inside the crowded bar. "We're posing as a married couple," he said, starting the engine at the same time.

"Married?" One elegantly arched brow rose. "That's the one thing I have absolutely no experience with. I'm not sure I can be convincing."

He glanced at her and grinned. "Just follow my lead, darlin'. That's all you have to do."

From the momentary look of confusion on her face, he guessed she wasn't sure how to react to the endearment. He hadn't called anyone *darlin'* in years, not since his fiancée had died. But since he and Carmen were going to pretend to be spouses, he figured using it would be particularly apropos.

"Sounds good, sugar plum," she drawled, dead-faced.

He laughed—he couldn't help it. It had been a long time since he'd been around a woman who could make him laugh. Pity she was a Vampire. But then again, he wasn't looking for a mate. "I think we'll work fine together," he finally said.

When he glanced at her again, her beautiful face wore a ghost of a smile.

"Here's how we're playing this," he said, all serious again. "Word has gone out in a certain group of people that the Sons of Darkness are looking to hire someone with a biology background. They're willing to pay big bucks. You happen to perfectly fit the bill."

"A biology background?" she snorted. "That's putting it mildly."

He continued on as if she hadn't spoken. "Your credentials and employment are right there for them to look up. You've never done any work with law enforcement, so there's no reason they'd suspect you."

"Maybe not, but what's my motivation? I'm well paid. I like my job. Why would I want to join their organization?"

Bracing himself, he gave her a sideways look. "You've just lost your job. That's your motivation. Plus, we've set it up so that anyone looking will believe you're massively in debt. You need to find work and find it fast."

"Lost my job?" She might have become a statue, she went so still. "Are you serious?"

"It's only temporary. We've got someone who pulled a few strings to make this happen. I'm sure you'll be fully reinstated once this is over."

Glowering at him, she sighed. "I'd better be. I love my job and I'm damn good at it."

"I'm sure you are. But look at it this way," he said. "You've got a chance to save the world. How many can say that?"

Chapter 3

Maddie could only stare. This guy, this *journalist*, had no idea what he'd just asked her to do. She couldn't, she wouldn't, and she needed to figure out a way to tell him that wouldn't arouse suspicion. Betraying her own kind, not to mention the other paranormal beings who frequented Broken Chains, was an act punishable by death.

"Jake," she said, swiveling in her seat to face him. "I can't. The private investigative agency I work for specializes. Your particular request doesn't qualify."

His jaw clenched. Slowly, he shook his head. "First off, I don't believe you. Second, I'm well aware you know what's behind that door. I've seen you go through it. With or without your help, I will find out what's going on."

Though she knew he had no idea of the magnitude of the danger he'd be placing himself in, she couldn't help but admire—just the teeniest bit—his dogged determination. Even though it completely mystified her.

"What is it with you and that door?" she finally asked. "Do you honestly think whatever is behind it is worth you being beaten within an inch of your life? Because I can promise you, if you keep pursuing this, that's what will happen again. Or worse."

"Wow." He stared at her. "Whatever the secret is that you're hiding, it must be something big. I can't believe you're threatening me."

"Not threatening. Warning." She let her gaze roam over him. Even with his battered and bruised face, he was still handsome. His angular features and the light brown tint to his skin made his brown eyes stand out. She liked his lean muscular build and narrow waist. In fact, if she'd met Jake Cassel under different circumstances, she'd have dated him.

Even now, despite him ditching her earlier and then stating he planned to continue on his dangerous and fool-hardy course of action, she felt a twinge of attraction.

A jolt of awareness struck her. She realized she had to do whatever it took to keep the truth hidden from him—and by doing so, keep him safe.

"Jake, look." She swallowed. "I'll do it. I'll take the job."

Instead of making him happy, he narrowed his eyes. "Why?"

That made her laugh. "What do you mean, why? I thought you wanted my help."

"I do."

"Yet you're still frowning."

"Because I can't shake the thought that you're some-how playing me."

Good instincts, though of course she couldn't say that out loud. Instead, she shrugged. "Up to you. We don't come cheap. I completely understand if you've changed your mind."

He tilted his head, eyeing her as if honestly trying to read her mind. "Do you have a card?" he asked.

"Of course." Luckily, she'd just printed up a batch. She kept several in the console, so she pulled one out and handed it to him. "You can call me if you change your mind."

He accepted it, put it in his pocket and stared straight ahead.

"Where to?" she asked. He gave her an address in a neighborhood near hers, but a few streets away. She drove silently, efficiently, keeping her concentration on the road. When they finally pulled up in front of a small yellow frame house, she parked. "I hope you get to feeling better soon," she said.

"Thanks." Still avoiding her gaze, he slowly and painfully climbed from the car. "I'll be in touch."

She watched him walk up his driveway, waiting to pull away until he'd disappeared into the house. Then, because it was her habit, she made a note of the address on a small pad she kept in her console.

As soon as she got home, she called Carmen. Her friend didn't answer, which made Maddie suspect the Vamp harbored some resentment over being stood up. Maddie apologized over voice mail, said she needed to talk to her about a potential new case and hung up. No doubt Carmen would disappear for a day or two, as was her wont. When Maddie and their other partner, Shayla, called her on it, Carmen always simply shrugged and told them to get used to it, because that's what Vampires did.

Simple chores, like pouring herself a glass of wine and reheating a leftover bowl of pho she'd picked up for lunch yesterday, brought Maddie a measure of calm. A creature of habit, she liked things to happen as planned and in a particular order. This made her feel secure.

Tonight she'd agreed to meet Carmen for an early

drink at Broken Chains. Everything had spiraled out of control before she'd even reached the iconic door. And while she hadn't intended to spend so much time tracking down Jake Cassel, she knew in her core that she'd done the right thing. There were procedures put in place—some of them primitive and violent—by those who protected their kind from discovery. Jake was lucky he'd only been beaten.

In fact, Maddie knew she actually had an obligation to uphold. Sipping her soup, she deliberated. If she made the call to the Pack Protectors—or, most likely, her brother, since he worked as one—they'd send people to round up the reporter. It wouldn't be pretty, it wouldn't be kind, and she wasn't a hundred percent sure Jake would survive.

Though calling her brother might be the right thing to do, she couldn't. Not yet. Instead, she'd keep an eye on Jake and try her best to protect him from harm. And from getting too close to the truth. If he'd actually hire her, that would make her task a lot easier.

She poured herself a second glass of wine and rinsed her bowl before putting it in the dishwasher. Carrying her wine to the living room, she clicked on the TV just in time to catch the evening news.

An ominous red banner was displayed across the scene. Breaking News. Apparently, there had been an explosion in one of the warehouses down near the pier. No one had been killed, there were three people injured and the police were looking for the suspects. It had not yet been called a terrorist attack and motive had not yet been determined. The warehouse had been believed to be empty, but firefighters said it was not.

When the camera panned the crowd, Maddie let out a little yelp of surprise. That woman in the group over to one side—tall, blonde and elegant—looked like Carmen.

Maddie hit the pause button on her remote and went back. Yep. She paused again. For whatever reason, Carmen was down near the pier. And from the looks of things, she wasn't alone. She stood arm-in-arm with a ruggedly handsome military-type man. He gave off a dangerous yet sexy vibe. He'd have to, she thought, to keep up with Carmen.

No wonder her friend hadn't answered her phone. Maddie couldn't say she blamed her. Jake made Maddie feel the same way—like going off the grid and getting to know him.

She found herself grinning when she thought of Jake. He didn't realize it, but she'd only told him the truth. While she knew what she was planning on doing walked a fine line as far as Pack law, she'd be careful. If, at any moment, Jake got too close to the truth, she'd talk to her brother, but right now she thought she could redirect Jake to some other story. The only problem was that she'd need to find one first.

In the years since moving to Galveston, Maddie had been on a lot of dates, especially when she'd worked as a police dispatcher. Human men, Shifter men, and even a Merman or two. Not a single one of them affected her the way Jake did.

Because she had an analytical mind, she sat down and tried to figure out what specifically attracted her to him.

It could be his dark good looks, but she'd dated many handsome men. She didn't know him well enough for it to be his personality or sense of humor, which brought her an odd sort of relief. Physical attraction was easily dealt with. She certainly wasn't ready for anything stronger.

The next morning, Maddie set to work. Taking her time, she snapped a camera phone pic of the sheet she'd printed out with The Shadow Agency's rates. She'd actually had to print out an amended list, as she couldn't send Jake the one that listed items like "Undersea Investigation," which was Shayla's area, since she happened to be a Mermaid.

After she'd sent the text to Jake, she tried again to call Carmen. She went straight to voice mail, which meant her Vampire friend had disappeared. With a sigh, Maddie left another message, knowing Carmen wouldn't call until she'd finished with whatever it was that she did when she disappeared.

Next, she phoned Shayla. Though her Mermaid friend had just returned from her honeymoon, Maddie really needed someone to talk to about this entire Jake situation.

Shayla answered and sounded delighted. "I was just thinking about you," she exclaimed. "I told Zach I needed some girl time with you and Carmen."

"Carmen's gone on one of her disappearances," Maddie said, relieved. "But I'd love to meet up with you for a drink at Broken Chains when you have time. I need to talk to you about something."

"I hope that's not as serious as it sounds," Shayla teased. "Either way, you know I'm full of advice, whether needed or not. Can you make it tonight around eight?"

"Perfect. I'll get there early to snag our usual table."

After ending the call, Maddie felt like a heavy weight had been lifted from her chest. Even though her friend wasn't Pack, Shayla understood all too well the intricate nature of keeping their truths hidden from humans. Heck, Maddie wouldn't have minded if Shayla brought Zach, her husband. Since Zach was also Pack, Maddie would definitely welcome his input, though she wouldn't have been able to speak as freely if it were just her and Shayla.

Trying not to look at the clock too often, Maddie

caught up on housework, went grocery shopping and checked her email. She heated up leftover pizza for her dinner, reapplied her makeup and tried to decide what outfit to wear. In the end, she went with a simple black skirt and light green sheer top over a black camisole. Though she usually wore ballet slipper–type flats, she tried on a pair of heels. In the end, she discarded them and slipped on her usual comfy shoes.

Dangly silver earrings and several cute bracelets and she was out the door an hour early. As was her habit, she parked near Pier 21 and walked back in the direction of the bar. The salt-scented sea breeze felt warm and familiar, reminding her how long it had been since she'd visited the beach. Now that tourist season was over, she needed to go. Fall was always a good time, even though her favorite time to meander down the sand was winter, when the colder water kept even most locals away.

As she strolled toward the bar, she found herself wondering where Jake hid when he did his surveillance. He'd claimed to have spent weeks watching the dead-end alley, but for the life of her she couldn't see where. This time, she'd pay special attention to her surroundings and see if she could spot him.

When she reached the alley, she slowly pirouetted. Regular protocol demanded those entering the alley check left and right, making sure no humans were in the vicinity before proceeding to the door. Now, in addition to that, she realized the abandoned warehouse across the street still had numerous windows that had not been boarded up, some with shattered glass. It would be a simple thing for someone like Jake to gain entrance and set up a camera in one of those windows. In fact, for all she knew he might be there right now.

Refusing to wave, she finally made her way down the

alley, knocked on the weathered door and waited. After a moment, it swung open and she stepped inside, then waited until it closed automatically behind her.

Because she was Shifter, the smells hit her first. Smoke and beer and whiskey, along with the various scents of other bodies. Next came the noise. Even though the band had not yet started playing, there was the low hum of voices, the clinking of glass and silverware, the scraping of chairs on the old wooden floor.

She sighed with pleasure. Of all the places she frequented on the island, this bar felt the most like home.

Wending her way through the crowd, she smiled when she saw Jason, her favorite bartender, had placed a small Reserved sign on her favorite table.

Waving at him, she took a seat. Immediately, he brought her a tall glass of wheat beer, her usual. She told him Shayla would be joining her, but not Carmen, and he nodded, whistling cheerfully as he walked off.

A shadow fell and she looked up, smiling. Her smile faded as she realized it wasn't her friend. Instead, a tall, muscular male Shifter stood glowering down at her.

"I'm not interested," she started to say, then gasped when he grabbed her arm in a painful grip.

"We need to talk," he said. "You've been seen with that human reporter. I'm a Pack Protector. I don't think I need to warn you of the severity of your crime against the Pack if you've revealed anything to him."

Nothing could have prepared him for the way Maddie affected him. After all, Jake considered himself like a bulldog. Once he fixated on a story, nothing got in his way. Nothing.

Not even a sexy redhead with a smattering of freckles across her nose. Then why couldn't he stop thinking about her?

When he'd asked to hire her, he hadn't expected her to eventually agree. After all, he knew she had secrets and they were tied in with whatever was behind that damn door. If his investigative reporting uncovered something illegal, something dangerous, he had to be prepared to take her down, too. This knowledge made his stomach churn.

Especially since he knew it could be worse than he'd originally suspected. When he'd seen the news of the explosion in a warehouse near Pier 21, he'd immediately thought of *them*, the mysterious group of individuals who met behind that strange old door.

Especially when, without any proof, the anchorman speculated that this might have been a terrorist attack. He'd said this as casually as if speaking about the weather. Sloppy reporting, Jake knew. Yet of course, this possibility made him wonder. Terrorists. What if a local cell of them met in that place along that dead-end alleyway? That would explain the reason for refusing to open the door and for the two men to jump him there.

No. He refused to play a guessing game. His journalistic integrity demanded facts. Without them, he had nothing.

The more he thought about it, the more he realized Maddie Kinslow might be his best chance at getting an actual lead.

He pulled out the business card she'd given him. *The Shadow Agency* was emblazoned across the top. Underneath that, *A specialized private investigation firm.* And then simply her name and phone number.

Specialized. In what? He turned the card over in his hand. To be fair, she'd tried to tell him her company handled only a certain type of clientele, though she hadn't been specific.

Deciding, he pulled out his phone and dialed her number. His call went straight to voice mail. He left his name and number, nothing else. Now to see if she'd actually return the call.

When his phone rang five minutes later, his heart leaped in his chest. "That was quick," he said after answering.

"Yeah, well…I've been worried about you." She made the confession in a husky voice that had his body stirring.

Ruthlessly, he tamped down the desire. "Don't," he snapped. "I'm fine. I just need a little time to heal and I'll be back to normal."

To his surprise, this statement made her chuckle. "I'll never figure out what it is about men that they think they have to be so tough. You forget, Jake. I was there. I saw you."

Instead of replying, he let his silence speak for itself.

"Okay," she said when he didn't respond. "What did you need? Why did you call me?"

Though he'd already begun to doubt the wisdom of his decision, he decided to go through with it. "I want to hire you."

Now she went quiet. He waited her out.

"For the same reason as before?" she finally asked. "Because you want me to help you find out what's behind the door?"

"Yes."

She sighed. "Are you absolutely certain you truly want to continue to pursue this? Because I can tell you this— it's dangerous. As in, you could lose your life, dangerous."

Deep down, he'd suspected as much, but hearing her

confirm it made his gut twist. "Are you involved in what-ever it is?" he asked.

"I can promise you, whatever you think you know is wrong," she said, without answering his question.

"Then enlighten me," he urged. "I've been watching that place for nearly a month. I've seen all the people coming and going. I've see you there numerous times, Maddie Kinslow. And you went inside. Why play games? Just tell me what you can and I'll find out the rest."

Again she sighed. "I wish I could, but then I'd have to kill you." She laughed, but he couldn't shake the feel-ing she wasn't kidding. "While I can't reveal the truth to you, even though it is such a minor thing, I can help you get a fabulous story."

"Are you offering me a bribe? Because it sure sounds like it." Now it was his turn to laugh, though without humor. "I have to say, the fact that you're actually doing that makes me even more eager to uncover the secret."

Silence.

"This is a bad idea," she finally replied. "Forget I ever offered my services. I wish you luck, Jake Cassel. Be-lieve me, you'll need it."

She ended the call.

He cursed. He'd gone too far and lost his chance. The beautiful Maddie Kinslow would be avoiding him now. What a shame, because he truly would have enjoyed get-ting to know her. Maybe it was all for the best. With such strong attraction sizzling between them, she'd probably have been too much of a distraction. Now he could focus solely on the story.

His phone rang again. "It's me," Maddie said, the sexy sound of her voice sending a shiver down his spine. "Look, I like you, Jake. I really do. But there is too much at stake here. People's lives, homes, families. Are you sure you don't want to at least consider my offer?"

"How can I when I don't even know what I'd be giving up?" He used the most reasonable argument he had. "Tell me what's behind the door and let me decide."

She hesitated. "Fine. There's a bar behind that door. Access is granted only to certain individuals. See? No story. Not even interesting."

"A bar?" He didn't bother to hide his skepticism. "What would possibly be so secretive about a *bar*?"

"The clientele. It's imperative that no one but certain… people are allowed in."

He had to give it to her. Her story had enough intrigue in it to interest him. And he knew it had to be—whatever, if any, part of it was true—the tip of the iceberg.

"Well?" she prodded after he didn't respond. "What do you think?"

Now he knew he had to play it cool. While he didn't entirely buy her story, in the end she was the best and only lead he had. If he "hired" her, eventually she might slip up.

"If your rates are reasonable, I'll definitely consider it," he finally said, trying to sound as disinterested as possible.

This time, he hung up first.

Pretending not to notice the man who'd been parked in the expensive car across the street and watching his house, Jake limped down his sidewalk to get the mail. The sun had begun to set and the breeze carried the smell of the sea. Bruised and battered didn't begin to describe how he felt today—more like he'd been run over by a large truck loaded with cement.

Late-model Mercedes, navy blue. Dark tinted windows, no plate on the front.

While he had no idea who his shadow might be, he

figured it had something to do with that dead-end alleyway and the door that wouldn't open for him.

Back inside the house, he glanced at the clock. If he planned to continue his surveillance, he'd need to head downtown soon. He'd taken great pains to ensure his point of entry into the abandoned warehouse would be hidden from any inquisitive eyes. And now he had no doubt they'd be looking.

He opened his laptop and checked his email. Finally, he really examined the message from Maddie detailing her company's rates. While he had no idea if these prices were competitive or not, it wasn't like he had another option. Maddie knew what went on behind that door. He just had to figure out a way to get her to tell him.

As dusk began to arrive, he knew if he wanted to leave his house, he'd need to shake his tail. If he got into his car and drove, the guy would certainly follow him. Normally he'd simply go out the back door, climb the fence that separated his yard from the guy behind him, and walk out onto the next street over. From there, it wasn't too long a walk to reach a bus stop, or if necessary, he could call for a taxi. But his bruised and battered body simply wasn't up to it yet.

Instead, he needed to get rid of the stalker. First, he called Maddie. But the call went straight to voice mail. Okay, he could understand that. It was after hours and he hadn't yet become her client.

Next up, he dialed the Galveston Police Department's nonemergency number. "I'd like to report a suspicious vehicle parked outside my house," he said. "I was jumped and beaten up the other day and I think the same individual has come back to try to finish the job. Could you please send someone?"

The dispatcher rerouted him to 911. After he repeated

his situation, he was told to stay inside the house and wait for the police to arrive. She asked him to stay on the line, so he did.

A moment later, a police cruiser turned onto his street and pulled up behind the parked Mercedes. The officer got out and walked up to the driver's-side window. He stood there a few moments, clearly talking to the driver. Jake hoped he'd asked for a driver's license and registration. If he at least had a name, he could do more research.

Finally, the policeman stepped back, lifted his hand in a friendly wave and watched as the luxury car drove off. One it had turned the corner, the officer walked up Jake's sidewalk and rang the bell.

Ending the call with the dispatcher, Jake hurried to answer the door. "Thank you so much, Officer," he began.

"You're welcome. But I wanted to let you know, there was no reason for you to be concerned. That was the mayor's son. He works for the City Planning and Zoning Department. He was parked on your street for business."

Though his insides froze, Jack managed to nod. "Good to know. Thanks again for coming out, Officer."

"No problem. I'm glad I could put your mind at ease." The policeman peered at him. "They did a hell of a job on you, didn't they? I hope you saw a doctor."

"I did."

"Good."

Finally the patrolman left. Jake closed the door behind him and made sure he locked the dead bolt. The mayor's son? Just how high up did this story go? If anything, this made him even more determined to get to the truth.

Moving as fast as he could, Jake hurried to his car. But before he even reached it, the navy Mercedes turned back onto his street and parked in the exact same spot.

Chapter 4

Carmen hid her surprise when Rick took her to the pier. Once the shrimp boats came in, sometimes the men would get together and drink and play cards or dice. An occasional prostitute worked one corner. Mostly, both tourists and locals avoided this place. It was nothing like Pier 21 with its popular restaurants and fish markets, close to The Strand. It wasn't even like Pier 19 or 20, with Sampson and Sons and Katie's selling seafood right off the boat.

No, this was further down, past a few abandoned, dilapidated buildings with cracked sidewalks and weeds. An overall sense of decay permeated the place. Once, smugglers had hung out here, with illegal gambling and gin joints and a whorehouse or two. Now, most of that was only a memory, though Carmen had been here once or twice during its heyday.

These days, this was where men went when they wanted to do things in secret, where the dim lighting and sense of anonymity made them feel at ease. It was an area she sometimes frequented when the craving for fresh, warm blood grew too strong. She'd become quite a pro at extracting just enough to make her target pass out, but without serious harm.

"Here." Rick's gravelly voice brought her back to the present. "In a moment, there's going to be an explosion. It will bring the rats scurrying from their holes."

She swung around and stared. "Why?"

"It's something I promised to do, as a sign of good faith. There's an illegal shipment of guns in one of these buildings. The Sons of Darkness needed a distraction so they could get them out. This will be a big one." He got out his phone and prepared to punch in a number. "Are you ready?"

"Sure." This got more interesting by the minute.

"Here we go." He dialed a number. A second later, a loud boom sounded and the ground shook. Someone screamed and someone else swore. Several people staggered toward them, some of them drunk, others in shock.

"I'm calling 911," Rick told them, holding up his phone. She watched, wondering if he really would since he didn't appear to be in any hurry to punch in the numbers. Maximizing time for the distraction, she guessed.

Someone else must have called, though, because sirens sounded in the distance, getting closer. The occasional straggler came down the sidewalk, one or two of them appearing shell shocked. Thick black smoke billowed from somewhere behind them, appearing to almost follow them as they fled.

"Do you think there were any injuries?" she asked.

"No one was seriously hurt," Rick assured her, sounding positive even though she didn't see how he could be certain. "The bomb was in a locked warehouse where we stacked some dry hay and bundled newspaper. Just enough to start a good fire with possible building collapse. It's far enough from the warehouse with the guns that no one will spot the crew moving the cargo. A perfect plan, if I do say so myself."

Since he sounded so pleased with himself, she felt the need to point out what seemed to her an obvious flaw. "But you destroyed a building. Most likely a historical one."

His jaw tightened. "That kind of collateral damage is better than people. Millions are at risk unless we do our job and get inside this group. I hope you understand that."

"I do." Before she could say anything else, the sirens grew closer. Lights flashing, two patrol cars pulled up the next street over. A moment later, a fire engine and ambulance arrived. Along with a growing crowd of people, they watched as Galveston PD cordoned off the street and sidewalk.

Soon a KHOU 11 news van arrived, which seemed awfully quick since they were out of Houston. They set up a reporter with her back to the mayhem, handed her a microphone and began filming.

"You do know in a few minutes that reporter is going to start asking people what they saw?" she said drily.

"That's good. We want to be seen. How else can I make sure Sons of Darkness know I was there?"

"You seem to have thought of everything." She shook her head.

"That's my job," he countered. "And I'm damn good at it."

Before long a couple of the other news stations sent their own crews. The crowd of onlookers continued to swell. News cameras panned the area. Rick grabbed Carmen's arm and made sure they were front and center, virtually guaranteeing them a spot on one, if not all, of the stations' evening news programs.

Since she'd spent most of her long, long life avoiding the spotlight, Carmen struggled with this. While she managed to keep her outward appearance cool, calm and collected, inside she battled the urge to step back and disappear into the large group.

But Rick's plan, she concluded reluctantly, actually made sense. If this was what was needed for them to gain entrance into that group, so be it. The idea that she— Carmen Vargas, Vampire—could make a difference in this world intrigued her. Plus, if she were totally honest, as she always was, she ached to get her hands on a microscope and take a close look at this new virus. Because of her expertise, the CDC had even contacted her several times, wanting her to come to Atlanta and work with them. She'd been tempted, but she'd come to value her friends and life here in Galveston, so she'd declined. Since they were no doubt involved closely in this case, she had a feeling that was how her name had been mentioned. For that, she considered herself lucky.

"Okay," Rick said, tightening his grip on her arm. "Time to go."

This time, she let him pull her away without questioning. He led her through the thick throng of people, up the sidewalk and to the still-crowded Pier 21 area. A couple had just gotten up from a bench along the walkway, and he hurried them to it.

"No matter what happens," he told her sotto voce, "show no expression. Just go along with it."

"No worries. I'm a master at that."

They sat. He put his arm around her shoulder, drawing her close. She let herself relax into the curve of his arm, liking the solidness of his muscular body. They pretended to be people watching. Despite the commotion going on a few blocks over, most of the ones strolling by her were fixated on having a good time.

"Mind if I join you?" The tall man wore a baseball cap pulled low over his eyes. Carmen eyed him coolly but didn't speak.

"Sure," Rick said, pulling Carmen closer to him so there was additional room on the bench. "Have a seat."

The stranger sat, staring straight ahead and ignoring him. Every sense alert, Carmen pretended not to be hyperconscious of him.

"Are you the biologist?" he finally asked, low-voiced.

Widening her eyes, Carmen nodded. "I am. Actually, I'm an infectious disease specialist. And this is my husband, Rick." The instant she spoke, she realized she hadn't asked if they were using assumed names or not. Most likely not, at least for her, since these people no doubt had wanted to verify her credentials.

"Rick." The man nodded, his gaze skittering from her to Rick and back again. "I'm Landers. The shipment was moved without a hitch. Thank you for your help."

"No problem." Rich shrugged, both his demeanor and his voice casual. "I did what you requested, and here we are. Are we in?"

"You're in." Landers stood, glancing left and then right. Finally, he focused on Rick and grinned. "Just so you know, we have several other guys who can do what you can do, but only one other biologist in our employ. Your wife is infinitely more valuable to us than you could ever be."

Carmen exhaled, recognizing the tactic. Divide and conquer. Except she knew this wouldn't work, not this time. "It's okay," she said, her tone lofty. "He likes that I make so much more money than he does. He jokes about being a kept man."

"Really?" Landers shook his head. "Well, there's none of that around here. Every single one of us has to earn our keep."

"And I will, I swear." Shooting Carmen a cross look, Rick shifted his weight from foot to foot. "You won't regret hiring me, I promise you."

"We'd better not." Was that a flash of pleasure across Landers's face? Carmen thought so, which meant she'd been correct. For whatever reason, Landers wanted to put a wedge in between her and Rick.

If that's what he wanted, she'd speak to Rick privately and make sure that's what he got.

"He follows orders well," she drawled, just for the hell of it. "Ask me how I know."

Rick flushed but didn't respond. This prompted another snorting laugh from Landers. "I'll bet he does," he sneered, leering at her.

"Now, can we possibly get out of here?" she asked, pretending to be uneasy with their location. "There are too many people around. If someone hears, they might have questions. Questions for which we will not have answers. I prefer to avoid collateral damage whenever possible."

Landers stared. "As if you've done this sort of thing before," he scoffed.

For an answer, she only lifted one perfectly shaped eyebrow.

Instantly, the other man's demeanor changed. "If you'll come with me," Landers said, "I'll take you both to meet the others."

"Lead the way," Carmen pronounced. "I'm looking forward to getting started."

* * *

Keeping his arm around Carmen, Rick followed Landers to a black Escalade with dark tinted windows. With shiny chrome accents everywhere, it was not the most inconspicuous vehicle. Who knew? Maybe they wanted it that way.

As they approached, the driver stepped out and opened the back door, motioning for Carmen to get in first. Moving with her usual fluid grace, she climbed inside. Rick followed her, trying unsuccessfully to avoid staring at the gleaming length of shapely leg her short skirt displayed.

Once the door closed, Landers got up front, riding shotgun. "It's about a thirty-minute ride, depending on traffic," he said.

"Off-island?" Carmen asked, frowning.

"Not too far, but yes. La Marque."

This surprised her, Rick knew. Surprised him, too. La Marque was a small town. Building a quality lab and running an operation of that size without attracting unwanted attention would be more difficult in a place like that.

As they drove, Landers turned around several times, making innocuous comments about the passing landscape. His frank stare assessed Carmen, as if weighing what options he had as far as trusting her.

Feeling the need to reassert the fact that he and Carmen were a team, Rick took her hand and clasped it firmly. Though he felt her briefly tense, her expression remained smooth and unruffled. And beautiful. He couldn't blame Landers for repeatedly checking her out. Hell, even Rick fought a constant battle to keep from staring at her.

Finally, they exited 45 and turned left, passing under the freeway and by the single motel, eventually leaving pavement for a gravel road. The houses here were small frame structures, and the flat landscape and sparse vegetation made everything visible.

For the first time, Rick wondered what they'd gotten into. He squeezed Carmen's hand, telling her silently to be ready in case this was some sort of trick. She squeezed back, cutting her gaze to connect with his to let him know she'd thought the same thing.

One more turn and they found themselves surrounded by pasture. Cattle grazed and vultures circled in the cloudless sky above. They continued on until they reached a black wrought-iron gate, which was closed. The driver punched a code into a keypad and the gates swung slowly open.

After turning in, they continued on to a low-slung stone ranch house. Nearby were several outbuildings, one of them a well-constructed barn that appeared to be new. There were black burglar bars over the windows.

Which meant that had to be the lab.

As they rolled to a stop in front of the house, two armed men stepped outside to greet them. Though inside Rick tensed up, he kept his posture and expression relaxed.

Again, the driver jumped out and opened the door, this time on Carmen's side so she could get out first. And she did, with an impressive display of leg. Her sky-high heels made her look both dangerous and sexy. Exactly his kind of woman, except for her being a Vampire. Too bad.

Head high, expression cool, she looked both of the newcomers up and down. Rick hid his smile.

Landers came around and told them to follow him. Once they'd gone up the steps onto the porch, someone pushed open the screen door and stepped out of the way. Rick reached for Carmen's hand as they went inside.

The small room had been sparsely furnished. Three

men looked up as they approached, though they all remained seated. Eyeing them, Rick wondered which of the three was the leader. Landers made the introductions in a clipped voice. The short, wiry man with the long white beard was Tommy. The bald guy who looked like a linebacker gone to seed was called Holt. And the thin, pale dude with the flat dark eyes was Gus.

They all dipped their chins in greeting. If Landers found it odd that no one spoke, he didn't show it. He motioned that Rick and Carmen should sit, so they took the empty spot at one end of the soiled couch.

"We got the shipment," Landers announced, filling the others in on the explosion Rick had engineered as a diversion. They listened carefully. Rick couldn't help but notice the way their gazes continually went to Carmen, as if they hadn't seen a woman in too long. For the first time since meeting her, he was glad she was a Vampire. At least he knew she could defend herself against any human male's unwanted attention.

"She's the biologist," Landers finally said, gesturing at Carmen.

"I'm thinking Sheldon's not gonna be real happy about her," Holt said, scratching his double chin.

"Maybe not," Landers replied. "But he could use the help. And look at her. What red-blooded man could stay mad in the face of such beauty?"

Though Rick's stomach twisted hearing this, he pretended not to care.

Carmen, however, apparently had heard enough. "I'm right here," she said, her voice clear and hard. "I can hear you, you know."

While Tommy and Holt fidgeted, each appearing embarrassed, Gus simply continued to stare. The hair on the back of Rick's neck lifted. Something was off with that one. He bore watching, in case he turned out to be especially dangerous.

Landers laughed. "True. I'm sorry, sweetheart. I'll try to do better."

"I'm not your sweetheart." Yanking her hand free from Rick's, Carmen pushed to her feet, eyeing them with clear disdain. "I've changed my mind about helping. I don't see anything here that makes me think you could actually pull off engineering something as complicated as a new virus."

Damn. What the hell was she doing? Did she really think these people were going to just let them go? Not likely, especially since they'd now seen their hideout.

"And," she continued, "even if this Sheldon person is some kind of biology genius, I fail to see how you could use something like this to your benefit. Thanks, but no thanks."

Though he had to tamp down his alarm, Rick stood, too. He hoped Carmen knew what she was doing. "Well, the boss has spoken," he drawled, while keeping his eye on the others to gauge their reactions. "I guess this means we're out."

"Not so fast." Landers placed himself squarely between them and the door. "It's too late. You can't quit now. You know where we are and you've seen all of our faces."

Rick decided he'd take a chance. "Maybe so, but none of that matters. We haven't laid eyes on your boss, so I'm thinking we're good to go. If you'd just pay me for the explosion, we can call it even."

Landers narrowed his eyes. "What do you mean, you haven't seen the boss? You've been dealing with me all along."

Unsure whether to laugh or take the other man seriously, Rick realized it would be prudent to play it safe. "You're in charge here?"

Immediately, Landers nodded.

"No, he's not," Carmen put in, her voice cool. "It's the quiet one, Gus. He's the leader here."

Landers froze. Judging by the panicked look he shot Gus, Carmen was right. Good instincts.

"Grab her," Gus ordered, his tone bored though his expression seemed furious. "Put her in my bedroom. It's time she and I had a private, one-on-one chat."

Rick stiffened, ready for whatever might happen next. To his relief, Carmen allowed Landers and Tommy to manhandle her, leading her from the room. The glint in her eyes told Rick she was actually enjoying this.

Rick started after her, but Holt, moving surprisingly fast for such a large man, blocked his way. "You wait with me. The boss will let us know when he's finished."

There was nothing Carmen loved better than taking down a power-hungry idiot who thought he could dominate her. While she knew she had to be careful so she didn't blow this important mission, there was no way in Hades she'd let this Gus person push her around.

His two henchmen shoved her into a large bedroom, dominated by an ornate four-poster bed. She pretended to stumble, but pivoted on her feet, ready to face the leader of the Sons of Darkness. As if. If only they had an idea of what a real son of darkness could be. Silly humans. They had no clue, nor would they ever.

Gus strode into the room and gestured at the other men to leave. Once the door closed behind him, he crossed his arms, his flat gaze hard. "Why are you here?" he demanded.

Since this line of questioning was not at all what she'd

expected, she took a moment to choose her reply. "For money," she said. "As I'm sure you're aware, I was let go from my job."

He continued to glare at her, as if by the force of his gaze he thought he could compel her to be truthful. Such a stunt might work on humans, but since she was a Vampire, she had to suppress the urge to laugh in his face.

"That's what I've been told, but I don't believe it." There was the slightest hint of a challenge in his even tone. "I've looked up your credentials," he continued. "You're one of the top three leading biologists in the United States."

In the world, she thought, but didn't say it. "I didn't believe it, either," she said, her voice sullen. "They accused me of stealing narcotics." Spur of the moment, but she thought it sounded realistic. "Among other things," she added, just in case. "None of it is true. I'm a damn good biologist." After all, she'd had centuries to hone her skills.

Looking her up and down, he grimaced. His flat eyes reminded her of some really ancient Vampires she'd met once. But this one was only human; she could smell the coppery scent of his blood and hear the steady thump of his heart.

As the silence stretched on, he continued to stare at her, no doubt trying to make her uncomfortable, but she refused to allow this. Instead, she stared right back and waited.

"Do you know what we're developing here?" he asked.

This time she didn't have to feign her interest. "Yes. A new virus. I admit, I find that fascinating. I'd love to be part of research like that."

"It's not research," he corrected her. "We plan to use it if we have to. Unless we receive what we want from the US Government."

Now they were on tricky ground. Rick hadn't told her how much of this she was supposed to know. "What do you want?" she asked, even though she already knew the answer.

"War with West Latvia," he immediately said. "I want that country's trade wiped off the map."

"But why?" And this truly was the part she didn't understand. "What are your reasons?"

"Russia." He spoke the name as if saying it should be enough. Still, she waited, not sure what he meant.

He sighed at her lack of reaction. "Russia trades heavily with them. It's a way to buy myself power."

"But why would you want power with Russia?"

This time, he laughed. "How about you just stick to biology? I don't have time to explain the intricate nature of politics to you."

His condescending tone had her clenching her teeth. But she kept her annoyance in check, aware the stakes were far too high for her to blow it on something so trivial.

"Money can buy power," she finally said. "I'm guessing you're aware of how much something like this would fetch on the international market?"

"We're exploring all options." He waved his hand in dismissal. "I can see how someone like you might be valuable to my organization. Your husband, though— I'm not sure I need him."

Alarm prickled along her spine, though she took care to show no reaction. Straightening, she tilted her head and eyed him the way one would look at a particularly noxious rodent. "My husband and I are a team. You can't have me without him."

He laughed. "You're not running things here, sweetheart."

This human was damn lucky she'd had centuries to learn how to control her anger. Even so, she felt that familiar flash of rage and wanted to crush him. Which she easily could, right here and right now, without blinking an eye.

"Again, I'm not your sweetheart," she drawled. "It's me and Rick or neither of us. Now, do we have a deal or not?" Bracing herself for Gus's reaction to her declaration, she knew she had to come up with a quick plan in case he decided to simply kill them. He had no idea he couldn't—the only thing that would end Rick was a silver bullet or fire. As for her, a stake through the heart. Beyond that, they were invincible. They could be hurt, true. But Rick's kind had supernaturally fast healing powers. She couldn't bleed if she hadn't been fed enough blood.

Instead of yet another staring contest, Gus laughed again. She detected a slight note of unease hidden in his pretend mirth. "You're a tough one," he said. "I will agree to take both of you—on one condition."

She nodded.

"No drug use while you're in my employ. Either of you. If I find out you indulged, I will kill you."

Finally, something that actually made sense. "Agreed," she replied. "As long as you leave my husband to me. I will need him at the lab, working as my assistant. He follows my orders really, really well. If he doesn't..." She lifted one shoulder delicately, letting her meaning sink in. "There are consequences to pay."

Chapter 5

Maddie stared up at the man, shocked at first. "How dare you," she said, her expression turning icy. "Do you know who my brother is?"

"Lady, your brother could be the President of the United States for all I care," he responded. "My job is to protect our Pack from discovery. You've been seen with that human who's been snooping around here."

Shaking off his hand, she spoke her brother's name. "Colton Kinslow," she said. "My brother is also a Pack Protector. Why don't you ask him if his sister would ever endanger the Pack?"

He stared at her, his expression still hard. "I'll call him and let him know what's been going on. I expect he'll be phoning you. Just be aware, we have our eyes on Jake Cassel. If we learn you have, in any way, enabled him to gain access to information that is off-limits to humans, you will be arrested and prosecuted to the fullest extent of the law."

Having said that, he turned around and stomped off. Frowning, Maddie watched him go. What the heck had Jake done now? As far as she knew, he'd been caught lurking around Broken Chains and beat up for it. Was there more he hadn't told her?

As if he knew she'd been thinking about him, her cell phone rang and the caller ID showed Jake's number.

"Well, well, Jake Cassel," she answered. "Were your ears ringing?"

"What? Never mind. Just call off your dog."

Perplexed, she wondered if he'd taken too many pain-killers or something. "I'm not sure I follow," she replied. "Maybe you should just lie down and get some rest."

Silence. For some reason, she could picture him dragging his hand through his hair. "Fair enough," he finally said. "I'm guessing you have no idea what I'm talking about."

"None whatsoever." Taking a long sip of her beer, she rolled her shoulders and tried to relax.

"Someone's parked outside my house, watching me. If I get in my car and drive anywhere, I know he'll follow me."

"Really? Have you tried it? How do you know for sure?"

Then she listened while he told her about calling the police and who the person claimed to be. When he got to the part about the stalker returning once the police had left, a shiver snaked up her spine. That and the fact that the Pack Protectors were actively interested in him meant there was more going on than she knew. Much more.

"I'm guessing you haven't told me everything," she said. While she couldn't inform him about the confrontation with the Pack Protector, she knew there had to be more to this than a case of a persistent reporter continually coming down the dead-end alleyway and trying to get Broken Chains' door to open. Other humans had tried in the past to no avail. No one paid them any mind, at least that she knew.

So what was so special about Jake Cassel? She got that he was a reporter, but he had no story. Even if he managed to make it inside Broken Chains—which he wouldn't—all he'd see was a bar with a bunch of people drinking and dancing. Like a private club. A human couldn't tell from looking at someone that they were a Shifter or a Vampire or a Merfolk. That was why all those different species were able to live side by side with humans, undetected.

And Broken Chains belonged to them, the nonhumans. It was their place, one of the few where they could go and relax and simply be themselves.

Sure, she found Jake Cassel attractive. It happened often. Shifters dated humans, Vampires dated Shifters, etc. Heck, her friend Shayla, who happened to be a Mermaid, had just married Zach, a Shifter. She was allowed to date Jake Cassel if she wanted. She wasn't permitted to let him find out her true nature unless they were in a serious, committed relationship.

One thing Maddie Kinslow believed in was following the rules. Though other private investigators might bend them once or twice, her father had raised her differently. He'd proven she could be a great PI without breaking the law. Did the Pack Protectors truly think she'd break Pack law and betray her own kind?

The silence had stretched out for so long she thought he might have hung up. "Jake? Are you there?"

"I am," he answered. "Just thinking. Where are you? Judging from the background noise, I'd guess a bar or restaurant. Do you mind if I join you? I need to get out of the house."

She nearly laughed out loud at the irony of that. "I'm sorry, but I already have plans. I'm meeting a friend. But even if I weren't, I think you really should consider staying in tonight and getting some rest so you can heal. Oh, there she is. I can see her crossing the room right now, so I'd better go. We'll talk later."

Not sounding very happy about that, Jake agreed and hung up.

"Shayla!" Maddie pushed to her feet, grinning from ear to ear. Every single man in the place watched as her stunning Mermaid friend made her way toward their table. With her silky mane of long black hair and her heart-shaped face, Shayla Dover-Cantrell tended to draw masculine attention. Even the large wedding ring on her left hand did little to deter their pursuit. Their other friend, Carmen, had a similar effect on men.

Reaching Maddie, Shayla enveloped her in a hug. "I know it's only been a couple of weeks, but it feels as if I haven't seen you in forever," she said, taking a seat.

"I know. How was the honeymoon?"

For the next several minutes, the two women caught up. Their waiter brought Shayla a glass of chardonnay, her usual beverage of choice, and a second beer for Maddie.

"What's he like, this Jake guy?" Shayla asked, eyeing her friend. "You really seem to like him."

Startled, Maddie had no choice but to laugh. "I do, you know. He's human and stubborn, but he seems to have a good heart. Plus, he's cute."

Her comment brought a grin to Shayla's face. "Too bad on the human part, since he can't come here."

Maddie hesitated, and then decided what the hell. "I

might as well tell you everything," she said. "He wants to hire me. For some reason, he's obsessed with getting inside Broken Chains."

As Maddie explained, Shayla listened, her expression changing from incredulous to dismayed. When Maddie finished up with how the Pack Protector had threatened her, Shayla shook her head. "You need to dump him," she advised. "Jake Cassel might be cute, but I don't think he'd be worth all that trouble."

"But don't you see?" Maddie protested. "He hasn't done anything that other humans haven't done over the years. You know as well as I do that we get at least one per month, wandering down the alley and trying to open the door. Yet he was beat up, probably by Pack Protectors, and left for dead. Now someone is staking out his house. I've clearly been seen with him, and now I'm being threatened. None of this makes sense."

Shayla tilted her head. "You're not going to back off, are you?"

"Of course not," Maddie scoffed. "How could I? You know me. I can't let a puzzle go unsolved, and that's what this is."

Shayla laughed. "Just be careful," she said, taking a sip of her wine.

"Always." Maddie noticed her friend glancing at her watch. "What's up? Is there somewhere you need to be?"

With a sheepish grin, Shayla shrugged. "Not really. I'm just missing Zach."

"You could have brought him. I wouldn't have minded."

"Really? He wanted to come, but I told him it was girls' night. I thought it might be good for us to come up for air." Shayla blushed, leaving no doubt as to what she meant.

Maddie pushed away the twinge of jealousy. "Someday," she told her friend, "I hope to find a guy who makes me feel the way Zach does you."

"Oh, Maddie." Shayla jumped up and hugged her. "You will. Wait." She pulled back, peering into Maddie's face. "Are you thinking Jake might be that guy?"

"Who knows?" Maddie took a drink of her beer to hide her confusion. "I suppose anything is possible. Maybe. Maybe not."

"Gut instinct." Eyes narrowed, Shayla watched her closely. "Let me hear what your gut instinct says."

Because they were such good friends, Maddie gave serious thought to the question. "I'm attracted to him," she finally answered. "Intrigued by him. I don't know how much of that is because of the mystery, though. To be honest, I wouldn't mind having an intense fling with him as well as getting to the truth of why he's considered so dangerous to the Pack. Beyond that?" She shrugged. "I don't know."

Apparently, her answer satisfied Shayla. "Fair enough," Shayla said, raising her wineglass in a toast.

They sat and chatted another hour, each having one more drink, until the band began to play, making conversation difficult. Finally, their glasses were empty and they settled up the tab. Arm in arm, they walked to the door and outside.

At the end of the alley, Shayla stopped. "Now what?" she asked.

"Now I walk you to your car or to get a cab, like always," Maddie replied. As a Mermaid, Shayla couldn't defend herself like a Shifter or Vampire could. Therefore, Maddie or Carmen or both always made sure she was never left unaccompanied.

"Oh, that…" Shayla blushed again, just as an SUV pulled up. "I texted Zach so he'd come and get me."

"That was quick," Maddie said, her tone dry. "Let me say hello to the lovestruck fool and then I'll let you two go on your way."

"Of course. But what are you going to do for the rest of the night? It's still pretty early. Maybe Jake would like some company."

Now it was Maddie's turn to blush. Unfortunately, when she did, she knew her pale skin turned the color of an overripe tomato, not all soft, appealing pink like Shayla's did.

Seeing the blush, Shayla chuckled. "I think you should find out if he would," she said. "Now come say hello to Zach so we can get home."

Maddie walked around to the driver's side and Zach rolled down the window. He tore his gaze away from his new bride long enough to smile at Maddie. "Do you need a lift to your car?" he asked. "I'd be glad to take you."

"Not tonight," she told him, lifting her head and sniffing the air. "With weather like this, I don't mind a walk." And since she was Shifter, she could easily defend herself if someone tried to jump her the way they'd jumped Jake.

Just thinking about him made her blush again. Luckily, Zach and Shayla were too engrossed in each other to notice.

Maddie said her goodbyes and watched as her friends drove away. Then, before she chickened out, she got out her phone and called Jake.

After ending the call with Maddie, Jake looked outside again. The car was still there. He thought about walking outside with a bottle of water and offering it to the driver, but in the end decided against that idea. His bruised and bandaged body and aching ribs warned him to be more careful.

Though he hated to admit it, Maddie was right. He

did need to rest and heal. Instead of giving the stalker something to do, he'd let him sit out there with nothing going on and be bored. At least that made Jake's mood improve. More than anything, he hated to feel as if he were powerless. After the childhood he'd had, he'd sworn never to put himself in that position again.

He pulled out his laptop and continued his research about werewolves. As far as he could tell, they were the stuff of urban legend. Lots of people claimed to have seen one, but there existed absolutely no proof. They were beloved by literature and filmmaking, and these days people seemed to regard them with a kind of benevolent fondness rather than any real fear.

Not for the first time, Jake doubted what he'd seen with his own eyes. Of course, he shouldn't. He was a trained reporter. Observant by both nature and calling. It wasn't likely he'd imagine something like this. Especially since he'd never even thought about werewolves at all until the moment he'd actually seen one.

When his cell phone rang, he almost didn't answer. But when from habit he checked the caller ID and saw it was Maddie, he did.

"Are you still awake?" she asked, a smile in her voice.

His heart skipped a beat. "Of course. What's up?"

"My friend had to go. Since it's still early, I was wondering if you still wanted company? I mean, I could come by if you'd like."

"I'd enjoy that," he responded, not bothering to pretend not to care. "We can talk about the case."

She laughed. "You definitely have a one-track mind. I'm not sure whether to be flattered or insulted."

Was she *flirting* with him? He swallowed, stunned.

"Come on over," he said, his voice as casual as he

could make it. "I've got beer. We can order a pizza if you want."

"Now you're talking. Text me the address again, please. I've got to walk to my car and then I can get on my way."

"Walk to your car?" He hoped it wasn't a long walk. A beautiful woman out walking alone made an easy target for some guy looking for trouble.

"Yep. It's not too far now. Just a couple of blocks. I'm near The Strand, so there are lots of people around."

He rattled off the address and ended the call. She'd said she was near The Strand. Had she been near the dead-end alley with the mysterious door? He resolved to ask her directly. After all, he saw no reason why they should play games.

Twenty minutes later, her headlights swept his front window. He hurried to the door, just in case the guy in the parked car decided to try and confront her. To his surprise, the stalker was gone.

"Hey there!" Smiling, Maddie greeted him. With her wavy red hair loose around her shoulders, she managed to look both innocent and sexy in her black skirt and green top, with a sleeveless back tank underneath. He noticed that even though she wore flat shoes, her legs seemed to go on for miles. As she got closer, a jolt of pure lust punched him low in the gut.

"Come on in," he said, stepping aside. As she walked past him, he got a tantalizing whiff of her perfume, which was floral and light. She took a seat on his couch and eyed his laptop, which he'd left open on the coffee table.

"Just doing some research," he told her. "Nothing too serious. Would you like a beer?"

"I'd better not," she said. "I had two at the bar. Just water for me, please."

When he returned from the kitchen, she was leaning close to his laptop, unabashedly reading what was displayed on the screen.

"Here you go," he said, handing her the water.

"Thank you." She flashed a brief smile before returning her attention back to the computer. "You're reading about *werewolves*?"

Something about her tone didn't ring right. "I am," he answered. "Fascinating topic. Do you know anything at all about them?"

She shook her head. "Only that they don't exist. I thought you were a journalist. I wasn't aware you planned on writing fiction."

"Ouch." Taking a swig from his beer, he sat next to her, close enough that if he moved his leg, they could bump knees. "I'm actually considering writing an exposé, attempting to prove their existence. I just need proof."

Now he knew he hadn't imagined that flash of alarm in her eyes. "That sounds interesting," she replied. But her voice contained little conviction.

"You think I'm nuts, don't you?"

"I mean, think about what you just said. Sounds really crazy."

"Maybe, maybe not," he argued. "But if I can get real proof, nondoctored video, people will have no choice but to believe me."

"I don't think they ever will. It's too far in the realm of myths and legends." She met his gaze, her expression troubled. "And even if werewolves were somehow real, what would be the point of making people aware of them? Can you imagine what kind of hellish reaction that would provoke? It'd be the Middle Ages and the Salem witch trials all rolled up into a modern-day frenzy to exterminate them."

Taken aback by her reaction, he wasn't sure how to respond.

"Our country is already divided enough," she continued. "But then you'd have to lobby for werewolf rights. There wouldn't be peaceful protests, because there'd be too much fear. And here in a state where carrying a gun openly is legal, I can see groups being organized to hunt them down and kill them. And for what? Just because they're different than us? Is that what you really want?"

"Wow," he said, scratching his head. "Where did all of that come from? How did we go from proving the existence of a supposedly mythical creature to worrying about protecting them?"

"Because, Jake, you have to think ahead to the consequences of your actions." Her green eyes were full of passion, and he could see her pulse beating furiously in the hollow of her throat.

"Consequences," he muttered. Though he was sore, though bruised and battered, he reached up and cupped her chin in his hand and kissed her. Slowly and thoroughly, exactly the way he'd been wanting to do since the moment he'd laid eyes on her.

He kissed her until she kissed him back, until she shivered. When her arms came up around his neck and she clung to him as if she wanted more, he gently broke off the kiss. Breathing hard, he let his forehead rest against hers. "You're something else, Maddie Kinslow. I've never met a woman like you."

Her generous lips curved at this, making him ache to kiss her again. Instead, he pushed himself back, putting some distance between them so he could think.

"Would you go to dinner with me sometime?" he asked.

"I don't think that would be a good idea," she answered. "Since you're going to be my client. I try not to mix business with pleasure."

"I'm thinking in our case, that's unavoidable." He smiled when he delivered what he knew to be the truth. "Look at how great we are together. Just a simple little kiss…"

"I'm thinking we shouldn't kiss again," she said. The lack of regret in her voice warred with her uncertain expression and her immediate blush. "That would be a simple rule to follow."

"Maybe," he allowed. "As long as I don't look at you, or touch you, or catch a whiff of your perfume."

The hitch in her breath told him how his words affected her. She swallowed, her eyes huge, her pupils dilated. "You make us getting together sound inevitable."

"Eventually. I'm confident of that. Not right now, when I can barely move my chest and stomach without pain. But someday, once I'm healed. Sooner rather than later."

Was that disappointment in her gaze?

"Since we're apparently being candid," she said, "you should know I find your confidence really sexy."

Damn. Another jolt of lust hit him. His body responded immediately and decisively. "And there you have it. Proof. When we do come together, it's going to be gasoline on a flame."

She flushed again. "Okay, I'll take your word for it. But right now, let's talk business. I sent you The Shadow Agency's rates. What do you think?"

"I want to hire you. But honestly, not if my doing so will come between you and me getting together."

"Oh, it definitely will." Even her quiet chuckle struck him as sexy. "So, what you have to decide is if you can be patient enough to wait until the investigation is finished."

Surprised, he considered her. "Knowing what you now do, are you still willing to help me investigate?"

"I think so. Are you still fixated on that door and that dead-end alley where I found you, or have you moved on to somehow proving the existence of werewolves?"

"Both," he answered promptly. "I think the two are tied together."

Rolling her eyes, she groaned. "Are you serious?"

"Yes, I am. I've been doing investigative reporting a long time. I've got a gut feeling that I'm on to something. And I've learned to trust my gut."

"You're not afraid of ridicule? It will happen if you continue to pursue this werewolf thing." Back straight, hands folded in her lap, she studied him.

"I have my reasons." He hesitated. "I'll go ahead and tell you, just so you understand. I don't want you to think I'm crazy, but I know what I saw." He took a deep breath. "After I became interested in that door, I started watching the alley. People went in and didn't come out for hours. Some of them stayed all night."

None of this seemed to surprise her. But then again, he reminded himself, she'd actually been one of those people he'd seen going in through that door. She knew more than she was letting on.

She didn't react when he pointed that out to her. "I can promise you that what's behind that door is infinitely less interesting than you think it is. It's a club, a private club. With drinks and music, just like any other bar. Except only members are allowed. Which is why I can go inside. I'm a member. Nothing nefarious is going on, I promise. You've been wasting your time."

"Have I? Then tell me why those two guys beat the crap out of me in that alley?"

"Who knows? Drunk bullies have been known to do

such horrible things outside bars all over the country. They might not have liked the way you looked at them, or—"

"Or my skin color," he interrupted. "I admit the possibility of it being racially motivated occurred to me. But I don't think so. They didn't call me names and the entire time, it seemed clear from the way they attacked me that it wasn't personal. More like they were defending something instead of lashing out."

"You really are observant," she mused. "If you're correct, then why do you think they attacked you?"

"To warn me away. Somehow, they figured out I've been watching them."

"Okay, even if I buy that explanation—which I don't— it doesn't make sense. There's a bar behind that door. Nothing more, nothing less. A private party place for members to go."

"I don't believe you," he said.

Hurt flashed across her mobile face. "Then I guess it's best if I go."

"Wait." Though he'd told himself he wouldn't touch her again, he grabbed her arm. "I have a good reason for saying that."

"For calling me a liar?" She shook off his hand. "Let's hear it."

"I've seen something," he told her, hoping she'd believe him. "I've spent a lot of time watching that alley and seeing people come and go. One night around three a.m., I saw a group of men leaving. They seemed drunk, which lends credence to your claim. They were pushing each other around, loud horseplay, like young guys do."

Crossing her arms, she watched him. "Go on."

"They'd gotten loud enough to cause a disturbance or, at the very least, attract notice to the place. So a big guy—must have been a bouncer—came out and told them to shut it down. That's when it happened." He took a deep breath, not sure how she'd take what he had to say next.

"One of the young guys changed into a wolf and tried to attack the bouncer. The other two had to pull him off."

Chapter 6

Rick knew in his role as pretend human husband, he needed to act at least slightly upset that Gus had not only taken Carmen to his bedroom, but that they'd stayed so long. Truth be told, he actually did feel a twinge of something—maybe even jealousy. Had playing the fantasy messed with his head? When the two of them finally emerged, he narrowed his eyes. "What were you two doing in there?" he asked, making his voice heavy with suspicion and crossing his arms.

Gus turned away from him, clearly not wanting to quibble. Rick let him go, focusing instead on the beautiful Vampire. "Well?" he demanded.

Expression grim, Carmen only shook her head. "Nothing untoward. We were discussing the terms of my employment," she said. "Needless to stay, we both had differing ideas. But we finally reached an agreement. Now I'm eager to get to work."

"Terms?" he asked, his gaze sliding from her to Gus. "I thought we'd already settled all that."

"No. We hadn't." Gus wasn't smiling, either. Whatever discussion that had taken place between him and Carmen must have been a doozy. But, judging from the way Gus was acting, it appeared Carmen had won. Good.

Then Carmen took Rick's arm and peered earnestly up into his face. "No drugs," she said, imploring.

"What?" He wasn't sure he'd heard her correctly.

"That's part of the deal," she continued, trailing one scarlet-tipped finger down his chest. "Neither one of us can use drugs while working on this project."

Ah. Now he got it. He'd need to tell her later that her acting skills were superb.

For the sake of their audience, he pretended disappointment. "Not even—"

"Nothing," she cut him off. "Or this deal's off. Got it?" Again she used her nail, trailing it up the side of his throat, making him actually shiver. "Don't make me have to punish you."

Punish him? That actually sounded interesting.

Fighting through an unexpected haze of arousal, he nodded slowly. He wasn't entirely sure what Carmen was up to, but he clearly had no choice except to go with it.

Watching them, Gus laughed. "You'll survive," he said, his good humor clearly restored. "I'll even allow the occasional alcoholic beverage. But nothing else. No pills, no needles, no smokes. Got it?"

Rick and Carmen nodded in unison. Rick kept his face expressionless while he worked furiously to get his body under control. He couldn't believe she'd made him hard with just a touch of her fingernail and a few drawled words. Damn.

"Good. Come on." Landers motioned for them to follow him. "I'll show you where you'll be staying for the duration."

Staying on premises? Not good. Rick cursed under his breath, realizing he should have thought of this.

Next to him, even Carmen tensed. Vampires didn't like to be confined, so this would be even worse on her. Especially if Landers put them in a room near his, where he could keep an eye on them at all times.

To his relief, Landers led them out the back door. "We have a small guesthouse set up for your use," he said, winking at Rick. "All our on-site employees have them. We prefer to keep you where we can see you, you know. Plus, the individual structure gives you two some privacy to indulge your little role-playing games or whatever."

Unable to bring himself to wink back, Rick nodded. "Thanks," he said. "We appreciate that."

And then he caught sight of the "guesthouses." Landers had stretched the meaning of the term to describe these. Several tiny buildings the size of storage sheds had been set up on the expansive property. They were at the most twelve by fourteen, made of wood, with a door and one window. For whatever reason, each had been painted a different color. There were yellow, green, red, blue, brown, white, and black.

Landers stopped at the yellow one that sat closest to the main house. "It's not big, but it has everything you need," he said as he unlocked the door. "Come take a look."

Rick and Carmen exchanged a glance as they followed him inside. He flipped a switch and stepped back, gesturing grandly. "See? All the comforts of home."

He wasn't kidding. Somehow, they'd managed to cram a miniscule kitchenette with a miniature two-seater table, a living area with a small love seat and a TV hung on the wall, and a tiny bathroom with sink, toilet and stand-up shower inside the roughly 168-square-foot building. Talk about a tiny house.

"Wait," Carmen said. "There's no bed. And there's not room on that couch for one person to sleep, never mind two."

"Oh, we thought of that." Grinning proudly, Landers gestured at a wooden wall. "You'll have to push the kitchen table out of the way, but there's a Murphy bed. It pulls down for you to sleep on it and goes back up once you're awake. Perfect space-saver."

One bed. Rick could read the dismay in Carmen's eyes, even as his body practically thrummed. He'd tell her later that he'd sleep on the couch. Unless she, as a Vamp, needed other arrangements. He realized he'd never really considered where or how the undead slept.

On top of that, he knew she'd need a steady supply of blood for nourishment. How the hell would she get that if she was being watched 24/7? He'd have to hope she could figure out a way. She was a Vampire, so no doubt she would.

"This will do," Carmen said, nodding at Landers. "When do I start work?"

"Tomorrow morning, at 0600 hours."

She nodded. If she found it at all odd that she'd be starting work before the sun even rose, she didn't show it.

Finally, Landers left.

"Come here," Carmen ordered, standing and holding out her arms. Heart thumping, he stepped into her embrace, instantly hard and ready. She leaned close, her breath tickling his ear. "They're probably watching and listening to us," she whispered, pressing herself so close to him that he knew she had to be aware of his arousal. "So this is the only way I can tell you what went on in there. They think we're drug addicts. Oh, and also that we're into S and M. I'm the dominant and you're the submissive."

"What?" He reared back, too shocked to think straight. When he realized what he'd done, he wrapped her in his arms and pressed his swollen body against her. Her swift intake of breath was a satisfying reaction. Two could play this game. "Why the hell would you say something like that?"

She smiled, a slow, sensual smile. "To make things interesting, of course. In reality, I needed a way to be able to come and go as I pleased, plus protect you." She licked his earlobe, which made him start slightly. "You may not realize this, but I'm valuable to them. Gus wanted to kill you. By assuring him that I had you firmly in hand, I was able to guarantee your safety."

He wanted to tell her he could take care of himself, or that such elaborate subterfuge was completely unnecessary. But she kept shifting her body, putting friction and pressure on his swollen anatomy, and he could scarcely think beyond the red haze of desire.

What the freakin' hell?

Finally, she released him. Her savage grin told him she knew of his discomfort. "I already informed Gus that I need you to assist me in the laboratory," she pronounced. "He agreed. I said I'd work much better if I'm not distracted by worry about you."

Begrudgingly, he had to admit she had a good plan. At least, that part of it. But there was one thing he felt he needed to make perfectly clear.

Snagging her arm, he pulled her up against him. "Why do you think I'm going to let you be in charge?" he murmured into her ear. Then, telling himself he only wanted to prove a point, he covered her mouth with his, hard and punishing.

She gave back as good as she got, standing her ground. The instant she opened her mouth, giving his tongue access, he realized he'd made a major mistake. She took, he gave, until he found himself so caught up in the taste and feel of her that he spiraled out of control.

Worse, he didn't care. He wanted, he craved, and with his hands tangled up in her hair, he would have given anything to push himself up inside her.

She laughed, letting him know she knew. "Not now," she murmured, her unsteady voice telling him she wasn't as unaffected as he'd thought.

In fact, the desire blazing from her heavy-lidded eyes came close to matching his own. "Checkmate," he said.

To his surprise, she nodded. "We'll need to tend to this fire before it gets out of control."

"I agree." With a savage ruthlessness, he turned and worked at getting himself back together. It had been a long time since a woman had aroused him so strongly. The fact that this woman also happened to be a Vampire shocked him.

His inner wolf, now fully awake and restless, paced and whined. Rick had to spend a few extra moments calming that aspect of himself, as well.

Behind him, Carmen waited silently. Rick sure as hell hoped she was having to pull herself together, too. If not, he definitely needed to up his game. No way did he intend to allow her to have the upper hand. No way at all.

Finally, he turned to face her. "What now?" he asked.

"I think we should go for a walk and explore the grounds," she said, using a normal voice. "I'd like to check out the landscape of where we're going to be living while working here."

"Sounds like a good idea." He held out his hand. When she slipped her slender fingers into his, he resisted the urge to tug her close. This would never work. He was good at his job, damn good. He refused to let lust be this big of a distraction. As soon as possible, they'd deal with it and get it out of their systems. Things would surely go back to normal after that.

Either way, he knew he'd enjoy finding out.

Damn that Shifter. Though smiling on the outside, Carmen fumed. She'd planned on having the upper hand, using her considerable sexual prowess to beguile and ensnare Rick Fallin. He might be a covert intelligence operative, he might work for the Pack Protectors, or both, but in the end, he was male. When she set her sights on a man, she knew exactly how to reel him in.

Except when she tried it on Rick, she found herself wanting him with an intensity that had shaken her to the core. Actually, she'd come perilously close to losing self-control. Talk about backfiring.

Maybe she'd simply gone too long without taking a lover. That had to be it. Which meant the solution was a simple one. She and Rick needed to have at each other, let loose the desire, and surely both of them would find their clarity of focus restored.

She would have done it right then in their small cabin, but she didn't want them to be on camera for anyone and everyone to view. And while she hadn't taken the time to search for any recording devices, she felt quite certain there were some. An operation as sensitive as this one wouldn't take chances with their assets.

Hand in hand, they walked outside. Rick leaned close and put his mouth against her ear, again sending a shiver of longing down her spine. "I feel confident this entire place is under heavy surveillance," he murmured. "Just so you know."

She nodded, her mouth suddenly dry. She couldn't tell when the tables had turned, and truly didn't understand why. For most of her long, long life, she'd used sex to control men. She hadn't really thought it would be any different with this one.

Until it was. Now she had two intriguing mysteries to investigate. The science of the new virus and Rick Fallin.

Both promised to be equally pleasurable. For the first time in decades, anticipation filled her.

As they strolled around the huge yard, they passed several other small sheds just like the one they'd been given to occupy. If any of these had inhabitants, no one came out to greet them.

Though at first walking around holding hands with Rick felt odd, eventually she began to relax. They had roles to play, after all, and role-playing happened to be one of her specialties.

Finally, they went past the last of the sheds. Careful to avoid the barn/laboratory, they continued on to where the mowed grassy area ended and the forest began. No one stopped them or confronted them.

"Do you still think they're watching us?" she asked. They'd ducked into the trees and walked to the edge of a fast-moving stream.

He frowned. "I'm not sure. It doesn't seem reasonable, but I don't understand why no one is making sure we don't simply continue walking until we're gone."

"Maybe we're not prisoners," she said.

"Hmph," he snorted. "I imagine security will be a lot tighter once you see what's inside their lab. There's no way they can risk you taking off and selling your information to the highest bidder."

"True." Contemplating pulling her hand free from his, she let it stay. There was something comforting in his touch. While she'd never been one to seek the softness of such coddling, she found she liked it too much to let it go just yet.

"Tomorrow is going to be a big day," he said, still keeping his voice low. "I'm wondering if once you get in there and start working with this virus, you can find a way to disable it."

Since she knew he had no idea how biology worked, she took pity on him. "Clearly, at least from what you've told me, it's already been developed and used. I'd have much better luck finding an antidote."

"That would be helpful, too." Facing her, he smiled. "I should let you know I have several concerns with how this is playing out so far."

She shrugged. "Don't worry about it. I'll try not to boss you around too much. Remember, like you told me, it's all for show."

"That's not what I'm worried about." His smile faded and his gaze darkened. "Think about it. As you pointed out just now, they already have their virus. What do they need an additional biologist for? What exactly are they going to ask you to do?"

"That's a valid question." Again, her anticipation was so strong it almost felt sexual. "Whatever it is, this is right in my wheelhouse. Someone like me could work for years without ever coming across something like this. It's fascinating. Honestly, I can't wait to report to work in the morning."

"You really mean that, don't you?" His serious tone matched the gravity of his expression. "This is really something you want to do."

"It is," she told him. "This is what I've worked for,

studied for, reinvented myself for. When I moved to Texas, I went back to school for this advanced degree. I did unpaid internships, whatever it took to increase my knowledge."

Wondering why she felt compelled to share all this, she took a deep breath and continued. "Eventually, I planned to work for the CDC in Atlanta. But since we Vampires live so long, when I met Shayla and Maddie, I decided it wouldn't hurt me to live in Galveston for a few more years. The one thing I have an overabundance of is time."

"I see." He squeezed her hand, his expression thoughtful. "You love your work."

"Yes."

"That's one thing we have in common, then. I love my job, too."

Since she'd just spilled her guts, she probed for him to reveal more. "What is it you do, exactly?"

When he didn't immediately respond, she nudged him with her hip. "Come on, you can tell me. We're partners, remember?"

Gazing down at her, he finally nodded. "I work two jobs in one. With humans, I'm in a specialized division of the FBI. One so covert, on paper it doesn't exist. With my own kind, I'm a Pack Protector. I'm sworn to uphold the safety of the Pack. They were thrilled when I got my other job. They like to have operatives right in the thick of things."

"I'm guessing if I ask you to tell me about what a regular day in your life is like, you're not going to do it."

A ghost of a smile flitted around his mouth. "Probably not," he admitted. "Actually, you'd be surprised at how boring it can be sometimes. Just routine paper pushing."

Skeptical, she smiled back. "I don't believe you."

The sound of shouting came from the direction they'd

left. As they both turned, several gunshots rang out. After that, silence.

"What the…" Rick tugged her hand. "Come on, let's get back. That didn't sound good."

As soon as they left the shelter of the trees, they started running. In a clearing between two of the little sheds, several people stood in a small circle. As Carmen and Rick drew closer, they saw one person on the ground.

The scent of blood drifted as they approached, making Carmen's fangs ache. She kept her mouth closed, holding on to Rick's hand so tightly he had to shake his slightly to make her let up.

"What's going on?" Rick demanded. "Where's Gus?"

"None of your business," Landers snarled. Brandishing a pistol, he waved it at the man on the ground, who wasn't moving. "Damn fool tried to blackmail us."

Several of the other men muttered, too low to hear their words, but no one confronted Landers. After all, he was the one holding a weapon.

At that moment, Gus strode out the back door of the house. "What's going on out here?" He paled when he noticed the man lying in a pool of blood.

"Sheldon was trying to blackmail us," Landers repeated. "He was carrying glass vials of his virus, said it had gone too far and he wanted the CDC to see them so they could work on an antidote."

Eyes bugging from his face, Gus pointed at him. "Where are the vials now?"

"Underneath him," Landers replied. Then, as he realized the implications of this, he swayed. "I'm not sure if they broke or not."

At his words, everyone else started backing away.

"Put away the gun, Landers," Gus ordered. "We've got way bigger problems to worry about."

Carmen finally spoke. "Everyone freeze. No one move. This virus. Is it airborne or must there be contact?"

Every single man turned to look at Gus. "I'm not sure," he allowed. "Sheldon handled all that."

Since she wasn't supposed to know that they'd already used it on someone in Houston, she thought fast. "Did you use any people as test subjects? If so, how were they infected?"

Gus swallowed again. Instead of answering, he turned on Landers. "This is all your fault, you dumb ass. We're right in the middle of the operation. Roscoe is going to be so mad."

"Even worse," one of the other men said, "is if this virus kills us all. Then what Roscoe thinks ain't gonna matter."

At the mention of the virus, several of them again started backing away. This time, Gus barked out the order for them to stay put. "If we're already infected, running away is not going to help. It'll just spread it."

"Again, I need to know how this virus is spread," Carmen interjected, her voice cool and steady. "Air or touch?"

This time Gus looked at her, his gaze hard and assessing. "The last guy who died from it had a dose put into his drink."

She nodded. "If that's the case, it's probably not airborne. Therefore, none of you should be in any danger."

One of the men cried out, falling to his knees. "Thank you, Lord." The others all wore similar expressions of relief.

"We need to dispose of the body," Gus said.

"I wouldn't touch him," Carmen replied. "If those vials are crushed under him, whoever moves him will be exposed to the virus."

Gus nodded, eyeing her with newfound respect. "What do you suggest?" he asked.

"It'll have to be controlled, as if working with the virus in a laboratory," Carmen replied. "I'll handle it, if you'd like."

"I would." Gus looked from her to Rick and back again. "Once you have, clean up and report back to me. Since this unfortunate incident, your job duties have changed. The man Landers just killed, Sheldon, was the creator of the virus. You're going to have to take over from here."

Unfazed, she nodded. "Well then, I sure hope he left detailed notes." Though sorry for the human's death, inside she was delighted at the change in circumstances. She'd have complete and utter control over the laboratory. And with no other biologist working with her, no one would have any idea whether she was working on an antidote or something else.

"What do you want to do with the body?" she asked Gus.

Something akin to respect flashed in his eyes. "Burn it. Less chance of contamination," he replied.

"All right. I'll need gloves, bleach, a large tarp and more vials," she told Gus. "Plus some gasoline or lighter fluid. Will you send someone to fetch this stuff for me? If not, I can go search the lab myself, but since I have no idea where anything is kept…"

"Tommy, bring the lady what she asked for. Everyone else, back to work," Gus ordered. "Except you, Landers. You're coming with me. If we have to explain to Roscoe what happened, you're going to have to do it. So you'd better start thinking about it, because if he doesn't like what you have to say, you're a dead man."

Once everyone had dispersed and they were alone

again, Carmen eyed the human body and sighed. "Poor guy. All that wasted blood," she said. "And on top of that, if this man really did create a new virus strain, he was a freaking genius. It's a shame his life had to end this way."

Rick nodded. "I agree. That Landers seems a little trigger-happy. He's one we need to watch out for."

Studying the situation, she nodded. About to ask him if he had any idea who this Roscoe person might be, she remembered the possibility of cameras and decided to wait until later. One thing at a time. Dispose of the body, catalog whatever vials of virus were still intact, and then figure out where to go from here.

"How safe is it for you to move Sheldon?" Rick asked. "I know you'll be okay, but what about me? If those vials are shattered—"

"According to what they said, you'd actually have to touch or drink the stuff to get infected. But just in case, maybe you should stand back, too."

He stared at her. She swore she could see his inner struggle. He didn't want to let a woman do such a horrible job alone, yet no one knew yet if the virus could kill a Shape-shifter.

"You forget I'm superstrong," she said softly. "In the interest of safety, I don't want you anywhere near this guy when I move him, okay?"

Their gazes locked. Finally, appearing reluctant, he nodded. "I don't like it, but you're right."

Tommy returned a moment later with everything she'd asked for. Shooting her a plainly hostile glare, he set it on the grass nearby and hurried back into the house.

After putting on the gloves, Carmen spread out the tarp, rolled poor Sheldon onto it and got busy cleaning up the mess. Luckily for everyone, all of the vials appeared to be intact.

Chapter 7

Jake's words hit Maddie like a punch in the stomach. This was worse than she'd imagined. Far worse.

"Let me get this straight," she said, hoping she sounded relatively normal. "You think you actually saw a man change into a wolf?"

"Yes." There was not a shred of doubt in his voice. "Not think. I really did."

Crossing her arms, she tried to calm her racing heart. "How much had you had to drink?"

"Nothing. Coffee is all I drink when I'm on stakeout."

Stakeout. Crud. If the Pack Protectors were to learn about this, they'd take Jake away for what they called reprogramming. While she wasn't sure what exactly that entailed, she knew it involved some form of brainwashing.

And then they'd try to locate the Shifter who'd been foolish enough to risk the discovery of their entire species. His punishment would also be severe.

"You do realize how crazy that sounds, right?" She kept her voice gentle.

He shrugged. "I don't care. If there are actual werewolves walking around among us, people need to know."

Once again, she had to tamp down the urge to argue, to explain what kind of chaos would ensue if people believed this. Her own kind, her *people* would be exposed and their lives placed at risk. Maybe she should wash her hands of this and call her brother, let the Pack Protectors take care of the problem.

Except she liked Jake. More than she should. In fact, the intense level of her attraction to him had once again resurrected her old hope that she wouldn't always be alone. That she might have found that special someone. *Mates*, her kind called them. Members of the Pack believed firmly that everyone had a true soul mate, someone who had been placed on this earth specifically to join with them.

Sometimes, when she looked deep in Jake's velvety brown eyes, she wondered if he might be hers.

Fool. It was way too soon to tell. And she refused to squander the possibility, especially when she thought she could convince Jake to give up on his desire to out her own kind. If she could figure out a way to make him believe it had been some sort of magic trick, sleight of hand, change in lighting and costume. All said, such a thing would make much more sense to a human than a werewolf. She shuddered internally at that word. Shapeshifters despised being called werewolves. It was considered insulting, reducing their complicated natures to nothing more than base instincts and superstition. Of course, Jake had no way of knowing that, nor could she explain. If they ever became serious, true mates, then she'd reveal her true nature, trusting that he'd love her enough to understand.

Love. Not yet. But perhaps. The possibility shimmered before her, a bright hope for the future.

She had to give them a chance. Maybe she could be a big enough distraction to cause him to lose focus. Because the alternative—Jake having his memory wiped clean—would mean he wouldn't remember her, either. They'd be over before they even got a chance to begin.

While she'd been lost in thought, he'd started pacing. "I know you probably think I'm crazy, but I haven't gotten to be an award-winning journalist by ignoring my instincts. I truly believe this could be the story of the century."

"Or you could lose any journalistic credibility you might have," she pointed out. "Look, I'm not trying to be harsh, but listen to yourself."

"I know what I saw." Judging from the stubborn set of his jaw, he wasn't going to budge on this. "If I can just get some video or even a few still shots…"

Before replying, she shook her head. "No one would believe it was real. They'd think you doctored the video. Have you considered that possibility? That what you think you saw was some magic trick or something? Involving a costume and just the right lighting."

Expression incredulous, he stared. "Not possible. You weren't there. This guy dropped to all fours. There were a bunch of sparkling lights, like fireflies, swirling around him. When the lights dissipated, his clothes were tattered and a huge, shaggy wolf stood where he'd been. It was unreal."

Whoa. Her heart sank even more. He'd just described exactly what happened when her kind shifted. She went on the immediate attack. "That sounds even crazier.

Sparkling lights? Maybe whoever used lights masked the switch. For all you know, someone was filming that thing. It could have all been an elaborate production, of which you were an unknown observer."

For the first time since introducing the subject, doubt flashed across his face. "I thought of that," he said. "I've already asked around to see if someone was shooting a movie, even a small independent film. I thought that would go a long way to explaining everything I saw."

Her momentary flash of triumph went up in smoke. "I take it you didn't find anything?"

"Nope. Not even a whisper. And you know how those film people are. Any media coverage is good coverage." He met and held her gaze. "Plus, they would have been members of whatever club you say is behind that door. They went in. They came out. Maddie, I'm an investigative reporter. It's natural that I'd try to explore every potential angle rather than immediately settling on the most difficult."

"Of course," she murmured. Still, she thought it couldn't hurt if she got someone to put out a fake story about filming a werewolf flick, even after the fact. At the very least, it would provide her with a better basis for arguing against Jake's confidence in what he'd seen.

"Anyway, whether you want to believe it or not, that's where I'm going to need your help. Surveillance. With two of us working on this, we have double the chance of catching it on film."

Seriously? "Nope. That's not going to happen," she said. "I'm sorry. But I withdraw my offer of assistance. I can't work with you. You originally asked me to help you find out what's behind the door and I did. I told you the truth. But this? Werewolves in Galveston? No. The Shadow Agency has a reputation to uphold."

He swallowed, looking down. "Those are all valid points. Maybe you're right. Perhaps I should rethink this idea."

Though she didn't know him well yet, she understood him enough to guess he didn't mean a word of his last few sentences. He had no intention of giving up on his quest. He just didn't want her getting in his way.

Which of course was exactly what she'd have to do. She just needed to figure out a plan. Otherwise, the next time the Pack Protectors got ahold of him, he'd lose his memory.

Why did everything have to be so hard? Just once, why couldn't she meet an attractive man, go out on a date or two, have amazing sex and have a normal relationship?

"I think reconsideration is a good idea," she told him, aching. "In fact, I hope you do. I'd really like to see you again. But if you keep on with all this insane werewolf talk, I don't know that I can."

Their gazes locked. Her breath came faster. She could feel her entire body yearning for him, craving his touch, his kiss. She looked down, afraid of what her eyes would reveal.

"How about this?" he asked, coming to stand right in front of her. "Please. Look at me, Maddie."

She raised her gaze to his. Again, her heart skipped a beat. She didn't understand how it could be possible to desire a man she'd just met as much as she did. What if he didn't feel the same way?

But the warmth glowing in his brown eyes hinted that he did. "Don't give up on me."

"I…"

"How about I prove my theory to you?" he said, his expression intense. "If I can do that, will you help me prove it to the world?"

More than anything, she wanted to say yes. But she couldn't bring herself to outright lie. She knew if, by some miracle, he was able to gather enough information to actually prove he'd seen someone shape-shift, she'd have no choice but to call her brother or one of the other Pack Protectors.

Betraying him would be a thousand times worse if they got involved.

The truth of what she knew she must do felt like a knife stabbing straight into her heart. She had to give him up, cut all ties. And then, if he continued on this dangerous path, she'd have to report him to the Pack Protectors. For the safety of her people.

But first, she thought she'd be allowed one indulgence. Just once, she wanted to make love with this amazing, beautiful man. One time, with him moving deep inside her body, holding her close with those strong arms.

She'd have to wait until after he'd healed, of course. But she'd give herself one night of lovemaking with Jake before breaking things off.

"You know what?" She pushed to her feet, wrapping her arms carefully around his neck, mindful of his bruises. "I'd really rather our relationship be personal rather than business anyway. You do your thing and I'll do mine. We won't talk about this werewolf stuff anymore."

His gaze darkened. "Personal sounds good."

Right before he kissed her, she felt a twinge of unease, wondering if she'd be strong enough to do what needed to be done when the time came. But the instant he covered her mouth with his, her doubt vanished.

This was what she'd waited for her entire life. She'd never known a man like him. His touch, the press of his mouth on hers, and she went up in flames.

She leaned into the kiss, into him, careful of his battered rib cage. She would have given much to have met this man under different circumstances.

"Nice try," he said against her mouth, grinning. "I have to admit, you're really good at distracting me."

She grinned back. "I like you," she told him, surprising herself. "A lot."

"Ditto. I think we should go out sometime. Like for drinks."

Drinks and sex, she thought, though of course she kept that to herself. One time and one time only.

"Sounds good." It took a lot of effort for her to sound casual. "Once you're feeling better, let's make plans."

"Soon, then?" A glint of mischief flashed in his eyes. "Like tomorrow? I'm sure I'll feel much better after a good night's rest."

"Will you?"

"Definitely."

Pleased that he seemed as eager as she felt, she smiled. "You just let me know when you're ready." In fact, it might just be the shortest date on record. A glass of wine and then they'd head to his place and go straight to the good part. A buzz of pleasant anticipation filled her.

"I will," he said. "I know exactly where I want us to go. Since you're a member, I'd like to visit that bar you told me about. The one behind the secret door. Surely members are allowed to bring guests."

Poof. Just like that, her giddy mood vanished. "We'll see," she said, unable to hide her disappointment. "I'd hoped we could move on beyond all that. Maybe start over, as if running into each other in the alley never happened."

"You don't want to go to that bar."

Throat aching, she shook her head.

"Hey." Hand under her chin, he raised her face to him. "I'm guessing you can't."

She took a deep breath. "No. Only members are allowed." If only he knew.

"What does one have to do to become a member?" he asked. "Unless it involves shelling out thousands of dollars, I'll do whatever it takes."

Since she couldn't tell him the truth, that one had to be born a Shape-shifter or Merfolk, or made into a Vampire, she could only shake her head. "And here we are again, with me stuck between a rock and a hard place."

Releasing her, he narrowed his eyes. "You can't even tell me the criteria of becoming a member?"

She sighed. Best to stick as close to the truth as possible. "It's sort of based on lineage. You have to be born into a certain family."

"You're kidding me, right? You're saying membership in a bar situated behind a beat-up old door on a dead-end alley surrounded by a bunch of run-down, abandoned warehouses in Galveston, Texas, is based on heritage, like some highbrow country club?"

"Yes." Gathering her things, she got ready to go. "I shouldn't have come here. This was a mistake. It's been nice knowing you." Her throat clogged up. Horrified, she hurried to the door. Damned if she would let him see her cry over something so silly as the loss of a potential relationship that had died before it could really even begin.

He let her go. At least, he followed her to the front door, but he didn't try to stop her or even walk her to her car.

The other vehicle was parked across the street from his house.

As Maddie headed toward her car, the other vehicle's

driver's-side door opened and a man got out. Under the glow of the streetlight, she could make out his features. A jolt of recognition had her hurrying to get into her car. Jake's stalker was the same Pack Protector who'd accosted her inside Broken Chains earlier.

Watching Maddie leave, Jake caught his breath when he realized the man stalking him got out of his car as she walked down the front walk. If that guy even made a move toward her, Jake would have to do whatever he could in order to stop him.

He grabbed the baseball bat he kept in his hall closet and returned to the front step. Since he didn't own a gun, the bat was the best he could do. At least he could use it to buy enough time for Maddie to get away.

Glancing at the other man, who remained by his car, standing partly in shadow, Maddie quickly got in her own vehicle and started the engine. As she backed out of Jake's driveway, her headlights illuminated the other car. She drove away. The man still stood there, swiveling his head to stare directly at Jake.

"What do you want?" Jake shouted, still clutching the bat.

Instead of answering, the man got in his car and hurriedly drove away, traveling in the same direction as Maddie.

Dammit. That creep was following Maddie. He had to warn her. Closing his front door, Jake dug out his cell phone and called her number, praying he'd catch her.

But she didn't answer. Immediately he tried again, cursing under his breath. This time, he went straight to voice mail, which could mean she deliberately wasn't taking his call.

Despite this, he tried a third time. When she finally

picked up, he didn't waste time on pleasantries. He told her what he suspected. "I think he's following you."

"That's possible." She didn't sound surprised or even alarmed. "There are headlights right behind me."

Suddenly suspicious, he took a deep breath. "Maddie, do you know that guy? Is he your boyfriend or your ex?" Or worse, her husband? After all, how much did he really know about Maddie? Not a whole hell of a lot.

"I don't know him. Not personally," she answered. "And I don't have a boyfriend or an ex. But I have seen that guy before. Don't worry, I'll deal with it."

"You can't go home," he warned her, hating the fact that right now, he was completely powerless to help her. "Drive to the police station, or some other public, well-lit place. I have no idea what he's after. I never suspected he wanted you rather than me."

"I don't think he does." Her enigmatic reply started his imagination again. "But I'm guessing I'm about to find out," she continued.

"What are you going to do?" He prayed she wouldn't try anything foolish. She was a short, small-boned woman and from what he'd been able to see of the stalker, that guy had both height and breadth. If he was crazy enough to follow a woman, who knew what else he might do?

"I'm going to have to let you go," she said, her calm voice at stark odds with his heartbeat hammering in his chest. "I'll call you when I'm home safely."

"Don't hang up," he urged. "At least leave your phone on so I can hear."

But he quickly realized he was only speaking to dead air. Maddie had already ended the call.

The next several minutes moved slowly and felt like an eternity. Jake hated being this powerless. The pain pill he'd reluctantly taken earlier made him feel woozy and dizzy, and he sure as hell figured he'd better not drive.

Yet what kind of man would he be if he left sweet Maddie alone to deal with that stalker? Debating, he realized he actually had no idea where Maddie lived.

He didn't even know whether she'd turned left or right after she'd left his street.

Still, he couldn't sit here and do nothing. Pain pill be damned. He had to at least try.

On his way to locate his car keys, the room spun and he had to sit down. Dammit. Masculine pride aside, he was in no condition to drive—he could potentially harm others.

Maddie was smart, he told himself. She wouldn't do anything foolish or put herself at risk.

When his phone rang twenty minutes later, he had to take a deep breath before answering.

"I'm home," she said, sounding cheerful. "Thanks for worrying about me."

"What happened?" he asked, keeping his voice level and calm. "Did you confront the guy?"

"No. I didn't see the need to. Instead, I just drove around. Went down the Seawall, which is still packed with tourists. Once I was absolutely positive that I lost him, I came home."

"That's a relief."

"It is," she agreed. "Now, if you don't mind, I'd like to get off the phone and chill for the rest of the night. And I saw how that pain pill affected you, so you probably could use some shut-eye, too."

"Where do you live?" He blurted out the question, wincing slightly as he did.

He could hear the laughter in her voice when she answered. "On Galveston Island," she said. "I wasn't Born On Island, but I got here as quickly as I could."

One of the first things he'd learned upon relocating here was how seriously the islanders took that status. BOI—Born On Island—was a source of great pride among them.

Her meager attempt to distract him might have worked if he hadn't been so focused on her safely. "I figured you lived on the island," he told her. "I'm asking for your specific address."

"Why?"

"Because tomorrow I'm not going to take a pain pill, no matter what. I want to come by and see you. And make sure your home is secure." He almost didn't add the last, but figured he might as well tell her the truth. "I'm worried about you, Maddie. Men who do that kind of stalking aren't right in the head. I'm not sure what he wants, but you need to understand he could hurt you."

She went quiet. "Thanks for your concern," she finally said. "I appreciate that you care enough to worry about my welfare. But I have lived alone a long time and I promise you, I can take care of myself."

Though the reporter in him wanted to press for specifics—did she own a gun, had she taken self-defense classes—he could tell from her cool, remote tone that she wouldn't appreciate him grilling her.

And maybe, just maybe, she had a valid point. Maddie was a competent, self-sufficient woman who ran her own business. She also, he reminded himself, had membership in the secret club that met behind the old door. He couldn't help but wonder if the stalker had ties to that place, as well.

"I'm sorry, but I have to go," she said. "I just wanted to let you know that I made it home safely."

"No contact with the stalker?"

"None. I made sure he didn't follow me home. Good night, Jake."

"Good night." After ending the call, he grabbed a pad of paper and a pen and started doodling. This technique helped free his mind, which he sorely needed to do right now.

Every gut instinct he possessed told him this was all connected. The guy he'd seen change into a wolf, the men who'd assaulted him, the "club" behind the door and the stalker. And perhaps even Maddie. For the first time he wondered if she'd been sent as a distraction.

While part of him scoffed at this notion, he couldn't discount it entirely. After all, she had happened upon him immediately after he'd been attacked. And she, a beautiful, sexy woman, was a hell of a diversion.

But then again, he thought, sketching the alley and the strange sign with no words and the door, she had refused to work with him if he tried to catch a werewolf on video. He'd think if her purpose was to negate the story, she'd have agreed and then done everything in her power to make sure he never got the opportunity.

Finally, with his brain growing even fuzzier, he knew he had to sleep. The effects of the pain pill threatened to propel him into unconsciousness there at the kitchen table, and he'd much rather be in his bed.

The next morning, Jake woke, the lingering after-effects of the narcotic making him still feel fuzzy. A shower and a strong cup of coffee did much to remedy that. Once he'd scarfed down some instant oatmeal, he made a second mug of coffee and carried it into the den. He booted up his laptop and logged into one of the chat groups he'd joined under a pseudonym. This one was comprised of people who'd claimed to have seen a werewolf. Jake had not yet posted his experience. He wasn't sure he ever would.

Reading some of the recent messages, he had to acknowledge Maddie had a point. Some of the comments bordered on mentally unhinged. Others spouted ideas ranging from conspiracy theories to alien invasion.

This was Jake's third time logging in. He'd hoped somewhere in the mishmash of random craziness, one or two nuggets of rationality would emerge. Apparently, this was not to be the case.

He logged out of the chat group and next checked his email. There were two legitimate employment offers, both needing articles written about a certain subject. One required photos also. The other did not. The fees listed were reasonable, so he accepted both of them. Knowing he now had legitimate work made him feel better about continuing to pursue what increasingly appeared to be an insane story.

Except he knew what he'd seen. He hadn't imagined it or dreamed it. There'd been no special lighting or costumes or tricks. A man had—somehow, someway—become a wolf. And then, after remaining a wolf for a moment or two, changed back into a man.

While logically such a thing didn't seem possible, Jake figured maybe all the legends about werewolves just might have originated in reality.

If he could obtain proof—real, solid, indisputable proof—such a story would be groundbreaking. He could change the world.

Except… He frowned, trying to picture a future in which werewolves were known to exist. Would fear and paranoia run rampant? Mass incarceration, people making accusations about anyone they didn't like? Werewolf hunts, people being made into second-class citizens just because they happened to possess a special ability?

In his line of work, he'd seen the face of much of humanity, and it wasn't pretty. Still, being a journalist was all about uncovering the truth. In this situation, that was what he intended to do.

Starting with what really was behind that door.

Chapter 8

As Rick watched the self-assured competence with which Carmen worked, a chill went through him. He'd known female special operatives who moved like that, all efficiency of movement, intent upon their task. They'd taken pride in claiming ice ran in their veins, and none of them had been a Vampire. Carmen put them all to shame.

He felt like a fool. Despite knowing exactly what kind of being Carmen Vargas was, he'd deluded himself into allowing the intense sexual pull of her to make him forget. No doubt she'd be excellent in bed, but he needed to remember it could never be anything more than that. Vampires were notoriously adroit at avoiding emotional entanglements. Perhaps because they had no beating heart.

Still, he liked her. Gutsy, smart and beautiful, all in one.

Once she'd carefully moved all the unbroken glass vials to a safe area, she finished rolling up the dead man and secured him in the tarp.

"For this, I need to be careful," she said, her voice low. "While I can easily drag him off by myself, if anyone sees me, it'll raise questions."

"Good point." A human woman of her size and shape would have difficulty moving a large, inert dead man. "Since nothing broke, I think I'll be okay helping you drag the tarp. Where are we going with him?"

"There's a fire pit in an area away from the little sheds and houses. I noticed it when we were walking earlier. It's not huge, but I think I can utilize it to burn this body."

Again, her clinical, remote tone gave him pause. Something must have shown on his face, because she shook her head.

"Would you rather be dealing with a hysterical, crying female?" she asked him drily. "When you live as long as I have, the one thing you're not afraid of is death. It's a shame, what happened to this man, but nothing I can do will change that."

"Point taken." He matched her tone. "Let's get this done."

"Do you mind grabbing the gasoline and the lighter?" she asked, pointing to where Tommy had placed the items on the ground.

"No problem." He grabbed the gas can with his right hand and stuck the lighter in his pocket. Then he took hold of the tarp, his left hand next to hers. When he gave a sharp tug, he could barely make the poor, dead Sheldon move.

Carmen shot him a look of disbelief. "Allow me," she said, and began effortlessly dragging the tarp away. To his chagrin, Rick could barely keep up with her pace. Of course, he was also carrying a five-gallon can of gas.

"Better slow down," he muttered. "Only a Vampire could move this fast."

Immediately, she complied. "Damn, you're right. I'm sorry. But look, we're almost there."

And they were. The fire pit sat less than twenty yards to their right. With a few more moves, they maneuvered the body into place. At her signal, Rick doused the tarp with gasoline.

"Hand me the lighter," she asked.

He almost declined. Almost. But then, because for whatever reason he didn't want to be the one who set a man he'd never known on fire, he passed the lighter to Carmen.

"You might step back," Carmen pointed out quietly. "You know what fire does to your kind."

Jaw tight, he didn't move. "Just do it," he said. "I'm far enough away."

With a shrug, she picked up a dry stick, dipped it in the gas and lit one end. Once she had a flame going, she touched it to the edge of the tarp and dropped it, simultaneously stepping back. There was no wind, so at least neither of them had to worry about that.

The blaze burned hot and furious. The awful smell made Rick want to gag, but he managed to maintain his stoic expression. Carmen turned away, as if to say she'd finished with this, but when he touched her arm and she looked at him, he realized tears streamed down her face.

Stunned, he froze.

"Sorry." She sniffed, swiping at her cheeks with her fingers. "This man had a brilliant mind. While death doesn't usually upset me, sometimes I just hate the complete and utter disregard humans have for life. If they only understood what a precious gift it is to be alive..."

Stunned, he nodded. Clearly, Carmen Vargas wasn't nearly as heartless as he'd thought.

They stood and paid homage to a man they'd never known, waiting until the flames settled down into embers, glowing amid the thick ash. Soon, with nothing else to use as fuel, those glowing bits of heat would fade also.

"We should have asked for a shovel," Carmen said. "I'd prefer to bury the ashes once this is over."

"I can go back and get one," he offered.

She jerked her head in a nod.

Once at the house, he started up the porch steps, intending to knock on the door. Instead, Tommy came outside and met him. "What's up?"

Rick explained what he needed. Tommy grunted, told him to wait there and went to the garage to fetch it. When he returned with two large shovels, Rick thanked him and started back toward Carmen.

"Do you need any help digging?" Tommy called after him.

Noting that the other man had waited until Rick had gone a fair distance, Rick told him no.

Once he reached Carmen and handed one of the shovels to her, they made short work of digging a hole. It didn't have to be that deep, because wild animals didn't go after ashes.

"There," he said, tossing the last shovelful of dirt on the mound and tamping it down. "That's done."

Expression solemn, she nodded. "Thanks for understanding a bit ago. Let's go for a walk. I need to move. Something, a bit of a distraction."

Since he could well understand this, he nodded. "Come on. The woods are waiting. I feel better when I'm among the trees."

On impulse, he held out his hand. After a second's hesitation, she took it. He didn't know about her, but right now he needed skin-to-skin contact.

Though it hadn't been that long since he'd shape-shifted, his inner wolf recognized the earthy scent of the forest and grew restless. Rick couldn't help but think about what a relief it would be to change into his lupine self, and run and hunt until exhaustion chased all thoughts from his head. Obviously, he couldn't, and wouldn't, not while the fate of the entire human race hung in the balance.

He imagined Carmen felt similar, in her own way. Vampires enjoyed their own form of hunting.

"That was unusually rough for me," she said once they were far enough into the forest.

"You took that guy's death harder than I expected."

"Maybe." She lifted one shoulder. "Humans come and go. Usually, their passing doesn't affect me much. But this…" Clearing her throat, she looked away. "While I didn't know Sheldon personally, I was looking forward to learning from him. He clearly had a brilliant mind. I wanted to find out what steps he followed in his creation or discovery of the new virus. I'm hoping at least they preserved his notes."

Intelligent and vulnerable. His heart squeezed. Damned if she didn't keep surprising him, making him like her even more, deepening the strong sexual attraction he felt into something he didn't dare guess at. Too dangerous.

Hand in hand with her, walking through the leafy shadows of the trees, he could almost pretend they were a normal couple, out for a stroll. Since this—being normal, with a regular life—wasn't something he'd ever wanted, much less thought about, the odd direction his mind had taken concerned him. Had to be because his libido seemed to be working overtime where Carmen was concerned.

He needed to focus on the case. Nothing else. The rest could wait until the unforeseeable future.

They came to a large boulder near the edge of the stream. He squeezed her hand, meaning to help her up. She grinned at him, pulled her hand free and then leaped to the top. Clearly a Vampiric move and one he couldn't replicate unless in his wolf form.

With a sigh, he climbed up the normal way.

"This is nice." Expression serene, she looked around. "I always thought I'd like living in the country, though I haven't, not since I was a small child. I like the lack of people. Plus, these pine trees have a nice scent."

"They do. Where did you live before you came to Galveston?" he asked, genuinely curious.

"All over," she replied, grinning. "East Coast, West Coast and several places in between. I stick to large cities, usually. My favorite is Chicago. And then Europe, before America became so populated. London, Paris, Rome." Her heavy sigh matched her wistful expression. "I really need to get back there someday. I was born as a human in London."

"Exactly how old are you?" he asked, mentally wincing at the brusque nature of the question. "Sorry," he added. "But I really want to know. Idle curiosity."

Where most women would have been instantly offended, Carmen just brushed her hair away from her eyes and studied him. "Why?"

"I'm intrigued. You're the first Vampire I've ever been even remotely close to. Most of what I know about your kind is hearsay."

"Seriously? In your line of work?"

"Sorry." He shrugged. "I'm a Shape-shifter. I work mostly with other Shifters and with humans. I've never worked with a Vampire until now. In fact, I've never even talked to another Vamp."

"You haven't missed much," she said, deadpan. And then ruined it with a huge grin. "Just kidding. Like anything else, being a Vampire has its good and its bad sides. Eternal life is a plus. Having to drink blood is a minus, though you get used to it. I miss real food, especially pasta. And a good T-bone."

"I'd never really thought about that," he mused.

"Most others don't. That's okay. But in case you ever wondered why we Vamps tend to stick to our own kind, there's part of your answer. It's easier being around others who understand where you're coming from."

Though he knew better, he reached for her hand again. "I think we're all like that. Even among my kind, we Shape-shifters tend to stick to our own beast. Wolves hang around with other Pack members, the big cats keep to themselves, and so on."

"Hmm. Maybe we have more in common than we thought." She squeezed his hand, the simple move sending a jolt to his midsection. "What else do you want to know? I guess I don't mind answering your questions."

"How about instead of me grilling you, you just tell me whatever you feel comfortable sharing." The notion that he truly wanted to know more about her worried him slightly, but right now he couldn't make himself care.

"I was thirty when I was made," she said, still smiling, her misty gaze faraway.

He waited for her to elaborate. When she didn't, he pushed. "What year did you turn thirty?"

Her smile faded. "I'm not sure I should tell you. I fear it will make you think differently about me, and I don't want that."

"I already know you're a Vampire," he pointed out. "And judging by what I know of your kind, I'm guessing you're at least a couple hundred years old. I'm just curious."

"Let's just say it's been a while and leave it at that." Gently pulling her hand from his, she fluffed her hair. "Call it Vampire vanity."

He wasn't sure whether he found her reluctance to talk about herself charming or stubborn. In the end, he decided it was a combination of both. "Interesting," he mused. "I never would have pegged you for being vain."

"Vain?" One perfectly arched brow rose. "I'm female. Why wouldn't I be vain?"

Her response made him chuckle. "Point taken. Beautiful women like you are usually vainer than most."

Her lack of reaction to the compliment disappointed him. But then again, no doubt she was well aware of the lure of her beauty.

The thought felt like someone had splashed ice water in his face. What the hell was he thinking, acting like some lovesick teenager who couldn't keep it in his pants? He had a job to do, as did she. The entire human race's survival was at stake.

"I'm sorry, but this is getting weird," he said, making his voice flat and his expression cold. "Whatever this thing is that's simmering between us, we need to put it aside until we've successfully completed this mission. Then and only then, we can explore it."

Her throaty laugh had him clenching his jaw. "I disagree. I think we need to have wild sex immediately and get it out of our systems, so we can focus on the task ahead. Shutting down this virus is going to be difficult enough without me being distracted. What do you say?"

* * *

Since it had been years, no, *decades* since she'd wanted a man with this much intensity, Carmen found herself holding her breath. She'd been bold, certainly, but she'd learned life went better if she simply asked for what she wanted. And in this case, she wanted him.

"Ms. Vargas, Mr. Fallin!" Landers's voice, high with panic, echoed through the trees. "Where are you?"

They exchanged glances. "Let's go toward him before we respond," Rick said. "No sense in giving away our hiding place."

Since she agreed with that, she nodded. "Come on." She jumped down from the boulder, smiling when he did the same.

They took off at a slow jog, heading for the path that led back to the field behind the house. Landers called out again. Since they were halfway there, Rick responded. "We're on our way," he shouted.

As soon as they burst into the clearing, the sight of several men waiting for them sent a shudder of warning up Carmen's spine. "Trouble," she murmured to Rick, who'd skidded to a stop alongside her.

"What now?"

Slightly winded, Carmen and Rick jogged to the others. "What's going on?" she asked.

"Where were you?" Gus's narrow-eyed gaze swept over them, his expression drawn and suspicious.

"We went for a walk in the woods." Carmen kept her voice cool. "What's up?"

"What did you do with the vials?"

"I moved them over by that shed." She pointed. They were no longer there. "I'm assuming Tommy came out and got them after bringing me the supplies I asked for. Why? Has something happened to them?"

Seriously, she hoped not. Those vials contained a deadly virus. How much more incompetent could they be?

Gus stared at her. "Are you lying to me?"

"Of course not. Why would I?" She took a step closer to him, making her own expression fierce. "What happened to those vials? Surely you understood they needed to be put back in a safe location in the lab."

Naturally, Gus looked away. "Yeah, I got that. I asked someone to do that. No one wanted to. They were *scared*," he sneered. "Finally, one of my newer guys said he'd handle it. Ted."

"And?" she prompted, unable to hide her impatience. "What happened?"

"Ted took the vials, got into a truck and took off. No one even realized he was gone at first. He got a fifteen-minute head start on us, but I sent two guys out looking for him."

"Fifteen minutes," Rick said, disbelief in his voice. "I'm guessing they haven't found him."

"Well, no." Fury blazed from the other man's eyes.

Carmen swore, using words she'd learned long ago from longshoremen on leave. "Do you realize what you have done?" she asked. "Do you have any idea?"

"Believe me, lady." Gus advanced on her, fist clenched. "I don't need you to tell me."

With a look, she dared him to touch her. Dared him.

Rick cleared his throat. "What does this Ted want with the virus? Has he asked for a ransom? Or is he planning to stage some sort of terror attack or something?"

Gus spat. "Probably money. He'd heard enough to know we were sitting on a gold mine. We'd just started negotiations with foreign countries. I'm talking millions." He clamped his mouth shut.

"What do you want us to do?" Once again Rick, sounding like the voice of reason.

"I don't know." For the first time, panic leaked into Gus's voice. He eyed Carmen. "If Sheldon left notes, can you recreate the virus?"

Careful to contain her excitement, she nodded. "I can. But why do you say *if*? Why wouldn't there be notes?"

"Because Sheldon might have destroyed them when he found out what we planned to do with his creation. That's why I had to shoot him, remember?" Landers said.

"Might," she pointed out. "I take it that means you don't know for sure?"

Gus and Landers didn't answer.

Worst case scenario—no notes. And the virus out in the open, in the hands of someone who might not realize the full extent of what he had. If this Ted were to get into an accident, the repercussions would be deadly.

"How much does Ted know?" Rick asked, apparently having similar thoughts. "Is he aware of how much danger he could be in?"

"Like I said, he's new." Gus shook his head. "I don't keep any secrets from my men, but I'm not sure exactly what he does and doesn't know. He was pals with Sheldon. In fact, Ted took his death hard."

Talk about giving them the important news last. Carmen and Rick exchanged a glance.

"When you say *pals*," Carmen said, "do you mean they hung out together after work? Or did Ted help Sheldon in the lab?"

Gus kicked the ground with the steel toe of his work boot. "Ted was Sheldon's assistant. He was supposed to be yours, too, once you started work. I imagine he knows more about the virus than all of us put together."

Blinking, Carmen closed her eyes. She didn't want Gus to see her fury, especially since Vamps' eyes tended to glow red when they were engaged. Mentally she counted to twelve, tamping down all emotion. When she felt even-keeled again, she glanced at Rick. He appeared stunned.

"It appears we've got one hell of a mess, gentlemen," she said. "If any of your men even remotely considered Ted a friend, they need to start working on contacting him immediately."

"What for?" Tommy asked. "Ted ain't stupid. He knows he'll be a dead man if he comes back here."

"Shut up," Gus ordered. "She's right. At least we have to try. Who was friendly with Ted?"

Though more than one man shifted his weight uncomfortably, no one responded.

Of course, this lack of response had Gus erupting into a string of curses that rivaled Carmen's earlier outburst. "Come on, now. At least one of you had to be friendly with the guy."

"Not really." Tommy again. "He hung out with Sheldon. He didn't talk much to anyone else. He even slept up at the lab like Sheldon."

Which meant Ted probably knew more about the virus than anyone else. She swallowed hard as a thought occurred to her. "Is Ted a biologist?"

"No. Before he came to work for me, he was a trash collector for the city of Atlanta, Georgia."

Atlanta. Where the CDC happened to be located. Coincidence? Carmen didn't believe in coincidences.

"Let me take a look in the lab," she said. "Now. Hopefully, I can find something to reveal the methods Sheldon used to create the virus."

Rick glanced at her and nodded. "I'll help."

They both knew in order to find an antidote, they'd need to know the composition of the virus. And especially now, time was of the essence. If Ted did something stupid, the repercussions—contagion, death and panic—would be almost instantaneous.

And not only the human population would be at risk. No one knew how this virus would act on Shape-shifters.

"Follow me," Gus said, reaching into his pocket and withdrawing several keys. He took off for the barn/laboratory. Carmen and Rick followed.

When they reached the entry door, Gus unlocked it and turned to face them. Now that he was away from his men, he allowed his worry to show. "I'm really afraid," he said. "Everything I was planning was controlled. I asked for war to be declared in West Latvia. For this, I would be paid one billion dollars. After that, we'd planned to put the virus on the open market and let all the superpowers bid."

"Wait," Rick interrupted. "Someone paid you to have war declared? Earlier you said you were doing it for power."

Gus shrugged, his expression unconcerned. "Money is power, don't you know?"

But Carmen wasn't having it. "How much of what you told us is actually true?"

"None of your damn business. Unless you want me to put a bullet in you like Sheldon, you'd best shut your mouth and get to work."

Carmen allowed a slow smile to spread across her face. "Go ahead," she said. "Shoot me. I'm your best chance—no, your only chance—of figuring out a way to recreate this thing. But if you want to be left with nothing while Ted holds all the cards, then go ahead. Pull out your gun and shoot me, right this instant. Otherwise, don't ever threaten me again."

Apparently, Gus hadn't expected her reaction. His mouth dropped open and his already squinty eyes narrowed before he recovered. He looked at Rick and shook his head. "She's crazy, you know?"

Rick grinned. "Maybe, but I can tell you she meant every word that she said."

"Really?" Gus pulled out his pistol and pointed it at Carmen. "Not so brave now, are you?"

Carmen couldn't help but laugh. "Go ahead. If you're going to shoot, do it."

Instead, Gus jammed his weapon back into his holster. "I didn't even take the safety off," he said. "Here." He tossed her the keys, appearing surprised that she effortlessly caught them. "Get to work," he ordered, spinning on his heel and stomping off.

Carmen waited until he'd left before going inside. "Strange man," she commented to Rick as she felt along the wall for the light switch. While she could see just fine in the darkness, she knew Rick couldn't. Plus, she needed to see in every nook and cranny if she was going to find those notes.

When the fluorescent lights kicked on, she turned around and gasped. A quick glance at Rick revealed he shared her surprise.

"This is…" She had no words. She'd expected at least a semblance of sterility, so necessary in a biological lab. But no. Glancing around at the piles of manila folders and haphazard pieces of paper, she grimaced. This looked like something used by a mad scientist.

A rat scurried across the floor, veering away when it saw them. Carmen gasped. "What the…?"

Rick crossed the room, lifting a pile of what appeared

to be rusted machine parts. "Maybe there's more. Another part, where Sheldon did actual work."

"I hope so." Privately, she had her doubts. In fact, she was beginning to wonder if this virus was actually real.

Chapter 9

The Pack Protector who'd been parked outside Jake's had made no attempt to follow Maddie home. Which meant he no doubt already knew where she lived. Great. Just great. Even more proof she was being watched. What she didn't understand was the logic behind it.

Maddie took pride in her reputation as someone who could be counted on to do what was right. *Reliable* and *loyal* could have been her middle names. Same for her family. Her father's reputation had been stellar, right up until the day he'd died. Having a brother who'd been promoted to a powerful position high up in the Pack Protector organization used to mean something. As in, someone like her would be considered above reproach.

Clearly, that was no longer the case. And she had no idea why. The simple fact of Jake hanging around the alley that led to Broken Chains didn't seem to be an adequate reason. There had to be more to all this. She needed to find out what.

Right now, she wasn't sure what to do, what course of action to take. The only thing she knew for certain was that she wanted to protect Jake as much as she could. Which meant she had to somehow dissuade him from the crazy idea he had about unmasking the truth about werewolves.

But how? He seemed so determined, so focused. So damn cute. Even his not-so-sly attempt to get her to take him into Broken Chains made her smile. She admired him for trying.

Her phone rang. Glancing at the screen, she groaned. Her brother. As if he'd known she'd been thinking about him. She could only hope he wasn't calling her in his official capacity as a Pack Protector.

"Hey, Colton." She put a lot of effort into sounding carefree. "How are you? It's been a long time."

Never one for pleasantries, he cut to the chase. "What have you gotten yourself into now, sis?"

She knew better than to bother trying to deflect. "It's nothing I can't handle," she said. "For the life of me, I don't understand why anyone would think this is a big deal."

"Maddie, if it's been elevated to enough of a threat that the Field Protectors are notifying me, then I'm not sure you can handle this. Now tell me what's going on."

With a sigh, she gave him the short version. "This human guy happened upon the alley leading to Broken Chains. He became obsessed with what was behind the door, especially since he saw a lot of people coming and going."

"And?"

The way he prodded told her he probably already knew the rest. But then again, if he did, the Protectors would have already rounded up Jake and taken him in.

No way was he finding out from her.

"One night two guys beat him up and I stumbled across him and helped him. He claims he's seen me go inside and has been trying to get me to take him with me. Of course, I can't."

"What did you tell him?"

She sighed. "That it was a private club for members only. He asked to go as my guest. So I told him that wasn't allowed. He keeps pushing. I keep refusing."

"Why?" Colton asked. "Why does he want to go inside so badly?"

"I think it's the lure of the unattainable. You know how you men are. Put something out there and tell a man he can't have it and he'll move heaven and earth. That trait must be built into the masculine DNA."

Colton laughed. "It sounds as if you like him."

"I do," she admitted. "He's human, but he's cute."

"He's also a journalist. A well-respected one. Did you know what?"

"Yes." Closing her eyes, she braced herself for her brother's reaction. "I think that's also the reason he wants to find out what's really behind the door. The journalist part of him believes it might be his next big exposé, like he'll uncover a terrorist cell or some huge, earth-shattering story." *Like the existence of Werewolves, Vampires and Merfolk.* Good thing Jake had no idea about the others.

"That's not good," Colton commented.

"No, but right now it's manageable. What I don't understand is why your field operatives are so worried about this. Don't they have better things to do?"

"That's their job." Colton's tone went sharp. "Worrying about the potential possibilities of situations like this."

A little taken aback, she swallowed. "Okay. I get it."

"Then I don't have to tell you to be careful, do I?"

"No, not really." Suspicious now, she waited. No way would Colton let her off this easily. But when he didn't speak again, she cleared her throat. "Can you call off the goon?"

Colton didn't even pretend not to understand who she meant. "He's there for your own safety."

"He threatened me. I didn't like that. If I didn't have you on my side, he would have scared the hell out of me."

"Threatened you how?" Colton's flat voice told her how little he liked her words.

"He felt it was his duty to warn me that the Protectors knew about Jake. And he advised me about the severity of my crime if I were to betray the Pack."

"That's standard protocol."

Disappointed in his dismissal, she sighed. "Intimidation tactics should never be the first line of offense. I'd think you'd know that better than anyone. What'd Dad always say?"

"To lead off with courtesy and respect." Colton could recite their father's creed as well as she could. "People are always more willing to help you if they like you."

She had him there, and he knew it. Still, she couldn't resist pounding the point home. "Exactly. Enough said. Maybe you should point that out to your goon."

"That's ridiculous," he protested. "Besides that, I don't even know which Field Protector has been assigned to your case."

"Oh, now I'm a *case*?" she asked. "And I know good and well that you can find out. That guy has been following me around, stalking Jake and bothering me at Broken Chains. I could understand if I was some known criminal. But no. I'm the sister of an upper-level Pack Protector. Surely that should buy me a little respect."

Colton laughed outright at that. "I'll see what I can do," he said, his tone dry. "But be aware, someone will always have eyes on the journalist. I don't care how cute you think he is, I want you to promise me you'll always be aware what a threat he could be."

"I promise. And Colton, if I see any indication that he'll be taken seriously, I'll call you immediately."

"Good enough," he replied, and then he ended the call.

Shaking her head, she scrolled over to check social media. She'd barely started to read her news feed when the phone rang again.

"What'd you forget?" she asked, not bothering to check caller ID. "Because, Colton, believe me, I get it. I understand."

"Colton? Who's Colton? This is Jake."

Yikes. Glad she hadn't said this out loud, she apologized. "Sorry, I'd just finished another call. What's up, Jake?"

Now he hesitated. "I think maybe we should talk in person," he finally said. "If you want to give me your address, I can swing by and get you."

"I'd rather meet somewhere."

"Of course you would." His tone had gone glum. "Listen, maybe this isn't a good idea. I shouldn't have bothered you. Especially if you're in the middle of something."

Was he *jealous*?

"I'm not in the middle of anything. I was just on the phone earlier. Colton's my brother," she said. "In case you were wondering."

"Okay."

He didn't sound relieved. Or skeptical. Or anything, really. Maybe she'd misinterpreted. Yikes! Now she felt embarrassed. "I just thought you might want to know."

She spoke fast. "In case you thought he was my boyfriend or something. Because I don't have a boyfriend."

Awkward silence. Gripping her phone, she wished the floor would open up and swallow her.

Finally, Jake laughed. "I get it. I'm glad you don't have a boyfriend."

Warmth spread through her at his words.

"But what I don't understand is why you don't want me to know where you live," he continued. "At least, that's what I surmise is the reason you don't want me to pick you up at your house. Do you think I'm going to start stalking you or something?"

Now she had a reason for the earlier silence and the reserve in his tone.

"Of course not." And she had to admit, he had a point. "I guess I'm just a private person." But she'd been to his house. And logistically, there was no reason why he couldn't come to her apartment. "You're right," she finally said. "If we're going to have a relationship, I've got to be more open."

There. She'd put it out there.

"I agree," he replied, to her relief. "I'll head that way if you'll give me your address."

She did. Once she hung up, she rushed around her apartment, tidying up. Mostly, she kept her living space pretty neat, but she couldn't help wanting to make it look perfect for Jake.

As nervous as if she was going on a blind date, she paced, unable to resist continually checking the window for the sight of his vehicle. Finally, common sense prevailed and she opened a can of Diet Dr. Pepper and carried it onto the front porch to wait. From here, she could see not only the parking lot, but the turn-in from the street.

She took a seat in her favorite wooden rocking chair, sipped her soft drink and willed herself to calm down. This behavior was not like her and she didn't like it. But just when she finally felt normal, she caught sight of his SUV pulling into the parking lot, and her heart rate kicked into overdrive.

Wiping her hands on the front of her jeans, she went inside and waited.

When he knocked, she opened the door. Jake smiled when he saw her, his appreciation sending warmth all the way to her toes. "Hey," he said.

"Hey yourself." She stepped aside. "Come on in."

As he moved past her, he looked around. "Nice place," he said. "Great location. You can almost see the ocean from here."

Since proximity to the beach had been one the reasons she'd chosen to lease this apartment, she grinned. "Thanks. I like the sound of the waves. It's soothing." Especially at night, when the traffic on Seawall Boulevard had died down.

"You look great."

The compliment made her blush, which was one of the curses of being a fair-skinned redhead. She couldn't help but let her gaze travel over him. Everything about this man called to her. From the light brown tone of his skin, to the angle of his masculine jaw. She liked his broad shoulders, narrow hips and the way he towered over her. He had a sensual mouth, the eyes of an old soul and a wicked grin. "So do you," she responded.

"Here." Oblivious to her decidedly carnal thoughts, he handed her a brown paper bag. "For you. Wine."

"Wine?"

"Yeah." He grimaced. "It's a nice chardonnay." Eyeing her, he appeared to realize something. "Do you even drink wine?"

"I have. Though I typically prefer beer." She checked her watch. "Since it's a little too early to drink this, I'll put it in the fridge so it can chill."

He nodded, practically bouncing on the balls of his feet, vibrating with energy. "I have news," he said.

"Just one second." All she could think about was how badly she wanted to kiss him. Needing to give herself time to regain her equilibrium, she carried the bottle into the kitchen and placed it inside the refrigerator. Reminding herself to breathe, she straightened her spine and headed back to her living room.

His intense gaze tracked her every move.

"Okay. What's your news?"

In response to her question, he dragged his hand through his short hair and inhaled. "Maddie, you're probably not going to like this, but I thought it was fair to tell you first. I've made contact with someone who says he can get me inside that club."

At first, his words didn't register. When she realized he meant Broken Chains, she shook her head. "I don't know what this person is asking for in return, but you need to be supercautious. There's no possible way he can do this."

Judging by the stubborn set of his jaw, Jake didn't believe her. "You don't know that," he said. "In my line of work, there's always a source who can do what others say is impossible."

"Oh, but I do know." Arms crossed, she shook her head, biting down hard on her anger. Not at Jake, never at Jake, but at whoever was trying to dupe him. "What's he asking you to pay him for this privilege?"

"Not too much," he hedged. "A thousand dollars."

"Ha." She snorted. "You might as well set a match to your money. He's just trying to swindle you."

"Are you always so negative?" he countered. "If I thought like you, I'd have missed out on numerous good stories."

"Negative?" Incredulous, she stared. "Try *realistic*. I can even guess how it all went down. You were doing your usual watching the alley. This person happened to run into you and struck up a conversation. He seemed nice, genuinely perplexed why you couldn't get in. Then, to prove he could, he left you and went inside."

Now Jake viewed her with open suspicion. "That's exactly what happened. How do you know this?" He narrowed his gaze. "Is he a friend of yours?"

"Nope. But I know a setup when I hear one. I grew up in a family of private investigators. I've honed my instincts." Plus, she knew, though she couldn't tell Jake, that if anyone were to take a human inside Broken Chains, they'd be set upon within minutes and killed. The Vampires would smell his blood and hear his heart, the Shifters would scent his humanness and notice his distinctly human aura, and the Merfolk would know by a look. Though this had never happened within Maddie's lifetime, she'd heard tales of a human once breaching the club's defenses. He'd been killed instantly.

The thought of such a thing happening to Jake made her shudder. And then she realized this could actually be the plan. Not only to relieve Jake of his money, but to get him inside. His death would neutralize the threat he posed. Would the Pack Protectors go that far?

Jake dropped onto her couch, his frustration showing in his face. "That makes no sense. In my world, when a journalist is looking for leads for a big story, sources sometimes show up with information and want to be paid. It's considered unethical, but sometimes the story is just too big. This guy did exactly that. What would be his reason for setting me up?"

Again, she stuck as close to the truth as possible. "Because only certain people can go inside that door. There are many who will do anything to stop an outsider—such as yourself—from entering. Can you give me a description of the guy?" She needed to know if he was a Shifter, a Merman or a Vampire. Right now, she was betting on Shifter. Probably another of her brother's employees.

Jake leaned back. "Sure. He was a big guy, like a football player. My first thought was to wonder if he worked as a bouncer. Shaved head, wore dark sunglasses. He did ask me if I'd seen anything unusual outside in the alley."

Her heart skipped a beat. "What did you tell him?"

"Nothing, of course."

Relieved, she smiled. He wouldn't be here talking to her right now if he'd told a Pack Protector he'd seen someone shape-shift. They'd have already dragged him away for reprogramming.

He had no idea how much danger he'd placed himself in.

"Where and when are you supposed to meet this guy?" she asked.

"Sorry, I can't reveal my sources." One corner of his mouth quirked. Hounds help her, but her mouth went dry.

"Seriously?"

"Yep. Obviously, I can't have you trying to ruin it for me." He patted the couch next to him. "Come here. Sit. Tell me about your day."

His rapid switch of topics, no doubt meant to throw

her off balance, amused her. Because she needed to buy some time to come up with a better way of explaining to him the impossibility of what he'd suggested, she sat. But she prudently kept a few feet of distance between them.

He chuckled. "Why are you way over there? I don't bite. Come here."

Staring at him, she swallowed. Her entire body tingled. She wondered if he realized the power of his sexy smile. Of course she slid over, inch by inch, until her hip bumped his. Even that small bit of contact sent a shiver of longing through her.

Talk about distraction techniques. He was good, she'd give him that. Except she had no idea if Jake even knew how he affected her.

But the warm glow in his dark eyes told her he did.

Determination set in. Two could play this game. Maybe this would be her only chance to convince him to abandon the idea of trying to get inside Broken Chains.

One ability Jake prided himself on was being able to read other people's reactions. And Maddie meant what she said. Not only did she worry about him being swindled, but she appeared truly worried, even afraid for him.

Why? Granted, she'd found him after he'd been jumped by the two thugs. He'd been caught by surprise that time. That wouldn't happen again—he wouldn't allow it. Not only did he now carry a knife, he'd looked into applying for his concealed handgun license and planned to purchase a pistol. Plus, he'd purchased—on the black market—a body camera similar to those used by police officers. It was on back order. He couldn't wait until it arrived. Once he had it, anything that happened to him would be sent to secure storage in his personal cloud, with a scheduled and timed release to all his social media accounts in exactly one day.

He'd taken, as the saying went, precautions. However, though he hadn't yet admitted it to Maddie, his always reliable gut instinct warned him to be wary of the entire thing. "Maybe you're right," he told her. "Something doesn't feel right."

Some of the tension drained out of her body. He could feel it, even though they were just hip to hip, shoulder to shoulder. "You were really worried about me," he mused, turning to face her. As usual, being this close to her sent his every sense into overdrive.

From the way her pupils dilated, she felt the same way.

"I was," she murmured, tilting her head. "I really wish you'd just let this obsession you have with Broken Chains go."

"Broken Chains?"

"Damn." Briefly, she closed her eyes. "I shouldn't have said that. I don't suppose you'd be willing to pretend I didn't?"

Since he suspected she already knew the answer to that one, he didn't immediately reply. Instead, jubilant, he leaned in and kissed her. What he'd meant to be a quick, celebratory kiss caught fire and turned into something more.

Arms wrapped around his neck, she kissed him as if she'd die without him. Her ardor fed his own, until he could scarcely breathe, never mind think. If she meant to distract him, he didn't care. Around her, rational thought ceased to exist. One touch and he craved more. One press of his lips to hers and he became so hard it was painful.

"Oh," she gasped, coming up for air. He barely let her inhale before claiming her mouth again.

Earlier, he'd given himself a stern talking-to. This constant craving for Maddie bordered on obsession. Definitely not healthy and, for a man in his position, and not safe, either. Being pretty sure she felt the same way, he'd resolved to talk to her about it.

Of course, every time he tried, they couldn't seem to keep their hands off each other.

Dimly he realized she was speaking. With his blood roaring in his ears, he'd missed the first part.

"Get it out of our systems," she concluded. "What do you think?"

"I..." He swallowed, trying to concentrate on anything other than how good her body felt pressed up against his and how badly he wished there weren't any clothes between them.

Clearly still unaware he had no idea what she'd said, she wiggled against him, possibly to underscore her point. He found himself even more aroused—something he wouldn't have believed possible.

"I want you," he managed, stating the obvious. "More than you can imagine."

"Um, no." She grinned, glancing at his spectacular bulge. "I can see that. And I want you. So, what do you say? Maybe if we go ahead and get it out of our systems, this attraction between us won't be so intense."

Relief mingled with desire as he finally realized she'd managed to put into words what he'd been trying to articulate.

As he reached for her in agreement, she eluded his grasp. Moving back, she lifted her T-shirt over her head, and then shimmied out of her denim shorts. Standing proudly before him in her black lace bra and matching panties, she was the most beautiful, sexiest woman he'd ever seen.

"Your turn," she said.

Glad she hadn't offered to help him undress—because he knew if she touched him right now, he'd lose his tenuous grip on self-control—he rapidly divested himself of his shirt. Removing his khaki shorts was a bit trickier, due to the sheer size of his arousal. Finally, he decided the hell with it, and stepped out of everything. He stood before her, naked, aroused and aching.

Her grin widened. Without taking her eyes from him, she made quick work of removing her bra and panties. The instant she was naked, he reached for her. She met him halfway and they fell to their knees together onto the couch. Skin to skin, finally, he let himself touch her in places he'd only dreamed of.

She guided his hand to her lady parts, warm and wet. "I need you inside me."

"Wait," he managed, with his fingers half buried inside her. "Not here. The bedroom." He wanted their first time to be in a proper bed.

Head back, eyes half-lidded, she moaned. "Only if you swear to keep touching me exactly the way you are right now."

"Oh, I can do better than that," he promised. "Let me show you."

They made it to the bedroom, limbs still intertwined. Separating from her, he went to the nightstand, found a condom and managed to pull it over him. She watched, her full chest rising and falling with her rapid breathing.

"Now I'm ready," he growled, reaching for her as she came around to the side of the bed. She pressed against him, so close he could feel the rapid beat of her heart.

He entered her as they fell back onto the comforter, already moving, moving inside of her. She enveloped him, he filled her, a perfect fit.

She moved with him, crying out in pleasure. When her

climax came and her body pulsed against him, he gave himself over to his own release, knowing with absolute certainty that one time would never be enough.

Chapter 10

When Carmen started to speak again, Rick held up his finger. "Let me sweep for bugs," he mouthed, pulling some sort of device from his pocket and walking around the room with it.

She nodded.

After making a thorough sweep of the room, he went again. Nothing like being thorough. After all, if the gang had bugged their living quarters, it made sense they'd want to listen in on their biologist as he worked in his lab.

But no, he found nothing. "It's clear," he told Carmen, letting his confidence show in his voice. "Maybe it's just us that they want to keep ears on."

"Yeah, maybe." Frowning, she turned in a slow circle, surveying the room, her slender figure and graceful neck reminding him of her stunning beauty. "After seeing this, I have to wonder if the bugs in our room are even active."

"Come on," he said, managing to stop himself from

reaching for her hand. "This is a big barn. Let's check out the rest of it."

"Fine." She strode past him, disgust evident on her beautiful face. "Look at this place. There's no way to avoid contamination. If anyone developed anything here, I'd be surprised. No, more than that. Shocked. I call BS."

While he didn't know anything about biology or laboratories, he tended to agree with her. Nothing about this place screamed *high-tech lab*.

They crossed the center of the barn, stepping around a rusted out old tractor, three or four semi tires, and a pile of junk. As they passed, a large rat scurried past them. Instead of screaming like a human woman would have, Carmen hissed and bared her fangs. For a split second, her eyes glowed red.

"Impressive," he said. "But be careful about who sees those."

Though she gave him a narrow glare, she nodded and continued moving, the stiff set of her classical features revealing her discomfort.

In the back section of the barn, they came to a locked door. Rick felt along the top of the sill, finding a key. "Lax security, too," he said, shaking his head. Once he'd inserted the key into the lock, he turned the knob. "After you."

At first, she didn't move. Noticing his quizzical glance, she forced a smile. "I'm bracing myself for more disappointment."

"Maybe we'll be surprised," he said, though he privately doubted it.

Carmen squared her shoulders and opened the door. She stopped so suddenly he nearly ran into her.

"Now this is what I expected," she breathed. "Take a look."

Moving around her, he stopped and stared. They stood in a small area that appeared to have been converted to a washroom. There was a sink, a soap dispenser, and a box of rubber gloves. Two white clean-room suits hung on the wall. Unlike the rest of the barn, this room was immaculate.

"There." She pointed. Separated by a clear glass wall, the next area over was even tinier, the size of a small elevator. Some sort of keypad blinked on the outside, and it appeared to be the only way to unlock the door. Someone had helpfully posted the code on a yellow sticky note taped up above the keypad.

"What the heck is that?" Rick asked.

"A decontamination area. The only way one can control contamination is to control the entire environment. I would be surprised if this isn't up to Federal Standard 209E."

Since he didn't want a long explanation, he didn't ask. "That's good, right?"

"Yes. Very good." But then her excited expression fell. "But look." She gestured. "They haven't been maintaining this. Once a clean-room has been built, it must be maintained, cleaned to very high standards. If it isn't, it's no longer considered clean."

He squinted, trying to see what she saw. "Where are you seeing contamination?"

"Everywhere. Look closely. Dust in that corner." She pointed. "And there, rat droppings. It's no longer up to par."

"I see." Pushing back his disappointment, he touched her shoulder. "How long ago do you think it became contaminated?" he asked. "Can it be brought back up to par quickly? Maybe it's just been since Sheldon was killed."

"No." She immediately shot that idea down. "From the

looks in there, this has been going on a while. I wouldn't be surprised…" She stopped, pushing him back. "There's a possibility that the virus is growing inside that room, unassisted. Since we don't know how it would affect you, I'm going to have to ask you to step away."

"No." He didn't have to even think about his response. "If I put on one of those suits, I'm protected, right?"

Expression reluctant, she nodded. "Assuming they're intact. Given the state of the rest of this place, it's probable they have rips or tears. I can't let you risk it."

"You're not in charge of me," he began.

"But I am." Her eyes flashed. "You agreed to those terms if I consented to help you. So, if I say I don't want you in the lab, you will remain out here."

Frustrated, at a loss for words, he did the only thing he could think of to do. He hauled her up against him and kissed her until they both were breathless.

When he lifted his head, she gave him a slow smile, her sexy eyes glittering. "Now that you got that out of your system, I need you to wait out here while I ascertain the risk inside the lab. Can you do that?"

"Now that you asked nicely, yes," he drawled. "Though I can promise you that I'll hate every minute of it."

"Sorry." Without a backward look, she crossed the room to the sink and began scrubbing up. Once she'd finished, she dried off and reached for one of the clean suits, checking inside to make sure there were no unwanted residents.

"Why bother?" he asked, confused. "If the lab is already contaminated."

"The less the better," she replied, pulling the garment up over her clothing and zipping it closed. Next, she grabbed a headpiece and put it on, making her look as though she wore some kind of bizarre spacesuit. Finally she pulled on gloves, after shaking them out first in case anything might have crawled into them.

Fully dressed, she stepped awkwardly forward, removed her glove and punched the code into the keypad, then slid it back over her hand while she waited for the door to swing open.

Inside, she stood absolutely still while water sprayed her and then wind dried her off. Despite himself, Rick was impressed. This small terrorist group apparently had big funding behind them, which meant the FBI knew only part of the story.

Once the machine had finished cleaning her, the door to the inner chamber swung open. Carmen stepped inside and turned slowly, surveying every bit of the place, inch by inch. From Rick's vantage point, he could make out a gleaming stainless steel table, a refrigerator and several empty glass vials, similar to the ones Sheldon had been carrying when he'd been shot.

While Carmen did her thing, Rick prowled the outer room. Even though she'd claimed the place had been contaminated, as far as he could tell, that would be only this outer room. The inner room where she was now appeared to be inaccessible except through the purifying room. The glass went all the way from floor to ceiling. And it appeared the outer barn wall had also been sealed off with the same kind of glass or Plexiglas.

He checked for bugs or cameras twice and found nothing. Either Sheldon and his assistant Ted had cleared the area, or they had never been there at all.

Something was off. First thing, Carmen could see no evidence whatsoever that this lab had ever been used for work. Any kind of work whatsoever. Which meant this Sheldon person had either brought the virus in with him, or the entire thing was some sort of elaborate hoax.

She frowned, trying to think. Rick had said there'd been a victim. And that the CDC in Atlanta had been working on identifying the virus and developing a cure.

Which meant a new virus did exist. But the likelihood that this group, the Sons of Darkness, had anything to do with creating it seemed nonexistent.

Then why? What could possibly be the reason for creating such an elaborate setup? Building a clean room wasn't cheap, and the fact that they'd brought her in to assist their existing biologist made no sense if they were aware Sheldon hadn't created anything. Clearly, Gus and his ragtag crew had no idea that anything was amiss.

However, Sheldon and his sidekick, Ted—well, that was another story. Damn, she wished Sheldon was still alive. Evidently, he'd panicked when he'd learned Gus was bringing another biologist on board. He'd known she'd find out the truth. So he'd staged a protest, not figuring the men would actually harm him. And when Sheldon had been shot, Ted had grabbed the vials and fled. Why? Because they contained the virus? Or, more likely, because they'd contained nothing at all.

Anger warred with curiosity. She made another sweep of the room, again noting that everything, every single freaking tool and beaker, appeared to be brand-new. Some still had the plastic on them.

Opening the refrigerator proved her theory beyond a shadow of a doubt. The pristine inside of the fridge housed nothing. And she'd bet there'd never been any contents. This entire thing—the messy barn, the expert attempt at replicating the clean room—all was a sham.

They were being played. Whether or not these Sons

of Darkness people were in on it or not, she had no idea, though she tended to think they had no idea whatsoever.

Furious, she strode through the door to the connecting spray, allowed it to do its thing and then exited. As soon as she was clear, she yanked off her headgear and gloves and made a face. "How certain are you that this place isn't bugged?" she asked, keeping her voice low.

Rick's brows rose at her tone, but he shrugged. "I'm sure. I did two sweeps while you were in there. I found nothing. It's clear."

Though she nodded, instead of blurting out the news, she went closer, putting her mouth against his ear so she could whisper. "This place is a setup. It's never been used as a working lab."

He froze. With her Vampiric hearing, she could detect the immediate increase in his heart rate. "You're positive?"

"Yes. I'm not sure if Gus and his crew know, but probably not. Otherwise why would they have brought me in?"

Turning slightly so that he faced her, he jerked his head in a nod. "That puts all of this in an entirely new light."

"It does," she agreed. "The question is, do we tell them?"

"Not yet." He checked his watch. "I think we've been in here long enough. We'd better go back. I want to see how this shakes out."

She nodded. They exited the clean area, moving slowly through the cluttered and filthy barn.

"At least now I understand why there aren't any notes," she mused. "Imagine how Sheldon must have panicked when he found out they were bringing in another biologist."

His grim smile told her he'd already thought of that.

"For now, we'll just play along like we know nothing,"

he said. "If these guys don't actually have the virus, if they never had it to begin with, that is an entirely different ball game."

"But it still leaves the question of where the virus came from to begin with."

"Exactly," he agreed. "Let me ask you. Is it possible that a previously unknown virus strain could appear naturally?"

"Emerging disease is usually a yet-unrecognized infection, or a previous one that expanded with a significant change in pathogenicity," she said. "Many so-called new strains originate in the animal kingdom." Noting the way Rick's eyes had glazed over, she shrugged. "But the CDC is well versed in all this. If they have reason to believe this thing was artificially created, then I have to think they're right. It's what they do. They have the brainpower and the resources to make these kinds of calls."

"That makes sense."

"Which begs the question. What's these guys' angle?" she asked.

"Or who is actually behind them pulling the strings?" Rick added. "Either this goes deeper than we originally thought, or this group is being played."

"And I'm thinking that's an answer you're never going to find out," Landers said, stepping from behind a stack of moldy bales of hay. He had a pistol pointed directly at Rick.

"I should have known it was you," Rick responded, his tone even, though his body had gone tense. "I'm guessing the others have no idea."

"Of course not." Motioning with the gun, Landers apparently wanted them to move forward. "They all think we're going to get rich. They have no idea."

Neither Carmen nor Rick moved. She exchanged a

quick glance with Rick because she was thinking of simply using her Vampire ability to move and snatching the weapon out of the puny human man's hands.

But Rick gave a miniscule shake of his head, letting her know that for now, she should see what Landers intended.

"You're going to shoot us and pretend we were escaping, aren't you?" Rick asked. "Kind of like what happened to Sheldon."

"Smart guy," Landers sneered. "But I have bigger plans for you."

"Oh, really?" Carmen kept her voice cool. "What would those be?"

"I need you to create a virus," he said. "You've got the lab and the know-how. I can get you anything else you need."

Her mouth fell open before she quickly snapped it shut. "Do you have any idea what you're asking? That's insane."

"Is it?" Landers waved the pistol from her to Rick. "I'm going to give you one week. If you don't have something by then, your husband is going to die."

"One week?" Not bothering to contain her disdain, she had to keep her lips locked tight to hide her aching fangs. If this fool had any idea how badly she wanted to snatch him up, clamp her fangs to his neck and drain him of every drop of his blood, he'd throw down the gun and run away. Naturally, he didn't and he wouldn't, not until he died.

"Carmen." Rick's quiet warning brought her back to rationality. "Maybe you should at least try to do what he's asking."

"Try? Try?" She rounded on him. "What he wants is impossible."

"Not for you," he prodded, gently reminding her that they needed to stall. At least for now. "Can't you give it a shot?"

Landers snorted. "Listen to the man. He's begging for his life."

Except he wasn't. Unless Landers had a silver bullet in his gun, he couldn't kill Rick. And since she had already died a long time ago, nothing short of a stake through her heart would do her in now.

Landers knew none of this. And if Rick wanted her to play along, then that's what she'd do.

"I guess I can try," she said, pretending to be deeply in thought. "I'll need Rick to assist me. I'll make a list of what I need and get it to you. Most important, I'll need a working computer and access to the internet."

"No can do." Landers didn't even blink. "I can't take the chance of you alerting the authorities. You'll have to figure everything out on your own, without the internet."

Clenching her jaw, she nodded. Apparently, Landers had no clue that what he asked was simply impossible. She had no idea how to even begin to create a new virus. It would have to come from a genetic mutation of an already existing one. She'd need access to research papers among other things.

Again, the clueless human thought she could work miracles.

"Oh, sure." She flashed a humorless smile, hoping her eyes hadn't turned red. "No problem. I'll get right to work. And don't worry about supplies. I'll have no problem creating a completely new virus out of thin air."

Either her irony was lost on Landers, or he was playing along for his own reasons. She'd bet on the former.

Landers nodded. "Perfect. I heard you were the best."

"True, I am." She dipped her chin with false modesty.

"Since you expect results so quickly, I guess Rick and I had better get to work immediately."

"One slight change in plans," Landers announced, his voice pleasant. "I'm afraid Rick will be staying with me until you have what I want. Insurance, you understand."

"No." Both she and Rick spoke at the same time.

"That's not going to happen," she said. "No Rick, no virus. That's nonnegotiable."

Landers waved his pistol. "Neither of you are in any position to negotiate," he said.

"That's it, I've had it." Carmen shot a quick glance at Rick, though at this point she didn't particularly care if he agreed or not. To her surprise, he gave a tiny nod, as if telling her to go for it.

Perfect. Grinning, she turned her attention toward Landers, who'd started to laugh at her frustration. When he saw her eyes, he choked.

"U-um," he stammered.

She moved. Before he could tighten his finger on the trigger, before he knew what hit him, she took him down. The weapon went flying—without discharging—and she left retrieval of that to Rick. She sunk her fangs in Landers's neck, drinking deeply.

At the first coppery taste of human blood, energy flowed into her. She hadn't realized, not until that very instant, how starved she'd become. Used to subsisting mostly on a diet of frozen blood, having her meal come fresh and warm was a gourmet treat.

As Landers went limp in her embrace, she looked up and saw Rick watching with a kind of revolted fascination.

"Is he dead?" he asked, his detached tone at odds with the look in his eyes.

"Not yet." She looked away, hurt stabbing her heart,

oddly enough. She'd long ago come to terms with what kind of being she was and refused to make apologies. She imagined Rick would be ten times more savage if she were to watch him as wolf, taking down a kill.

"Maybe you should leave him alive," Rick suggested. "Won't he turn into a Vampire if you kill him?"

Considering, she swallowed. He was right. The last thing she wanted to do was to create another Vamp. Doing such a thing came with heavy repercussions. This was never to be undertaken lightly. Which made her wonder. Had she become so crazed by the taste of fresh blood that she hadn't thought things through?

"What will happen to him if you stop right now?" Rick pressed. "If you let him live, how much will he remember?"

"Nothing." She glanced down at the still-swooning man in her arms. A single drop of bright red blood glistened on one of the puncture holes in his neck. The sight made her fangs ache, but she ruthlessly shut down that craving.

"For humans," she continued, "this process is perceived as sexual. I'm not sure how he'll remember it, exactly—I've never stuck around long after drinking from a person. Most likely he'll believe it to have been a particularly sensual dream."

Though he merely nodded, her words sparked a glint of something in Rick's gaze. He hid it quickly, turning to survey the junky barn. "We need to come up with a quick plan," he said. "I'm not sure, but I'm gathering from what Landers said that none of the others were in on this scheme. But then again, we don't know for sure."

After gently easing Landers to the floor, she stood. "I know what I want to do. We need to get out of here and go after Ted. Once we catch up with him, we'll know if these Sons of Darkness ever even had a virus."

"I agree," Rick said immediately. "If not, we've got to find out who's using this group as a cover-up. And where the virus is."

"Exactly. I wonder how close the CDC is to figuring out an antidote."

He took her arm. "That's some more information I'll find out once we're clear of here. How do you propose we escape?"

Laughing felt good, so she did. "That's simple. You change into your wolf self and run. See if you can keep up with a Vampire at full speed."

After a moment, he laughed, too. "I doubt I can, but it'll be close. My wolf side will appreciate the opportunity to try."

"Perfect." The fresh blood had energized her, making her feel as if she could do anything. "If you change now, go ahead and strip first. I'll carry your clothes for you so you'll have something to put on when you change back."

He eyed her and then nodded. "Good thinking. At first I thought you just wanted to see me naked."

"That, too." She saw no point in lying. "Another time, I'd definitely take advantage of that. But we need to hurry. There's no telling how long it'll be before someone decides to come looking for us."

Without hesitation, he removed his shirt, then kicked off his shoes. As he undid his belt and prepared to take off his jeans, she couldn't look away. Despite the circumstances, and maybe because of the fresh blood flowing in her veins, the simple act of him getting undressed aroused her.

The luck of bad timing. In a few seconds, he stood before her in all his magnificent male nakedness. He scooped up his clothes and shoes, bundled them together and handed them to her. She couldn't help but notice that his body was also aroused. And large. Very large.

"I've never seen a Shifter change form before," she said, her husky voice betraying her.

"Then you're about to." Dropping to all fours, he winked at her and then initiated the change.

Firefly lights surrounded him, twinkling as brightly as miniature stars. Fascinated, she watched as his bones began to lengthen and change shape. His human features blurred, elongating, and fur started to rapidly take over his previously smooth skin.

The multitude of lights swirled, hiding him momentarily. When they abruptly vanished, a massive and dangerous-looking wolf stood in Rick's place.

Nonplussed, she stared. Then, gathering her composure, she headed toward the door. "Are you ready?" she asked.

Wolf-Rick made a rumbling sound, a cross between a growl and a bark. For whatever reason, that lupine voice filled her with a fierce joy.

She opened the barn door and stepped out into the warm sunshine. After sidling past her, Rick took off, streaking away in the direction of the woods. She inhaled, glanced once at the house and took off at full Vampire speed.

Chapter 11

Held tightly in Jake's arms, Maddie felt a sense of contentment steal over her as she marveled at how powerful their lovemaking had been. She felt…changed. This had been more than just a simple slaking of physical need. It was like their souls had connected. They'd fit together as if their bodies had been made for each other. Even now, after all that, Jake didn't seem to be in any hurry to let her go.

He was unique, that's for sure. One of a kind. Hers.

Mate. Unbidden, the word flashed into her consciousness. She instantly rejected the thought. She'd never been prone to romantic fantasies or notions and she had no intention of starting now.

Sheesh. Give her a taste of some mind-blowing sex and she went all mushy. Luckily, Jake had no idea.

Turning her head to look at him, she caught him studying her, his brown gaze as warm as melted chocolate. "What?" she asked, curious.

"You're amazing, you know that?" His grin took her breath away and made her stomach flutter.

"So are you." She used a brisk tone to cover up how he made her feel. Too fast, too soon. Scooting out of his arms, she grabbed a T-shirt and pulled it on. "I don't know about you, but I'm starving. How about we get dressed and go grab something to eat?"

"Sure." He yawned, not sounding particularly enthused. "I guess I could eat."

She almost offered to go get them something and bring it back, but that felt wrong. Too…girlfriend-like. No, they needed to get moving so she could feel normal again.

"Great." Jumping up, she headed toward the bathroom. "Let me get cleaned up and then you can have a turn."

The hot shower brought back rationality and eased the tightness in her chest. After drying her hair, she applied a light touch of makeup, got dressed and opened the bathroom door.

Sauntering past her fully naked, Jake seemed completely aware of his effect on her. He grinned as she caught her breath. She could breathe again once she heard the shower turn on.

This. Had. To. Stop. She'd vowed never to let any man turn her into goop, and it wouldn't be starting now with him. Surely she could enjoy fabulous sex and a friendly relationship without becoming *that* girl. Right?

When he emerged, his short hair still damp and his shirt unbuttoned, the stab of longing she felt was so strong she had to look away. "Are you ready?" she asked, her tone too bright.

"Sure. We'll take my car."

While he drove, Jake kept glancing sideways at her, one corner of his mouth quirking in a half smile.

"What?" she asked again, battling the urge to smile back.

He shrugged. "Don't take this the wrong way, but I really like you."

Secretly pleased, she nodded. "Ditto."

"But," he continued, "just because we made our relationship physical doesn't mean I'm going to abandon the chance to get inside that club of yours."

"Seriously?" She groaned. "Well, I've said all I can say. Don't blame me if you end up getting fleeced."

They pulled into the parking lot of her favorite Mexican restaurant. After he parked, he turned in his seat to face her. "Wouldn't it just be a lot easier if you could take me inside yourself?"

She shook her head. Not wanting to ruin a perfectly good evening, she opened the car door and got out. Maybe in his line of work, he'd learned if he kept pressing, he'd get results. Not this time.

As she reached for the door to go inside, someone opened it for her. Not Jake, as he'd just now gotten out of the car. But another man, and one she recognized. The Pack Protector who'd been parking outside Jake's house. The same one who'd confronted her inside Broken Chains.

"You." She glared at him. "My brother said he was going to tell you to back off."

"Really?" His smug look infuriated her. "Well, he hasn't yet. I see you're still slumming around with the human."

Right about then, Jake noticed something was going on at the entrance and came hurrying up. He glanced blankly from Maddie to the other man, clearly not recognizing him.

"Is something wrong?" he asked, directing his question to Maddie.

"Nope. This man thought I was someone he knew.

That turns out to be wrong." She gave a hard smile at the Protector. "Now if you'll excuse me," she said pointedly.

Immediately, he stepped out of the way, having no choice. She knew enough about how Pack Protectors operated to understand he wouldn't start something here, in a popular restaurant filled with tourists.

But why hadn't Colton called him off? Knowing her brother, he'd simply gotten busy and the thought had slipped his mind. She'd text him and remind him.

"Are you okay?" Jake eyed her. "Whatever you and that guy were discussing looked pretty heated."

"Did it?"

"Yes. You can tell me all about it once we're seated."

Of course mild deflection didn't work on him. She figured once his journalistic instincts were roused, he'd pursue it until he had his answer.

Part of her—the private investigative side—admired this. It was sexy, even. However, the Shape-shifter side found it not only annoying, but dangerous. No matter how much she liked Jake, she had to protect her people.

The hostess led them to a booth. As Maddie slid into the seat, she sighed, bracing herself for an onslaught of questions.

"Hey." Jake reached across the table and took her hand. "Are you sure that guy wasn't your ex?"

"My ex?" Reminding herself that she'd promised not to lie, she shook her head. "No. He's someone who knows my brother."

"I take it your brother is a bit overprotective?"

A server delivered a basket of chips and two small bowls of salsa. Right after that, the waitress appeared to take their drink order.

Maddie ordered a margarita. She figured she'd need a little help in order to relax.

After they placed their food order, Jake sat back and studied her. "You're a very private person, aren't you?"

"I guess." She shrugged. "But you also tend to forget to put your reporter side away."

"What does that mean?" His frown told her he truly didn't understand.

"You ask a lot of questions."

Was that hurt flashing across his handsome face? Telling herself she must have imagined it, Maddie reached for another chip and dipped it into the salsa.

He waited while she chewed. Then, leaning forward, he met her gaze. "How else am I supposed to get to know you? I know nothing about you, really. I know you have a brother. Whether he's older or younger, I have no clue. Where he lives, if you two are close, those are the sorts of things people in a relationship should know."

In a relationship. Stunned, she took a sip of her margarita. As usual, she knew honesty was always the best policy. "Is that what we are? In a relationship?"

Again he flashed that devastating grin. "Unless you want to be acquaintances with benefits, then yes." His casual shrug fooled no one. "Up to you."

Their food arrived just then, giving her a few seconds to decide how to respond. "You're right," she finally said. "We should try to get to know one another better. I guess we kind of went about this backward, but that's fine." Spearing a chunk of her enchilada, she smiled. "Tell me about yourself. Where you're from, if you have siblings, all of it."

Over the course of their meal, in between bites, she learned Jake had been an only child, born and raised in Terrell. After graduating from Texas A&M University in College Station, he'd moved to Houston to take a job as a special correspondent for KHOU. His parents were both still living out near Tyler, and he visited them a couple of times a year.

For her part, she told him she had one older brother, and that they'd grown up in Missouri City, where her father had run a private investigative agency he'd taken over from his father. "When he died, my stepmother sold the agency right out from under me," Maddie explained, taking care not to sound too bitter, though she was. "I'd hoped she'd at least give me a chance to buy it and continue my family's legacy."

"So instead you started your own." His eyes gleamed with interest. "That's admirable."

She felt a warm glow at his praise. They'd both cleaned their plates and he was debating whether or not to order sopaipillas when her cell phone rang. Normally, she would have ignored it, but caller ID said Carmen.

"Sorry, I have to take this," she told Jake. "Hello?"

"Hey," Carmen said. "Are you home? We're on our way over."

No explanation for her disappearance, though Maddie hadn't really expected one. "First, I'm not home. I'm in a restaurant, eating dinner. And second, you said *we're*. Who's with you? Shayla?"

"No. Shayla's still with her new husband. You know that." Carmen's typical impatience rang in her clipped words. "How soon can you get home? Rick and I need someplace to hide where no one will think to look. That means Broken Chains is out."

"Hide?" What had her Vampire friend gotten herself into this time? And did it have something to do with that new case she'd mentioned taking on?

"I'll explain later," Carmen said. "Can we come to your place or not?"

"We're just finishing up our meal," Maddie replied, keeping her voice calm. "Jake and I will be home shortly. You know where I keep the extra key. Just let yourself in." She ended the call before Carmen could protest.

Across the table, Jake waited, his expression curious.

"Well, you said you wanted to get to know me better," Maddie drawled. "That was one of my best friends. She and a guy friend of hers—someone I don't know—are on their way over to my apartment. How'd you like to meet them?"

Jake put down the dessert menu and grinned. "Sounds great. Let me take care of this check and we can get out of here."

By the time they pulled into her apartment building's parking lot, Maddie figured Carmen and Rick—whoever he was—were already inside. Since she'd been wanting to come up with a distraction to keep Jake away from his earlier disastrous plan, she figured this one would be as good as any.

Either way, her invitation to meet her friends appeared to make him happy. As they walked up the sidewalk and climbed the stairs to her apartment, he turned to her and planted a quick kiss on her mouth.

Surprised and pleased, she smiled up at him, her lips tingling. "What was that for?" she asked.

"Just because."

She decided *just because* felt wonderful.

As she unlocked her front door and stepped inside, she saw Carmen sitting on the couch, next to a dangerous-looking, handsome man whose aura proclaimed him a Shape-shifter. They both jumped up when Maddie and

Jake entered. Introductions were performed all the way around. Maddie couldn't help but notice the protective way Rick Fallin eyed Carmen. As if she was his to protect. Even stranger, Carmen allowed it. In all the time Maddie had known the Vampire, she'd never seen her even come close to allowing a man, any man, to have the upper hand.

She also couldn't help but see the narrow-eyed glares Carmen directed at Jake.

"Maddie, do you have a minute?" Grabbing her arm, Carmen propelled her into the kitchen. "What's the deal with the guy, Jake? We have a lot of sensitive information to discuss. Why would you bring a human around and let him hear all this?"

"Because I need a distraction." Talking quickly, Maddie filled her friend in on everything that had been going on, except for the fact that she and Jake had made love. "If he keeps on pushing, he's going to end up either dead or with his memories erased. I thought if he had an actual story, he'd drop the other. I'm hoping you can help with the story. Highly edited, but still."

"I see." Expression thoughtful, Carmen finally nodded. "And you feel this is somehow your responsibility?"

"Yes. I like him, Carmen. A lot. He has…potential."

"Okay, okay." With her usual elegant grace, Carmen combed her fingers through her short platinum hair. "Rick's a bit freaked out, so let me talk to him."

"I'll do it," Maddie replied. "He's a Shifter, so I can make him understand."

"I'm not sure you can." Carmen seemed doubtful. "I know you don't know what's going on, but it involves a deadly virus, a terrorist cell and a dead junior senator."

"Wow. I'm intrigued and impressed," Maddie said.

"That's way more interesting than what's been going on in my life. Jake will eat this up."

Carmen tilted her head, frowning. "I don't know. If he's a reporter, maybe letting him hear about this isn't a good idea."

"Does this situation involve humans?" Maddie asked. "Because if it does, it wouldn't hurt to let him know. This could be the scoop of the century."

"And you think it would force him to abandon his other story about Broken Chains?"

"Yes. And about proving the existence of werewolves." Maddie shuddered. "I don't have to tell you how awful that would be. Especially once the Protectors got a hold of him."

"No, you don't." The frown smoothed out and vanished. "Come on then. You talk to Rick. If he's okay with it, then we'll let Jake hear a slightly sanitized version of our case."

When they emerged from the kitchen, they found Jake and Rick deep in conversation about baseball. It appeared they were both Houston Astros fans, though Jake also liked the Texas Rangers.

Joining the two men, Maddie exchanged a glance with Carmen. She'd need Carmen to lead Jake away on some pretext so Maddie and Rick could have a quick talk.

Both Jake and Rick turned to stare as the two women emerged from the kitchen. They were both stunning, though in different ways. Carmen's platinum blond, pale-skinned look seemed edgy and sexual, while Maddie had a more wholesome sexiness that Jake much preferred.

For whatever reason, Jake could tell Carmen wasn't thrilled to have him there. He wasn't sure why, at least not yet. He had no doubt he'd find out before the end of the evening. Carmen seemed really…direct.

In fact, she made a beeline over to him. "Do you have a moment to speak privately?" she asked, her husky voice full of confidence that he wouldn't turn her down.

Jake glanced at Rick, who shrugged. Maddie gave him an encouraging smile. "She doesn't bite," she said.

For whatever reason, both Carmen and Rick found this comment hilarious. "Inside joke," Rick finally said.

"Yes. Sorry." Carmen wiped at her eyes. "Will you talk to me?"

"Sure," Jake answered. "Lead the way."

She took him into the kitchen she and Maddie had just left. Though he could make out the quiet hum of Maddie's voice, he couldn't discern what she and Rick might be speaking about.

"How do you know Maddie?" Carmen demanded, folding her arms across her ample chest. Immediately he forced his gaze back to her face.

"Didn't she tell you when you two were in here a few minutes ago?" he shot back, wondering why she seemed so antagonistic.

"Maybe. But I want to hear it from you."

He decided instead to use a different tactic. "If you're worried about your friend, don't be. We both know what we're doing. We're adults. I won't hurt her."

Carmen didn't immediately respond. She just continued to eye him, her stare both bold and frank. "You're pretty," she pronounced. "I see why she likes you."

He grinned. "Pretty, huh? While I'm not sure if that's a compliment or an insult, I'll take it as a compliment. So, thanks."

When she didn't smile back, he shrugged. "Well. Nice

talk. We'd better get back in there and rejoin the others." He turned and started to leave.

"Wait."

What now? Slowly, he swung back around to face her.

She took a deep breath. "In a few moments, you're going to hear some sensitive information. Information I don't feel you need to know. But Maddie believes you're a good reporter and will do well with this story. Understand that we're all trusting you. There are lives on the line here. Don't mishandle this."

Though he had no idea what she meant, he nodded. Her use of the word *story* had his journalistic instincts on full alert.

"Assuming," she continued, "that Rick's okay with filling you in."

"Interesting," he said. Because it was. "Are you ready to go and find out?"

"Sure." Now she seemed indifferent. He couldn't help but wonder if her mercurial mood changes were normal for her. Or if he just rubbed her the wrong way. He'd ask Maddie later.

When they emerged from the kitchen, Maddie and Rick appeared to be arguing, though they both kept their voices low. They immediately stopped when they saw him.

"We need a few more minutes," Maddie began.

"No." Rick dragged his hand through his hair. "We don't. I'm good. Just be careful."

"I will."

Now every journalistic instinct Rick possessed had flared to full alert. "Let me go out to my car and get a pad of paper and a pen," he said. "I also have a little voice recorder, if that's okay."

"No recordings," Rick pronounced. "You can write

stuff down. This is very sensitive information. You'll need to give us your word that you'll handle it responsibly."

"Of course I will." Jake didn't even hesitate. "You don't become an award-winning, respected journalist by cutting corners. I'll report the facts without embellishment."

Rick and Carmen exchanged glances. "That might be a bit difficult. We don't actually know all the facts."

If anything, this intrigued him even more. "Let me grab my pad. Just a second." He dashed out the door and jogged to his car.

When he returned, the other three now seemed to be arguing among themselves. Again, everyone went silent the instant he stepped into the room.

"Guys, if you keep doing that, I'm going to get a complex," he joked.

Maddie was the only one who smiled. "Come on in, Jake. Sit down. They've decided Rick will tell you the story. Since I haven't heard it either, it'll be news to me, as well."

"Perfect." He made his way to the couch and sat, motioning to the spot next to him. Maddie didn't hesitate to take it, plopping down right next to him, close enough that their hips bumped.

He could get used to this. The fleeting thought made him smile at her, before he turned his attention back to Carmen and Rick. They both had chosen to remain standing.

Rick cleared his throat. "What we're going to tell you has to be off the record, at least for now. Agreed?"

"Agreed." Jake loved when people began with *off the record*. Things tended to get really interesting then. And although sometimes that meant he couldn't ever use what he'd been told, every now and then when *off the record* became *on the record*, the payoff was great.

"Perfect." Rick and Carmen exchanged a glance. "Where should I begin? There's a small cell of domestic terrorists who call themselves Sons of Darkness."

"A motorcycle gang?"

"Nope." For some reason Carmen appeared to find this funny. "Not even close."

Rick glared first at her and then at Jake. "Are you going to let me tell this story or not?" he asked her.

"Go ahead." She waved at him, covering her mouth with her other hand.

He shook his head and then continued.

Jake listened to the rest without interrupting, jotting down notes. When Rick finally finished, Jake nodded. "Interesting. I have a few questions." He looked pointedly at Rick. "Assuming I'm allowed to ask questions."

"Ask away."

"Considering that this group had a fake lab and, most likely, no virus, how do you know this virus even exists?"

Again Rick and Carmen exchanged looks, giving the sense that they weren't revealing everything. "The CDC is working on it. What we don't know is if this Ted person has an actual virus or not. If not, then the thing is currently completely contained inside the CDC lab in Atlanta."

For the first time since Rick began his explanation, Carmen spoke. "Most important, there's the matter of whoever really created the virus. I'm a biologist who specializes in diseases. I was excited when they contacted me and wanted me to join their operation, even if I'd be working undercover with the FBI. I welcomed the opportunity to learn from a scientist who, while he might have been evil, also appeared to be brilliant."

"Because he came up with a new virus?"

"Exactly. You have no idea how rare that is. And if I worked side by side with him, then I'd be more likely able to develop an antidote." Carmen's animated expression fell. "But that didn't happen. We thought it was this Sheldon out at the Sons of Darkness compound. He's dead, so we can't actually ask him. And while it's possible he might have stumbled across the perfect combination by accident, from the looks of the lab, that's highly unlikely." She grimaced. "In fact, I can state with 99.9 percent certainty that no virus was developed in that lab."

"So what are you going to do now?" Jake asked.

"That's where you and Maddie come in," Carmen said. "She's a private investigator and you're a reporter. You two should have enough skills between you to locate the missing guy—Ted—and find out what he does or doesn't have."

Jake turned to look at Maddie. Judging from her closed-off expression, she wasn't too keen on the idea.

"I'll have to think about it," he said, nudging Maddie with his knee to let her know they'd discuss it later. "But I have to ask, why are you telling me this, off the record?"

"Because once a solution is found, think of the story. It won't be off the record any longer. And you'll have an exclusive."

"Put that way," Jake replied, grinning. "It's an offer almost too good to be true."

"I'm in," Maddie said suddenly, startling him. "I personally enjoy a challenge."

She met his gaze, a challenging look on her face. "Well?" she demanded. "What do you say?"

Something still felt off. But he trusted his instincts and

knew he'd figure it out eventually. "Working together, right?"

Maddie nodded.

"Then I'm in, too," he said.

Chapter 12

Rick almost felt sorry for the reporter. No one could help but notice the way Jake and Maddie looked at each other, or the way sparks seemed to crackle between them. But then again, Rick could actually relate. He felt that way about Carmen. Too quickly, too soon.

Especially now that she'd seen him shape-shift into wolf. That knowledge alone boggled his mind. Among the Pack, such a thing was forbidden with other species—unless they were mates.

Mates. He'd never really given the idea serious thought. In fact, he wasn't sure he even believed in the concept. If he ever mated with anything, he'd have to say he was mated to his job. Most definitely it wouldn't be a Vampire.

Yet Carmen was…different. The more time he spent with her, the less Vampire-like she seemed. The initial impression, of her blazing hot sexiness, had become enriched with her dry sense of humor and mocking wit. He liked her, he had to admit. And while he found himself craving her, he knew enough about couples and partnerships to realize that wasn't enough.

"What's your plan?" Jake asked, bringing Rick out of his reverie.

"We're going after Ted, of course," Carmen put in.

"Okay. But what about these Sons of Darkness people? It seems to me you went through a lot of trouble to develop undercover identities. I get that you fled their hideout, but wouldn't it make more sense to continue to work with them?"

Jake had a valid point. Rick glanced at Carmen, who shrugged.

"The thing about them," Rick said, "is that we got a real inkling that they are a front for something else, something worse. The entire plan about starting a war in West Latvia to anger the Russians didn't make sense to begin with. And this was even before we realized they didn't have the virus."

"And most likely never had the virus," Carmen continued.

"But don't you want to know what's behind them?" Jake pressed.

"You'd better believe we do." Rick didn't bother to keep the impatience from his voice. "And we will find out, eventually. What matters right now is the virus. It's out there somewhere. We've got to find it before it's released into the general population and starts an epidemic."

"Meh. I'm skeptical." Jake directed his words to Carmen. "One body with a virus doesn't prove the existence of more, am I right?"

"Well, it's highly unlikely to mutate on its own. Plus, we've already confirmed that someone fed the virus to the victim, most likely in a drink or meal he ate at a restaurant right before he became ill." Carmen sighed. "So unfortunately, while I like the way you think, we pretty much are guaranteed that someone, somewhere, developed this virus."

"And has more," Rick said.

"Exactly. And has the capability of making a large enough supply to cause a pandemic."

Pandemic. Even nonscientific types like Rick hated that word. Maybe he'd seen too many movies, but the thought made him shudder.

Especially since they didn't have an antidote.

"Rick," Carmen said, touching his arm. "I'm going to call the CDC again, just to make sure they don't need me."

"Okay." He didn't tell her that he'd already checked, before recruiting her. She might be one of the top biological disease specialists around, but there were others. And some of them had connections. The CDC considered their staff full. Who knew—perhaps something had changed.

"While you do that," he said, "I need to make a few calls and find out what my boss wants me to do now that we've left the group. I haven't given a full report yet anyway."

Already scrolling through her phone, Carmen waved at him as he stepped outside onto the apartment balcony to talk privately.

As Rick had suspected, his boss wasn't happy.

"You what?" Special Agent in Charge Olson Ferring roared. "Do you know how long it took to get you set up for this undercover assignment?"

Then, without giving Rick a chance to answer, he continued. "You get back in, make contact with them. Come up with some sort of plausible story for doing what you did."

"Just a minute," Rick interjected. "You haven't heard the full story." And he proceeded to tell him the lab hadn't truly been used, that the biologist named Sheldon had been murdered, and someone named Ted had run off with vials that supposedly contained the actual virus.

Olson went silent for a full five seconds. When he spoke again, he'd lowered his voice. "Do you believe that he might actually have it?"

"We're not sure," Rick responded. "It seems highly unlikely, but there's still a minute chance."

"In that case, I want you two back in the group. Back undercover immediately. You need to hunt down and find Ted and those vials. Being part of the Sons of Darkness will afford you better protections in that world than if you go on your own. Understand?"

Rick allowed that he did and ended the call. He turned to go back inside, but Carmen stepped out onto the balcony instead and closed the door behind her.

"You look glum," she commented. "I'm assuming your work wasn't happy with you?"

"Nope." He relayed the conversation.

"Seriously? That's not so bad." She shrugged. "Especially since we'd planned to do that all along."

"No, we just involved that reporter," he said, jerking his head toward inside the apartment. "That *human* reporter."

When she put her hand on his arm, his entire body tightened. "It's okay. Maddie will make sure he stays protected. Let them search, too. The more eyes out there looking the better."

"Maybe. Though we need to let them know it's dangerous. Since Maddie's a Shifter, I have no doubt she'll be all right. But that poor human. He's already been jumped on by two Protectors in the alley outside Broken Chains."

She grimaced. "I heard about that. But this case will get him away from all that, at least for a little while. And if Maddie is willing to work to keep him safe, why not? You know as well as I do that sometimes reporters have ways to access information outside regular channels."

She did have a point. "Fine," he said. "Let's go back in and inform them. Then you and I need to get on the road. I'm going to have to call Gus and grovel in hopes he'll take us back."

"Oh, he will." The confidence in her voice made him smile. "Especially when you tell him what we discovered in the lab and that we want to go after Ted. I can pretty much guarantee that."

Side by side, they headed back into the apartment.

Still seated next to each other on the couch, Maddie and Jake looked up when they entered.

"That looked like a serious discussion," Maddie observed. "Is everything all right?"

Rick explained, careful to keep from focusing too much on Jake. He didn't like working with humans and preferred to work with other Shifters as much as possible, especially on dangerous cases. Humans were too... fragile. They slowed him down and distracted him, especially if he had to worry about keeping them from getting killed. They could be headstrong and impulsive and unpredictable.

Maddie needed to understand this, as well. Rick would talk privately with her before he and Carmen left.

By the time Rick finished his explanation, Jake practically vibrated with excitement. Rick had to like the guy's enthusiasm.

"Sounds good." Jake rubbed his hands together. "My

favorite kind of investigative journalism. I've got to get busy and do some research. I assume you don't want me to directly contact the CDC?"

"No." Both Rick and Carmen answered at once.

"Okay. I have back channels."

Though they glanced at each other, Rick and Carmen let that one pass for now.

"Do you have a moment?" Rick asked Maddie.

Though she lifted one brow in surprise, she nodded. "Out on the patio?"

Once there, he reiterated what he and Carmen had discussed. "Not only will you have to keep an eye on him, but you'll have to keep the two of you safe. Do you think you can do that?"

She grinned. "I relish the challenge."

"Good luck." The words came out gruffer than he'd intended.

Instead of taking offense, she laughed and hugged him. "You're a decent guy, Rick Fallin. I like you."

Not sure how to react to that, he simply nodded and turned to go back inside.

But she wasn't finished. She grabbed his arm. "Carmen likes you, too, I can see."

Hounds help him, but he fell for the bait. Turning slowly, he eyed the female Shifter. "Sometimes I have to wonder if she does. Because with all that Vampire aloofness, sometimes I have my doubts."

Her grin widened, telling him his casual tone didn't fool her at all. "You make a great team. I think with you two as partners, you'll solve this case in no time."

Partners. Now he really felt foolish. Glad she didn't know he'd been thinking romantically while she meant in a working relationship, he nodded. "Good to know. I'm hoping we will in time."

She laughed again before pushing open the door and stepping inside, with him following right behind her.

Carmen and Jake were deep in conversation. As he approached, Carmen looked up and winked. "I was just telling Jake how the CDC works. I took a tour there and did quite a bit of research when I was thinking about seeing if they would hire me a few years ago."

Rick made a big show out of checking his watch. "Sorry, but we need to get on the road."

"Give us just five more minutes," Jake pleaded, finally looking up from his notes. Apparently, he'd been scribbling furiously into a spiral notebook the entire time Carmen had been talking. "This information is really going to be beneficial in writing the story."

Rick frowned.

"It's fine, Jake," Carmen said, her voice as cool as the icy glare she directed at Rick. "I don't have to ask his permission to do anything. You'll have your five minutes and more if I feel it's necessary." Her tone contained a warning.

Since Rick didn't want to start this leg of their assignment off on bad footing, he didn't even attempt to argue. "Let me know when you're ready," he told her, escaping again to the balcony, where he could breathe the fresh air. Her mercurial mood change confused him. He didn't know if it was because she was a Vampire or if it was some feminine thing. Either way, he had no clue. He just wanted to get on the road. Like ten minutes ago.

Though maybe some alone time would do him good. Hopefully, Maddie wouldn't feel a sudden urge for more conversation.

To his relief, she didn't follow him. A quick glance back showed she'd joined the discussion with Carmen and Jake. Good. Because right now, Rick needed to get his head back in the game and stop obsessing over the gorgeous and sexy Vampire when he needed to figure out a way to relate to her only as a teammate, a partner. Nothing more, nothing less. Now was definitely not the time to allow himself to get distracted.

The one thing Carmen would never permit was for a man—any man—to boss her around. This was why she'd set up the working dynamic with Rick in the beginning. Her nature would not allow him to be in charge. She wasn't sure when this strong belief had taken place, but because she'd spent nearly her entire human life under first her father's then her husband's heel, she'd spent nearly a century after being made a Vampire exploring her strength. She'd vowed to remain independent and strong and so far, she had.

Damned if she'd let a bit of sexual attraction cut the legs out from under her.

After Rick's directive, she stretched things out and kept talking to Jake for fifteen more minutes rather than five. From the corner of her eye, she could see Rick standing out on the balcony, his back to the room while he gazed out into the darkness. For whatever reason, this made her feel vaguely guilty.

Finally, she took pity on him and wrapped things up with Jake. "Good luck," she said, uncoiling herself and pushing up off the sofa. She squared her shoulders and lifted her chin as she made her way to the balcony.

Stepping outside, she waited for Rick to turn. When he didn't, she touched his arm. "I'm ready now."

He swung his head to look down at her, the tightness of his expression revealing his leashed emotions. "I don't like playing games," he told her.

"Games?" she drawled, her tone mocking, unable to

help herself. "I wasn't playing a game back there. I told you up front early on that you weren't going to be the one in charge. You can't come and interrupt my conversation— it was important, too." Surely he could see the validity of her point.

A muscle worked in his jaw. "We needed to get going."

"Did we? Please. A few more minutes wasn't going to hurt anything."

She had him there and he knew it. But that didn't mean he liked it. She'd lived long enough to understand how it was with men and their pride.

"Look." Placing her hand once again on his arm, she felt the way his muscles bunched and tensed. There was power there, leashed yet fierce, and she liked that. "Don't take this personally. It's more my thing than anything else. I find it difficult to let a man call the shots."

"Ever?"

Judging by his incredulous tone, he found this hard to believe. And she had to admit, it did sound kind of ridiculous.

She shrugged to cover her confusion.

"Carmen," he pressed. "Are you saying that you always have to be in charge? Every single time?"

His question made her frown. Put that way, it made her seem both egocentric and bossy. Not to mention far too controlling. "I don't know. Aren't you making too much of this?"

He sighed. "Maybe," he answered, much to her surprise. "And I think you are, as well. If we're going to be partners, there's got to be a give and take. I promise, there will be times when I'll know or see something you don't, and I'll bark out an order. I'd do the same whether my partner was male or female. It isn't sexist. It's survival. Teamwork."

"There's no *I* in *team*," she joked.

He didn't even crack a smile. "I'm serious. I know for a fact that I won't be able to work with you if you're going to do the exact opposite of anything I say, just because you have control issues."

Since she wasn't sure how to respond to that, she did the only thing she could think of to distract him. She pressed her body up against his and kissed him.

As usual, instant sparks combusted. Except after a few seconds, she realized they were all on her end. Rick didn't react at all. In fact, after the first initial shock, he closed his mouth and took a step back. "Not fair," he said quietly. "You no longer get to play that card."

For whatever reason, this made her want to cry. Which infuriated her. She'd gone centuries without shedding a tear over a man and she wasn't going to start now.

"You are absolutely correct." Her clipped tone revealed her emotions, though she figured he didn't know her well enough to realize how truly upset she was. "From now on, we're just partners."

Her declaration didn't appear to impress him.

"Just partners?" he repeated. "Only if you tell me you understand that we have to be equal. Sometimes you might have to do as I say. Other times, it will be reversed. Unless you can see that, I don't think we can work together at all."

Stunned, she took a moment to swallow her injured pride. Intellectually, she knew he had a point. "I agree," she finally managed, wincing as she spoke. Then, she tried to lighten her eat crow moment with a bit of humor. "What do you know? It seems you actually can teach an old Vampire new tricks."

He laughed at this, his eyes crinkling at the corners.

"Come on, then. Let's hit the road. My SUV is parked nearby."

The rush of warmth she felt in her chest at his smile was like nothing she'd ever experienced. In fact, if she hadn't been a badass Vampire, she would have been frightened at the things this Shifter made her feel.

They rushed through their goodbyes, though Carmen hugged Maddie a bit tighter than usual. "Be careful," she whispered.

"I will," Maddie whispered back, her gaze sliding past Carmen to land on Jake. "And I'll do my best to keep him safe."

Carmen peered at her friend, wondering if the warm glow in Maggie's eyes meant she had strong feelings for the human man. She bit back the urge to utter a warning, still stinging from her earlier conversation with Rick.

Heading out, she caught herself shaking her head. Ever observant, Rick eyed her but didn't ask. He led the way to his vehicle and opened the passenger door for her. Once she'd climbed inside, he went around and got in, then started the engine. He backed out of the parking space and pulled out into the street.

"Now, what's the plan?" she asked. "How are we going to get back in with Gus and his guys?"

"I'm hoping a phone call will do it," he said. "But I need to buy a disposable phone. I can't take a chance on them tracing my number, especially if they decide we have to pay for running away."

"Why would they decide that?" Perplexed, she stretched. "They need us more than we need them."

"How so?"

"Think about it. How many biologists like me do they have access to? They need to recreate the virus, especially if they can't find Ted. Or worse, if they find Ted and learn they never had the virus after all."

"Which means they've been played."

"Or someone is pulling their strings still," she continued. "The question is who."

"Another possibility," he said, glancing at her sideways as he drove. "They could be aware that they're pawns or a shell for whoever is behind the big picture. Their little terrorist cell really hasn't done much other than funnel some guns to other terrorist groups. They're on the ATF's radar, but they've held back at the FBI's request. We've been hoping they could inadvertently lead us to whoever is pulling the strings."

Carmen nodded. "And all of this has something to do with West Latvia. Someone wanted a war with them, for whatever reason."

"Exactly. That is another bit of info we need to find out. Why?" He grabbed his cell, keeping one hand on the steering wheel. "I'm about to call Landers. Even though he pulled a gun on us and you bit him, he's the only one I have a number for."

"He won't remember much," Carmen promised.

"Good. I'll put it on speakerphone so I can drive. Feel free to chime in if you come up with anything you think will be helpful."

"I will."

But it turned out she didn't need to. As soon as Landers learned it was Rick calling, he put Gus on the phone.

"Where the hell are you?" Gus demanded. "Landers told me some bullshit story about you hightailing it out of here after seeing the lab."

"Was he acting on your orders when he confronted us at gunpoint?" Rick asked, his voice hard. "Or when he told Carmen to get to work while he intended to hold me hostage?"

Silence.

"So, yeah," Rick continued when it became apparent Gus wasn't going to answer. "And when we saw your lab had never been used, we figured it was in our best interests to go."

"I see." Gus had now become a man of few words.

"Were you aware?" Rick pressed. "About the lab, I mean? And if you were, then is it safe to assume Ted stole worthless vials?"

"I wouldn't assume that," Gus said. "It's entirely possible he and Sheldon had the virus, even if they weren't actually the ones to develop it."

Carmen perked up at this, though she didn't speak. Not yet.

"Explain," Rick prodded.

"Before I do, I need to know what side you're on. Are you still in?"

"Yep. We're definitely in," Rick hastened to reassure the other man. "But we need to know if we should even bother trying to hunt down Ted and see what's in the vials."

Again a moment passed before Gus spoke. "We didn't know they weren't working in the lab. One of Sheldon's strict criteria was that we stay out. Believing he needed space and time to develop large batches of the virus, we did as he asked."

"Where did you find him?" Rick asked.

"We didn't. He found us." Clearing his throat, Gus sounded uncomfortable. Unusual for him. "Actually, someone sent him to us."

"Who?"

"I'm not at liberty to say." On that, Gus sounded firm. "I need you to find Ted."

Carmen and Rick exchanged a glance. Since this was exactly what they'd hoped he would say, she figured Rick would wrap up the call.

Instead, Rick asked a question. "Why? What are you hoping we will find?"

"The vials," Gus barked. "The damn vials. We don't need that stuff being released among the public. Not yet."

Not yet. Chilling.

"You've got to give me a bit more information," Rick pressed. "You believe Ted does have the genuine virus. I need a logical reason why."

"No. You don't. You follow my orders, not the other way around. Understand?"

Nudging Rick's arm, Carmen nodded. Clearly, Gus felt Rick had overstepped. She had to agree. Rick never would have acted like this when they were at the group's location.

"Yes." Voice surly, Rick shook his head and made a face at Carmen. Careful to hide her smile, she gestured that he should continue.

"I'm sorry," Rick muttered. "What Landers did pissed me off. And the one thing both Carmen and I despise is being lied to. When we saw the lab and realized it had never been used in any way, we thought we'd been duped."

The words he hadn't said echoed in Carmen's mind. They still were being played, though they weren't supposed to understand that. And truth be told, they didn't. At least as far as the reason why.

That's one of the things they'd have to find out. After they stopped the virus from taking out an entire country or more.

Chapter 13

Even before Carmen and Rick left, Maddie wanted to jump Jake's bones. Once they were gone, she could barely control herself. Unfortunately, he had no idea. He'd asked to borrow her laptop and had immediately become engrossed in research. He kept his spiral notebook open and used a pen to continue to make furious notes.

She'd never seen him like this. He was on fire. Determined, enthused and sexy as hell. With her body aching and throbbing, she couldn't take her eyes off him.

Oblivious, he continued to simultaneously type and jot stuff down. She watched him, burning.

How was this possible, that he made her so hot just being in the same room? And conversely, the fact that he hadn't even the slightest clue made her want him even more.

Should she attempt to distract him or simply wait him out? As she mulled this over, considering all the delightful ways she could entice him, he looked up.

"Maddie? Are you okay?"

She blinked. "Um. I'm not sure."

"What's wrong?" Expression concerned, he immediately pushed up out of his chair and sat down next to her on the couch.

It took every ounce of any willpower she possessed to resist him. Instead, she slid sideways so her head rested on his shoulder.

To her immense relief, he put his arm around her. "I've got a distant cousin who works for the CDC in Atlanta," he said. "I've emailed him and let him know I'm working on a story—I didn't get more specific than that—and asked him if he'd mind answering a few questions."

"Great." If she turned her head slightly, she could nuzzle his neck. She loved the scent of him. Human male, spearmint and something else, something earthy and musky that called to her primal wolf self.

He glanced down, catching her about to go for it.

"You're beautiful," he mused. "And sexy and sweet and smart and..."

Unable to resist any longer, she pulled him down to her for a kiss. The instant their mouths connected, the fire that had been simmering low in her belly erupted into a blaze, consuming them both.

Out of control, they shed their clothes. Naked, skin to skin, she let her fingers explore every inch of him. His hands were all over her also, his touch driving her to madness. She tried to climb on top of him, but he was having none of that and pushed her onto her back instead.

"Slow down," he ordered. "I want to savor this."

Part of her thrilled at the way he took charge. And when he used his talented mouth to taste her breasts, her skin and, finally, the throbbing spot between her legs, she lost all capacity to think.

The first climax came quickly, rocking her world. And then, while her body still quivered, he rose up over her and pushed himself inside her, filling her completely. Then, to her surprise, he held himself perfectly still while her last spasms clenched and released him.

She caught her breath, a quick gasp of air before he covered her mouth with his, letting her taste her own nectar on his lips. Suddenly, she felt desperate to have him move. She squirmed and arched her back, rotating her hips as she urged him on.

He groaned. "Maddie…"

Grinning, she pushed harder, up and down, until he used his hands to still her hips. "Wait." He spoke through clenched teeth. "Give. Me. One. Second."

But as he ground out the last word, he apparently lost whatever grip on self-control he had. With a roar, he released her and drove himself into her, hard and deep and fast.

She met each thrust halfway, baring her teeth, feeling so savage it felt like her wolf self had taken over her human one.

As the tension built within her, Jake cried out and shuddered. This was enough to send her once again over the edge. Together, as one, building upon the other's pleasure, they reached new heights. Though even in her own mind it sounded corny, she felt as if they'd blazed a path directly to the stars.

He held her while their breathing slowed and their perspiration-slick bodies cooled. For once in her life, she allowed herself to snuggle close, something she usually avoided. But with Jake, cuddling felt right. Especially after…that.

"Amazing," he murmured, kissing her forehead. "You're absolutely—"

"Shhh." She cut him off with a lingering kiss. She'd wait to move until he fell asleep, which in her experience with men seemed to happen within twenty minutes after sex.

But not Jake. Instead, he gently disengaged himself and padded to the bathroom. She watched him, admiring his toned naked body, until he closed the door and she heard the sound of water running.

While he cleaned up, she got up and collected her own clothes.

A few minutes later, he emerged, still naked. He gathered his clothing, picking it up from the floor, and got dressed right there in front of her. She watched him with interest, amazed when she felt another twinge of desire.

"I hate to make love and run," he said, grinning. "But I've got tons of research to do on this story and I know I won't get much done with you to distract me."

Amused and bemused, she nodded.

"Bye." He pressed a quick kiss on her lips. "Lock up after me."

And he was gone. She turned the dead bolt and headed toward the bathroom. The pleasurable way her body ached made her smile.

After a hot shower, she fixed herself something to eat and tried to decide how to occupy herself for the rest of the evening. While Jake was all hot on the trail of this story, she knew Carmen and Rick planned to handle it on their own. Her job was to keep Jake out of harm's way. If they happened to learn any useful information along the way, even better.

She made scrambled eggs and toast and ate standing up.

Now with Jake long gone, the edgy restlessness that had simmered all day returned. She roamed her small apartment, a completely different type of ache filling her. Not sexual, as Jake had thoroughly taken care of that need. When she finally realized what it was, she actually laughed out loud, shaking her head at her own foolishness.

She needed to change. It had been far too long since she let her inner wolf come out and play. She'd take care of that now.

Decision made, she grabbed her car keys and headed out. Nothing like a good hunt to help improve one's perspective on life in general.

Because there were limited places on the island that would be deserted enough to shape-shift safely, she headed north toward the mainland. Since she had plenty of time, she drove all the way to Clear Lake City. The wildlife preserve. There was one of her favorite places to let her wolf run free.

Once she arrived, she parked. Since it was now dark, the lot was empty. All the tourists had gone on to other, more well-lit pursuits and the locals knew better than to roam around this place at night. The only others she was likely to encounter now would be actual wildlife or other shifters.

Grabbing her empty backpack from the passenger seat, she started up one of the hiking trails. She'd learned a long time ago that it was better to bring something she could store her clothing in. That kept out insects and damp and who knew what else.

A creature of habit, when she reached her favorite spot, she set the backpack down on a fallen tree. Since the complete and utter darkness made it impossible to see anything farther than her own hand, she listened. Nothing but the normal sounds of nocturnal animals doing their usual thing.

Satisfied she was alone, she removed her clothing, once again marveling at her body's pleasant aches. After stowing everything in the backpack, she tucked it into a hollow in the side of the downed tree.

Then she dropped to all fours, relishing the feel of the damp earth beneath her, and initiated the change.

As her bones elongated and changed shape, sparkling lights surrounded her like a thousand fireflies. While sometimes shape-shifting could be painful, this time she felt only pleasure. When at long last her body was no longer human, she lifted her snout and sniffed the air.

Damp earth, wet leaves. A nearby rabbit or two. Even an owl lurked somewhere on a branch nearby. As wolf, she relied on her sense of smell the most.

Her wolf eyes immediately adjusted to the darkness and she could make out the ghostly shapes of trees and plants. She began to move, relishing the strength of her lupine body, loving the way her claws sank into the moist soil.

The hiking path stretched out ahead and she began to run, stretching herself out to her full length. The landscape blurred as she reached full speed, her paws thundering on the trail.

Only when she'd burned up her reserve of energy did she allow herself to slow. At the point where the path reached a small pond, she wandered near the water's edge and sat. Again she checked the scents drifting on the wind. Sifting through them—the usual rabbits and mice—she lifted her head when she located deer spoor. It had been a long time since she hunted such a large animal. Deer were usually brought down only by packs, a group of Shifters who'd become wolves together for the express purpose of hunting.

Which meant she'd take a pass on deer meat tonight.

She'd go for something small or maybe even skip hunting altogether.

It was enough to be wolf again. She'd forgotten how much changing centered her, made her feel whole again.

Returning to the clearing by the downed tree, she laid her belly on the damp earth and breathed deeply. Humans couldn't seem to understand the connection between the earth and her creatures. When she was in her human form, that knowledge felt abstract and distant. But as wolf, she could feel the energy linking her to all other creatures, and to their home.

Since dwelling on such philosophical matters wasn't what she usually did as wolf, she sighed and initiated the change back to human. Again, the sparkling lights, a few flashes of pain, and she finally lay naked on the forest floor.

Wincing, she got up, shaking herself as if by doing so she discarded any last, lingering remnants of wolf. She reached into the tree truck and pulled out her backpack, dressing quickly. It wasn't until she'd turned to head back to her car that she realized something was different. Every Shifter, upon returning to their human form, experienced an almost overwhelming sexual arousal. Mated pairs often took advantage of this, as did younger, unmatched, sexually adventurous singles. Those who were alone simply suffered through it until it passed, or pleasured themselves.

But tonight, Maddie felt…nothing. Correction—she felt sated. Apparently, making love with Jake earlier had satisfied even her deepest primal urge. Interesting. While she knew she should probably try to figure out how this could be possible, she put the thought away for later.

Jake refused to allow himself to dwell on how amazing making love with Maddie had been. But try as he might, he couldn't stop thinking about her as he drove home.

This story! The endless possibilities—from saving the world, to being the first journalist to be able to share the inside details! More than exciting, the thought was intoxicating.

While he still hadn't forgotten his earlier obsession with the mysterious door at the end of the dead-end alley, he'd put that on the back burner for now. Something like that couldn't come close to this, which might be the story of a lifetime.

One of his favorite songs came on the radio, and he cranked it up, singing along. Up ahead, the light turned green as he approached the intersection, which felt magical. At least until he'd gotten halfway through and the speeding truck hit him broadside on the passenger door.

The force of the impact spun him around, his vehicle going up on two wheels. As he fought to control the steering wheel, he thought he might actually roll, and braced himself. Instead, miraculously, the car landed back on all four tires, spinning once more before crashing into the guardrail. The shriek of metal on metal made an inhuman wail as the vehicle screeched to a stop.

Stunned, Jake maintained enough coherent thought to kill the engine before unbuckling his seat belt and attempting to open his door. The door wouldn't budge. And even when he turned the key in the ignition, the electric window refused to open.

One step at a time. The next rational move would be climbing over the console and trying the passenger door. He did and to his relief, it opened. He climbed out, suddenly dizzy, squinting and trying to locate the vehicle that had hit him.

There, engine still idling, a large box truck sat in the middle of the intersection, likely right at the same spot where it had hit him. Why hadn't it moved? Was the driver injured? Jake started to head that way and check, but a shiver of warning crawled up his spine and he paused. He knew enough to trust his instincts, even if they didn't seem rational at that exact moment.

He glanced north and then south, east and west. No other cars. The road seemed abnormally quiet for this early in the evening. Was it his imagination, or did the large truck appear menacing?

No matter what, he didn't have it within himself not to check on the driver. He couldn't leave a potentially hurt person alone without help, so he was going over. Before he did, he quickly dialed 911 and gave his location and a brief description of what had happened. Even though the dispatcher encouraged him to remain on the line, after informing her that he was going to check on the other driver, he ended the call.

When he reached the box truck, it didn't appear there was anyone in the driver's seat, though the window was open. He eyed the shoulder and the grassy embankment, wondering if the driver had been ejected. A quick search didn't reveal a body, so that meant the driver remained inside the cab.

His legs felt surprisingly wobbly. Shock, most likely. In fact, when he looked over his shoulder at his car, he seemed to be looking through a thick haze. Damn.

When the paramedics arrived, he'd be sure to have them check him out.

Again, he faced the box truck, stepping up on the running board and reaching for the door handle. He intended to use it to pull himself up and look inside. Instead, someone hit him over the back of the head and he crumpled to the ground.

When he came to, the violence of his headache made him groan. The metal floor beneath him bounced and jolted him. Disoriented, at first he couldn't figure out where he might be, or remember what exactly had happened. It all came flooding back to him—the accident, the truck and, last, being attacked. And now, judging from the sounds and motion, he was in the back of that same box truck with his hands and legs bound by what appeared to be duct tape, heading down the highway.

This made no sense. As he struggled to clear the cobwebs from his brain—as well as battle the knifing stabs of pain—he tried to find the logic. That was the first thing he always did when pondering the why behind a story. Some things were obvious, like a terrorist driving a rental truck into a crowd of pedestrians. Others were not quite so clear. Like this. Why would anyone target him?

He thought back to the night in the alleyway near Harborside Drive. The one that led to that mysterious door. He hadn't staked out the place in a while, and the accident tonight was nowhere near that area. Heck, this time he hadn't even been on the island. Yet it all seemed to be tied to that alley, that door. He'd been beaten, stalked and now abducted.

The truck hit a particularly large bump in the road, sending him bouncing. The swift spike of pain in his head made him wince. Though he couldn't reach up and feel the back of his head due to the ties, he'd bet he had a good-sized knot there.

Since he could tell it wasn't in his pocket, he guessed they'd taken his cell phone. At least he'd managed to call 911, so the police would be aware he was missing.

Maddie. His stomach lurched. No one would know to notify her. Would she think he'd simply taken off, intent on chasing their story on his own? He wasn't like that, not at all, but she didn't know him that well. Even worse, she'd believe he'd disappeared right after making love, which ranked up there as inconsiderate.

Once more, he tested his bonds. The duct tape had been wrapped around his wrists numerous times and it held tight. The same went for his feet, though he had a bit more wiggle room there. Didn't matter. He had to get his hands free.

Though he twisted and clawed, trying to reach an edge of the tape proved futile. Instead, he began looking around the darkened interior of the cargo box to see if there was anything—a sharp corner, an edge—that he could use to cut through the tape.

But there wasn't anything else at all. Except…on the back door. The handle that was used to raise the door. He wasn't sure how sharp the edge would prove to be, but it was better than nothing.

Gingerly, shuffling on his knees, he made his way over there. He sat with his back to the door and uttered a quick prayer. Then, pressing hard, he pushed his bound hands against the handle.

The tape caught and held. The metal wasn't sharp enough to cause a tear, even if he tried sawing back and forth. He attempted it anyway, desperate to get his hands free before the truck came to a stop.

After several minutes and numerous tries, all in different positions, Jake lowered his aching arms and admitted defeat. As he shuffled back to the front corner, he spied some sort of loop built into the side of the box. Clearly it had been designed to act as a tie-down. Since it was round, he knew it would be of no use to him. Just in case, he checked the one on the other side.

Jagged. Unable to believe his eyes, he scooted over. The bottom edge of the loop had broken off, just an inch or so of it, but enough to create a sharp shard. Like a home-made shiv, he thought, giddy and dizzy at the same time.

He backed up, caught the duct tape on the edge and yanked his hands down. Again and again he did this, until finally he felt the smallest tear.

Hope gave him energy and he worked furiously, putting every ounce of his flagging strength into getting free. The first tear grew, a bit at a time. Since there were several layers, as soon as he cut through one, he started on another.

Eventually, he had torn through enough to separate his hands. From there, it was a matter of simply removing the tape.

Except he decided to leave it on. Now that he had full use of his hands, it would give him a better advantage if his abductors still believed him to be tied. And he'd need every advantage he could get. Next, he removed the ties on his feet, though he made sure to leave the duct tape wrapped on each individual ankle. If he kept his legs close together, the initial impression would be that his bonds remained.

The truck made a sharp turn, nearly sending him flying. He scooted back to his corner, keeping his arms behind him as if he was still bound.

Judging from the sounds and feel, they'd left pavement and now traveled on a gravel road. Which had to mean they were getting closer to their destination. He couldn't help but wonder if they meant to kill him and bury his body out in the country, where no one would find it. He set his jaw grimly. He wasn't going down without a fight.

Finally, they slowed. Jake braced himself, wondering how many there were, and if he had a fighting chance.

As the vehicle shuddered to a stop, the driver killed the engine. Jake listened, waiting for conversation, something to tell him if there was a single assailant, or two or three. He heard nothing. Nothing but the sound of footsteps on gravel.

Someone raised the door with a squeal of metal. Jake blinked against the sudden brightness, momentarily confused. They hadn't driven long enough for the night to become day, had they? He supposed it depended on how long he'd been unconscious.

"Get up," a harsh voice ordered. Male, and somehow familiar.

As his sight adjusted to the light, Jake blinked. He recognized his assailant. "You," he said, struggling to his feet. "You're one of the guys that jumped me in that alley."

"Good for you," the man said. "Now less talk and more movement. Get up."

Though not an easy feat with his ankles supposedly bound, Jake managed to hobble toward the door on his knees. He knew he had to get up, but had to be careful not to reveal the fact that he'd managed to remove his bonds. He needed to keep his eyes open for an escape possibility. As soon as one presented itself, he'd take it.

With a muttered curse, his captor reached up and hauled Jake the rest of the way out of the truck. Because he let go before Jake's feet connected with the ground, Jake fell. Seizing the opportunity, Jake allowed himself to roll, putting a few more feet of distance between himself and the other man. Who, at least at this very moment, appeared to be alone.

Better odds, at least. Even if his captor outweighed him by at least forty pounds, Jake bet the other guy couldn't outrun him. Especially if he got a good head start. The only problem would be if he guy was armed.

With that sobering thought, he decided to adopt a wait-

and-see attitude. If an opportunity presented itself, he'd definitely respond, but he wouldn't take foolish risks.

Plus, he had to admit to being curious about what this guy wanted with him.

A second later, he was glad he hadn't tried running. Two more guys the size of pro football linebackers appeared, seemingly out of nowhere. Flanking him, they lifted him up and carried him into a long cinder block building. Down a dimly lit hallway, and into a better lit room that resembled a police interrogation setup.

"Sit," guy number one growled.

The two goons deposited Jake in a metal chair. Carefully, he kept his ankles close together and, though his arms had begun to ache, his hands behind his back.

His captor stood on the other side of a battered wooden table and glowered at him, silent.

The door opened and another man strode in. Tall, with a thick head of dark hair, everything about him spoke of confident authority. He nodded at the first man, who immediately vacated the room.

As soon as they were alone, he faced Jake, his calm, gray-eyed expression unsmiling. "Explain yourself."

"I would if I knew what I'm supposed to be explaining. I have no idea what you want from me," Jake replied. "I haven't been back bothering your precious alley, if that's what this is about."

"That is where this began," the guy in charge said. "Let me introduce myself. I'm Colton Kinslow. I'd like to know what you're up to behind my sister's back."

It took all of three seconds for the name and the statement to register. "You're Maddie's brother?"

"Yes. And we've picked up enough chatter to know you're involved in something big, something top secret.

Something someone like you has no business being involved in."

Someone like you. The words made Jake bristle. All his life, there was always that one person who made assumptions about him due to the color of his skin. To blacks, he wasn't dark enough. To whites, he was too dark. With his mixed parentage, he personally thought his skin tone was the perfect compromise between the two. Clearly, not everyone felt that way.

Something of his thoughts must have shown on his face.

"I'm not talking about race," Colton explained.

Jake crossed his arms. "Then what did you mean?"

For the first time, Colton appeared uncomfortable. "I can't explain. Not at this time. Let me just say that we consider you quite a bit more vulnerable than Maddie, Carmen or Rick."

He knew their names. Fully alert now, Jake wondered if this guy, who claimed to be Maddie's brother, had something to do with the virus. If so, then Jake had just lucked into the middle of the action without even trying.

Now all he had to do was keep himself alive.

Chapter 14

They drove until Rick started seeing double. While he wasn't sure if Carmen wanted to drive, he knew he had to get some rest.

"I can drive," she said when he asked her. "But I'd prefer not to. At least not tonight. How about we find an inexpensive motel and catch a few hours of sleep? We can get back on the road at the crack of dawn tomorrow."

Relieved, he took the next exit, pulling up in front of an unassuming two-story motel that looked both inexpensive and clean. He went into the office, paid for a single room and emerged with a card key. Per his request, the room was on the ground floor near the back. Of necessity, he always had to consider if there might be an urgent need to escape.

The small room appeared neat, though the decorating looked like it had been last updated in 1982. Two full-sized beds with a nightstand in between them, a small desk-like table with a chair, plus a faded blue recliner were the extent of the furnishings.

"Not bad," Carmen said, gliding around to inspect everything. She flicked on a light in the bathroom, and smiled. "I'm going to take a shower."

"I'll go after you," he replied, even though images immediately assailed him of them both naked in the shower together, water running down their slick bodies. Shaking his head, he pushed these thoughts away, turning on the television to help distract him.

Ten minutes later, her short blond hair still damp, Carmen emerged. "Your turn," she called out. "Nothing like a nice hot shower to make you feel better."

Oh, he could think of a few other things that would work, but he wisely kept them to himself.

However, the shower did reenergize him. Toweling off, he emerged to find her engrossed in some talk show on the TV. She held a little plastic bag with a straw in one hand. Though it looked like a child's juice pouch, upon closer inspection he realized it contained blood. Of course. Since blood was how she got nourishment.

His stomach growled, reminding him it had been a while since he'd eaten. He went to the curtain, peered outside and spotted the huge illuminated sign of a fast food restaurant next door. Hopefully, it would still be open.

After telling Carmen he'd be right back, he walked over and ordered a burger, fries and a chocolate shake. He brought those back to the room and sat at the desk and ate. Still watching her show, Carmen glanced over her shoulder at him, gave him a thumbs-up sign and continued sipping her own meal.

When his cell phone rang, Rick's first thought was that Gus had thought of something else. But instead, he found himself once again on the phone with Olson, his Special Agent in Charge. He listened to what the other man had to say with mounting disbelief.

When he finally ended the call, he had to sit in silence for a moment and let what he'd heard sink in.

Carmen waited, impatience plain on her face. "Well?" she finally asked. "What's up? I'm guessing whatever it is, it isn't good. At least, judging by what I heard on your end."

"The CDC called my boss." Rick tried to keep the panic from his voice, not sure he succeeded. "They are about to release a public health warning."

Her head snapped up, instantly alert. Inhaling, Carmen nodded. "About the virus?"

"Yes. They're calling it a plague."

She froze. "Where is the outbreak? Please tell me not a large metropolitan area."

"Not yet. West Latvia."

"The very country in Europe where the terrorists behind this were wanting to start a war. What the hell?"

"Exactly." His stomach roiled. "Casualties are increasing by the hour. Apparently, there's a twenty-four-hour period from infection to death."

"What's the fatality rate?"

"My boss said 100 percent. This thing seems unstoppable."

She'd started shaking her head before he finished speaking. "Nope. We can't let that happen. How close is the CDC to an antidote?"

"No idea. All I know is that they don't have one."

"Yet." The fierceness in her voice matched the shine of determination in her beautiful eyes. "Do they want me to go there and help?"

"No. They want us to go back to the Sons of Darkness hideout and use the lab. They're sending us samples of the actual virus. Oh, and they found Ted. Looks like he really did have the virus."

"Is that where they're getting it, then?"

He hesitated. "Sort of. Ted must have had the real thing. I don't know what happened, but he got infected. He got really, really sick, and fast. He's as good as dead. They're having another Vampire transport him to you."

"Brilliant." She shot to her feet, her gaze glittering with excitement. "Working with a live subject will be much more intense. In fact, that should help me get quicker results than lab work. We need to keep him alive for as long as possible. When do we leave? I'd like to get on the road."

He stared at her, aware that he hadn't yet told her everything and not sure if he should. "Wow. That's not quite the reaction I expected."

"Why not?" She appeared the most animated he'd ever seen her. "I fail to see a downside. I mean, I feel bad for poor Ted, but he kind of brought this on himself. He was dead anyway. You know Gus and Landers would have taken him out if we'd brought him back."

"True. But at least it would have been quick. From what I understand, he's suffering greatly. All the victims suffer. And then they die."

"Well, this way, at least he will have done something good for his fellow humankind," Carmen pointed out, eyeing him curiously. "But how on earth are we going to explain this to Gus?"

"That's easy. Ted—in an airtight, sealed container— is going to be delivered to us. We're to take him back to Gus's lab."

"Perfect," she exclaimed.

He only grimaced.

"I'm sorry." Carmen squeezed his shoulder. "I take it you're not a fan of the idea. Can you explain why?"

"I'm not." Still he struggled with how to find the right

words to say what his bosses wanted him to do. Finally, he decided to just say it. "And my reasoning is purely selfish. This virus is deadly, and I'd love for you to find an antidote. But…"

"But?" Arms crossed, she waited.

"But, so far all of the victims have been human, and no one knows how it interacts with Shifters." He took a deep breath. "Because we really need to find out, they're offering me up as a test case."

At his words, all the animation vanished from her face. "They?"

"The Pack Protectors. My real job."

Expression thunderous, she took a step toward him.

"Why would they do such a thing? You're a valuable agent."

"Because they don't have anyone else. I know about it. They're trying to slam the lid shut on any leaks until they know more. If word got out to the rest of the Pack Protectors…"

"There'd be a panic."

"Exactly." He scratched his head, wishing he could feel honored or relieved rather than horrified. "We can't have the ones who are sworn to protect all Shifters worried about this…plague."

"Then why release a public health warning at all? Seems contradictory to me."

"They have to, at least for the humans. A thing like this can't be kept hidden. The human press is starting to notice. People are dying. You know as well as I do that most Americans tend not to panic when an epidemic occurs on a faraway continent. But at least they'll be aware. And when it starts to spread to other countries, it won't come as a total shock." He looked her square in the eye, hoping he seemed calm and resolute. "That's why this is so important. You've got to develop an antidote."

Arms crossed, she began to pace. She finally came to a stop right in front of him. "No. I won't do it. I won't be able to do my best work if I'm worried about you."

His heart skipped a beat but he kept his face expressionless. "You have to. If the worst happens and I become infected, I'll be collateral damage. This is too big, too important, to let the life of one Shifter get in the way."

She didn't react. "Surely you don't believe that."

"I do. And you should, too." When she didn't respond, he shrugged. "And we don't know for certain that the virus can kill me. So far, only a silver bullet or fire can do that. Otherwise, I might get sick, I can get wounded, but I always heal. I'm hoping it will be the same with this virus."

"But you don't know," she cried out. "I'd rather you don't get involved."

For the first time since taking the call, he smiled. "Me, too. But I have my orders. And either way, we have no choice. We leave in the morning."

"What if I refuse to go?" she asked.

"Then I'm traveling without you." One of the worst bluffs he'd ever made. She had to know how badly they needed her and her scientific expertise. Without it, he was just a shape-shifting guinea pig.

Her eyes widened. "Seriously? Because you have to know there's no way in hell I'm letting you go in this without me to at least try to protect you. We're partners, remember?"

"Yep." He grinned. And then, because who knew what was going to happen to him once they reached the lab and took delivery of Ted, he pulled her into his arms and kissed her. Thoroughly and slowly, taking his time.

When he finally raised his head, they were both breathing hard.

"Yes," she said. "Not that you asked." And she kissed him again.

Hungrily, greedily, they clung together. Somehow, they shed their clothes, or at least enough of them to matter. Still standing, they were skin to slick skin. Carmen, so pale, so smooth, arching her back for him to taste her breasts. His body had become so hard it was painful, pulsing with need and desire. Almost frantic now, he pushed himself up and into her while they still stood, her back against the wall.

Inside, her body sheathed him like a glove. Wanting to prolong the moment, he gritted his teeth and tried to slow down, to contain the urgency. But Carmen, making sexy sounds low in her throat, became a wild woman. Shoving up against him, rotating her hips, she fought to make him go faster. "Hard and deep," she ordered, raking her nails down his back. "Now."

If control had been tenuous before, he now found himself clutching frantically to what tattered shreds remained. Four seconds in, he gave up, and abandoned himself to the mindless pleasure of making love with Carmen.

Fast and furious, they came crashing together, each meeting the other halfway, as if racing for an as yet unclimbed peak.

She cried out, a guttural sound, a cross between a moan and a scream. Determined not to be the first to lose control, he tried to focus on other things, anything but how amazing he felt inside her.

But when she climaxed, her body clenching around him, his self-control shattered. He let himself go, riding the waves of pleasure right alongside her.

They clutched each other close until their breathing slowed. He would have bet a million bucks that Carmen wasn't the type to cuddle after sex. But when she burrowed into his side, snuggling up against him, he gladly held her. He'd never really thought about what a Vampire's body would feel like, but Carmen felt warm-blooded, just like a human or Shifter. Weird, but great.

"What am I going to do about you?" she mused, her lips against his chest. "I don't want to lose you. I really like you."

He couldn't help but laugh. "I like you, too. And we'll figure out something. What matters more than anything is you figuring out an antidote."

When she didn't respond, he looked down at her. She'd fallen asleep. Astounded, he studied her, memorizing her exquisite features with his gaze. He couldn't really afford to let himself go soft. Allowing that sort of weakness could get him into trouble.

Still holding Carmen, he let himself doze.

Somehow, morning arrived without either of them moving apart.

Now that she and Rick had allowed themselves to do what both had been circling around for days, the air should have been much clearer. When she woke to realize that she'd somehow managed to have fallen asleep in his arms, she nearly pushed him away and leaped out of the bed. But something about the serene look on his handsome face as he slept stopped her.

Usually, she wasn't a big fan of Shape-shifters. But Rick wasn't an ordinary Shifter. And there was no way in hell she was going to let him endanger himself by acting as a Shifter guinea pig for a deadly new virus.

She needed to have Rick ask his boss if he could send

her the CDC's notes. It would be extremely helpful to know what they'd tried and failed. This would save her tons of time.

"Hey." Rick's voice, gravelly from sleep, drew her attention.

She shifted, twisting herself slightly toward him.

"Hey yourself." Immediately, she realized he was magnificently, spectacularly aroused.

And of course, they indulged themselves in a replay of last night's lovemaking. This time, they were much more leisurely about it, allowing each other the luxury of a slower, less urgent exploration.

After each taking another quick shower, they packed up and got back into Rick's vehicle. He ran through the drive-thru next door, ordering a breakfast sandwich and coffee after asking her if she wanted anything. She brandished another shelf-stable bag of imitation blood and declined.

When she asked him about getting records from the CDC, he liked the idea and sent off a quick text to his boss. He got an immediate response, confirming that his request would be met ASAP.

"Perfect." Carmen sat back, wrinkling her nose at the smell of grease and cheese. "I don't know how you can eat that," she said. "It smells terrible."

"To each their own." He nodded toward her blood. "Next up, I need to call Gus and tell him we're on our way back with Ted. The special team delivering it to us will meet us near Kemah."

"It's going to be interesting to see how they react once they learn Ted's been infected with the virus."

He glanced at her and grimaced. "I imagine they'll stay clear. Or they will if they have any sense at all."

Making the call while he drove, after the initial greeting, he didn't say much. Finally, when Gus apparently took a breath, Rick explained he'd be bringing back an infected Ted. "He's terminal," he said. "Just like everyone else who's contracted this virus. You need to take steps to make sure no one else gets infected. We'll be taking him back into the lab."

Rick listened a moment long before ending the call. He glanced at Carmen and shook his head. "They've brought in another biologist."

Her heart sank. "Did he say who?"

"No, he never mentioned the name or anything about credentials. Just that we'd have someone else helping us work with the virus."

"I don't like that," she murmured. "Not at all. But since we weren't given a choice, I hope at least they found someone with excellent qualifications."

The exchange in Kemah went off without a hitch. Rick pulled over down a winding country road. A few minutes later, a black Ford Expedition pulled up. Two men wearing full hazmat gear got out, went to the back and opened the hatch. Rick did the same with his vehicle.

They transferred what looked like a large plastic cocoon and had Rick sign off. Then they drove away.

"That was weirdly efficient," she commented.

"Yeah." Now Rick seemed fidgety, uncomfortable. He made no move to get back in the driver's seat and she couldn't say she blamed him.

"He's sealed up tight," she told him. "Besides, this virus isn't airborne. You'd have to touch him or have him cough on you to become infected. It's safe."

He nodded, eyeing Ted's body. "How can he breathe in there?"

Pointing at a loop of plastic tubing, she gave a short explanation of the air circulation system. "It's enough to keep him alive. Even though we're not sure how long he actually has to live."

When he winced, she apologized for sounding callous. "I've already shifted into my scientist mode."

Finally, he climbed into the vehicle. Once she'd done the same, they took off, heading for the Sons of Darkness compound.

They arrived in the early afternoon. Only Landers came out initially to greet them. Rifle at the ready, he circled around their vehicle as if he expected them to start throwing out vials of the deadly virus.

After he'd made two complete circles, he gestured for Carmen and Rick to get out. Slowly, keeping their hands where he could see them, they did.

Carmen stared at Landers, fantasizing about how easy it would be for her to snatch that rifle away from him. But of course she didn't.

A moment later, Gus and another man—one she didn't recognize—emerged from the house.

Gus grinned as he made the introductions. Landers stood off to the side, glowering at all of them.

The new biologist's name was Scott. He smelled of cigarette smoke, perspiration and rotgut whiskey.

While she wasn't entirely sure what to make of the human man, she kept her doubts hidden. She'd been able to sum him up in one look—or smell. His hands shook and his bloodshot eyes were far too bleary. Drugs or alcohol, probably both, and that answered her other question. Why he was here instead of at another, more reputable lab.

"Carmen here has a reputation as one of the top biologists in the country," Gus said. "The two of you working together should be able to replicate the virus."

"I worked for the CDC for twenty-seven years," Scott bragged. "It wasn't my fault they let me go."

Right. Wisely, she didn't voice this thought out loud. He'd been caught drinking or doing drugs on the job, had failed a random drug test or had made the kind of mistake that could have been disastrous while under the influence.

She glanced at Rick, who stared straight ahead, distaste plain on his handsome face. This nearly made her laugh, but she throttled that, instead resolving to speak to him later about perfecting a better poker face. Of course, since he was a seasoned undercover operative, the possibility existed that he wanted Scott to know how he felt about him.

"Considering that the virus has broken out in West Latvia," Carmen interjected, "is it possible someone obtained a blood sample or tissue sample? That would definitely help us get quicker identification."

Scott laughed, a bit maniacally, she thought. "I managed to snag a test vial from the CDC lab before I left. They have several, all locked in high-security areas. When I found out they intended to let me go, I took it while my clearance was still good."

Finally, the man had said something interesting. And judging from the rapt expression on both Gus's and Landers's faces, they were enthralled.

"That should help," Rick commented, his voice level. A quick glance at him revealed he'd managed to once again mask his feelings.

"Definitely," Carmen drawled. "As long as you're careful and don't allow yourself to get infected. That would be unfortunate. And deadly."

For a brief second, Scott appeared uncomfortable.

"Yeah, that's true. But that's what he's for." And he pointed to Rick.

Carmen froze. "What do you mean by that?" she asked, her voice ice. What did he know? And how?

Scott grinned, malice shining in his small eyes. "They promised me a living test subject." He turned to face Gus and Landers. "Am I wrong in thinking it's him?"

Carmen turned. The glare she directed toward Gus left no doubt how she felt about that possibility.

"One of my men will do it," Gus finally answered. "For now, Rick is going to act as your assistant."

Careful to hide the relief that flooded through her, Carmen nodded. "That's what I thought." Though she now had a sneaking suspicion that Gus might be lying. She couldn't imagine any of his men willingly stepping in.

"I'll send someone along shortly," Gus continued. "Right now, why don't you all get to work. We've got to get this right before the CDC comes up with an antidote. Whoever does that first holds all the cards."

"They aren't even close," Scott said confidently.

"What about replicating the virus?" Carmen wanted to know. "What's their progress on that front?"

Scott shrugged. "They're still working on that, too. Pretty frantically, let me tell you. Once that thing crosses the ocean to other continents…"

The thought made her shudder. The human population would be swiftly decimated. And since no one yet knew if Shape-shifters and Merfolk were immune, the virus could possibly ravage the paranormal community, as well. This would leave Vampires. And the thought of a world full of only Vamps sounded like a grim place indeed.

"We've got to figure this out," she declared, allowing

eagerness to leak into her tone. "Let's get started immediately. We need to move Ted from the vehicle to the lab."

Though Scott appeared appalled at the idea, Gus nodded enthusiastically. "My thoughts exactly. You two, get
to work right now. And Rick, your job is to find them
whatever they need."

Rick nodded. Only the way his jaw tightened gave
away how much he hated being ordered around by Gus.

As for herself, Carmen had to carefully mask her excitement. Finally, the brand-new lab would be used. Add
to that the fact that she would be able to get her hands
on the actual virus and things couldn't have been better.

Scott grunted and began shuffling off toward the barn.
Following, she wondered if he'd been working in the lab
alone and unsupervised. Originally, she'd planned on
trying to work around him. Now, though, she'd begun to
reconsider. He might seem incompetent, but he had been
working at the CDC and had access to the latest develop-
ments. She'd pick his brain for those. And who knew?
Maybe they could actually work together and solve this
puzzle.

However, if either of them succeeded in developing
an antidote, there was no way she'd be turning that over
to the Sons of Darkness. Not only would that make them
the most powerful group on earth, but it would be a betrayal of all humanity.

Chapter 15

The next morning, Maddie puttered around her apartment while waiting for Jake to call. Knowing him, he'd stayed up late doing research on the internet and had slept in. If she didn't hear from him by nine, she planned to call and wake him up. She wanted company for a late breakfast.

On her third cup of coffee, and a bit jittery, she watched the clock. Out of necessity, she'd made herself a single piece of toast and slathered it with peanut butter since she'd needed something to settle her stomach.

At five until nine, she gave in and called him. His phone rang and rang and rang, finally going to voice mail. Which meant he was most likely still asleep.

Her conscience warred with her grumbling stomach. She could be nice and let him sleep, or she could continue to dial his number until his ringing phone finally woke him.

Having no choice, she went with choice number two.

Again just ringing and no answer. She hung up and immediately called again. This time, someone picked up on the third ring.

"Maddie?" a familiar voice asked. "As least that's what shows on caller ID."

Stunned, at first Maddie couldn't find the right words. Instead of Jake, her brother Colton had answered. "What are you doing with Jake's phone?" she asked, even as a horrible realization dawned on her. "Please tell me Jake's not in Protector custody."

"I can't tell you that, because he is," Colton replied. "Sort of. Actually, he's in my custody. Which is, as you know, much safer for him than if he'd been taken in to headquarters."

While he did have a point, this still worried her. She swallowed. "Why? What did he do?"

Her brother sighed. "As you know, we've been keeping an eye on him for a while."

"Right, but I thought you were backing off once I told you I was handling him."

"I always have a backup plan," he chided. "You know that. So we've been watching him. Turns out he was seen meeting with one of our other operatives, a guy who's been working deeply undercover."

"Rick Fallin?" she asked.

Either because he liked her to think he knew everything, or because he already knew the answer, he didn't ask her to elaborate. "He refuses to tell me what he's doing with him or, for that matter, you."

Poor Jake. She grimaced, keeping her thoughts to herself. Colton could be formidable when he wanted to be. She was impressed that Jake had resisted giving anything up.

"You aren't torturing him, are you?" She put a threatening note in her question. "Because so help me, if you touch one hair on his head..."

Colton chuckled. "No torture. Come on, Maddie. I'm not a savage. This human hasn't broken any laws. Yet. He's just come onto our radar one too many times. We need to find out what he knows."

"I think you should ask Rick Fallin. He's one of your own, plus he's fully briefed on everything." It dawned on her that this entire situation might be a bit above her brother's pay grade. No doubt Jake had reached the same conclusion and that was why he'd gone silent.

"You know," Colton mused, "that's exactly what Jake said. How are you involved in this, little sister? You've been seen with him numerous times and you were spotted with him and Rick and another, unknown woman yesterday."

Now she went silent. And then, she tried to salvage everything the best way she could think of. "Jake is my... boyfriend," she said, wincing internally at the actual term. "He might even be my mate."

"He's human," her brother protested immediately. "Please tell me you aren't serious."

"Since when did you decide to be against Shifters mating with humans?" she asked, honestly perplexed since such a thing was very common. The children who resulted from such unions were termed Halflings. While not as invulnerable as full-blooded Shifters, Halflings were much more resilient than humans. They healed much faster, for one thing.

"I'm not, but this is *you*," Colton responded. "My baby sister. I've been hoping you'd meet another Pack Protector."

Disappointment warred with anger. "Let's cut to the chase. You need to let Jake go."

"Really?" His icy tone matched hers. "Let me remind you that I don't take orders from you."

"Maybe not. But this could be a matter of not just national security, but Pack security. I'd suggest you contact Rick Fallin or his superior and clear this through them. I have a feeling that you're going to have to put Jake back where you found him."

"That won't be so easy," he grumbled. "Since that was at the scene of an automobile accident."

Her stomach clenched. "Is he okay?"

"He's fine." Colton paused. "His vehicle isn't. I believe the police department towed it."

"Tell me where he is and I'll come pick him up." Though she felt frantic, she kept her voice calm and cool.

"Not yet. I'm not quite done talking to him. This new info you've given me has brought up totally different questions."

"Like what?" Though she still sounded collected, an edge had crept into her tone.

"I'm going to find out what his intentions are toward my baby sister." And Colton laughed, the exact same way he used to when they were just kids and he'd managed to pull one over on her.

"Don't you dare," she began, and then realized her brother had already ended the call.

Next, she did what she had to do. She dialed Rick.

Of course, he didn't pick up. Most likely since he was back undercover.

Then she tried Carmen, just in case. The call went straight to voice mail. Of course. But it had been worth a shot.

Her doorbell rang. She froze. These apartments enforced a strict no solicitation rule, so she doubted it was someone selling something.

She rushed over to the peephole and peered out. And silently groaned. It was that same Protector who'd been staking out Jake's house.

She decided not to open the door. Colton hadn't said anything about sending someone over. She had the uncomfortable feeling that this guy might be acting on his own. For whatever reason.

He rang the bell again, once, twice, and a third press in rapid succession. Judging by that, she thought he seemed agitated. Not a good thing.

Running for her phone, she punched Redial, praying Colton would pick up again. Instead, it rang and rang before going to voice mail.

She cursed. Her apartment was on the second floor, so the only other exit would be the balcony. While she could probably figure out a way to get herself down, she wasn't nuts about leaving her apartment available for that man to rummage through and trash.

And for what reason? The more she thought about it, the angrier she got. If the intruder had been human, she would have been confident in her ability to fight him off. But since he was also a Shifter, it would be tougher. Not impossible, just unlikely.

Crash. The front door shuddered. She swore. Damn fool was trying to break through her door.

"Stop!" she yelled. "What the hell do you want?"

"I need to talk to you," he hollered back. "It's urgent."

"I just got off the phone with my brother, Colton Kinslow. If there was anything I urgently needed to know, he would have told me."

"He doesn't know," the man replied. "Please. I'm begging you. Let me in. I promise I won't hurt you."

Right. Because she was so gullible that she'd believe

what a stranger who was actively trying to break into her apartment said.

"Go. Away. I'm dialing 911."

He groaned. "Don't. Please. I work with Rick Fallin's unit. Your brother isn't authorized to know about this. Rick is being set up."

Now he had her interest. "Set up how?"

"Let me in and I'll tell you."

Stalemate.

"I'm sorry," she finally said. "I don't trust you. Go away. Or call Rick yourself and warn him."

"I tried. He's undercover and not answering his phone."

Since that was correct, she again reevaluated. Then, finally deciding to take a chance, she opened the door. "I warn you," she told him. "You try anything stupid and you'll have an epic battle on your hands. I might be a smallish female in my human form, but my wolf is fierce."

Nodding, he stepped past her into her apartment.

"May I?" he asked, gesturing toward her couch.

"Sure." Standing near the door, she eyed him when he lowered his large frame onto her sofa.

"Sorry, it's been a long day. They'd kill me if they knew I was here."

"They?" she asked.

"My unit. Rick's being betrayed by the very people he trusts to have his back. I refuse to do that to him, so I'm here trying to warn him."

"He's not here. He only stopped by last night."

"I know." He rubbed his chin. "They're tracking him. This was the last place he visited before going back undercover."

"Which means—" she swallowed hard "—there's a very real possibility they know you're here right now."

He nodded.

Great. Now it seemed entirely probable that the crazy in her living room might be hunted by other deadly and determined Pack Protectors. It hadn't been too long ago when that organization had gone through a major purge, ousting the corrupt and cruel Protectors and reconfiguring with honest, decent agents.

Or so they'd said. Now, with this man telling her Rick was being set up, she had to wonder.

"They had Rick pick up a body that had been infected with the virus," he continued. "A guy that had escaped from the group Rick's pretending to be part of."

A chill snaked up her spine. "Go on."

"They're going to ask Rick to be their guinea pig, to see if the virus works on Shifters. The thing is, they already know. Apparently, this thing doesn't just kill humans. It's deadly to our kind, too."

She swallowed hard. "That's bad. If it is fatal to us, it's probably lethal to Merfolk, as well."

"Probably," he agreed. "But there's no reason for Rick to sacrifice himself when they already know the answer."

"Who's *they*?" she wanted to know.

"People in the higher echelon of government. Not just our country, but internationally. They are Shifters and Vampires, and who knows what else. The one thing they're not is human. They have..." Gesturing, he appeared briefly at a loss for words. "A master plan," he finally continued. One that originally involved the extinction of humankind."

At that, Maddie narrowed her eyes. She wasn't entirely sure she could take this guy at his word. "Are you saying that a Shifter created this virus?"

"Yes. The one thing he didn't expect was for it to be able to harm his own kind."

"But why?" This, as far as she was concerned, was the million-dollar question. "None of this make sense. Our people have gotten along with humans for eons. Why change?"

"Power," he answered. "Some say a Vampire is behind all this. It's sort of logical, since Vampires will be all that are left once the virus decimates humankind, Shifters and Merfolk."

While she still wasn't entirely convinced she believed him, clearly *he* believed he spoke the truth. "Who all knows about this?" she asked.

"My unit—Rick's unit. One of our guys accidentally intercepted a communication stream between two men who are on the high council. Now that we have access, we've continued to monitor the chatter."

She nodded. "And you're confident this information is accurate?"

"Yes. One hundred percent." A muscle worked in his jaw. "We've got to warn Rick. It's imperative that he play along without endangering himself. We don't want to alert the ones behind this before we can take them down."

"Take them down?" she repeated, wondering why it felt like she'd walked onto the set of a television drama.

"Yes." Mouth tight, he shook his head. "The less you know the better. Suffice it to say, this is bigger than just finding an antidote. It's about power. Whoever can control that virus can control the world."

And whoever came up with the antidote would have the most power of all.

Finally, she nodded. "I'll continue trying to reach Rick or Carmen." Still uneasy, she walked to the door and held it open. "And you go back to doing what you were before you came here."

The hint to leave couldn't have been any clearer. To

her relief, he nodded and took it. As he stepped outside, he turned and faced her. "May I have your phone number? That way we can stay in touch."

"I'm surprised you don't already have it," she said, only half kidding.

"I do." He smiled. "I'll text you so you have mine."

And he left.

Judging from what he could hear of Colton's side of the phone call, Maddie's brother wasn't pleased with what he was hearing from her. And while Jake wasn't sure what Rick would want Colton to know, it wasn't his place to reveal anything. One of the hard rules of successful journalism was to keep one's head down and avoid revealing anything too soon, especially information about the source. Which, in this case, would be Rick himself. If, as Colton claimed, the two men knew each other, then Colton could simply speak to Rick directly. That way, Rick could fill him in at his own discretion.

When Colton concluded his call and walked back into the room, Jake worked hard to keep his face expressionless.

"That was interesting," Colton said, grimacing. "Now I've got a whole other set of questions for you."

"I couldn't help but overhear. Are you seriously about to ask me my intentions toward your sister?"

To Jake's surprise, the other man grinned. "Maybe," he allowed. "Are you two dating?"

To his dismay, Jake felt his face heat. "That's none of your business."

Colton laughed. "I'm going to need to make another phone call," he said, thumbing through the contact list in Jake's phone. "What, no number for Rick Fallin?"

"I don't think he's in a place right now where he can

receive calls," Jake responded, even though he had no idea where Rick might be. "I suggest you call the Special Agent in Charge at whatever FBI office he works out of."

"FBI?" The notion appeared to surprise Colton. "Uh, yeah. Sure. I'll call them." He started to put down Jake's phone and then reconsidered. "Here," he said, walking it over and placing it on the ground next to Jake. "And you can take the rest of that duct tape off. I saw you'd managed to cut through it. Pretty enterprising. Kudos on that."

Jake nodded. "Thanks." Feeling slightly foolish now, he brought his arms around to his front, rubbing his aching wrists. As he began peeling off the remaining duct tape, Colton left the room to go make his call.

Once he had all the tape off—both hands and feet— Jake stood and began walking around, trying to get the blood flowing back in his arms and legs. He had to admit to feeling relieved knowing he wasn't in any real danger. Though he still didn't understand why Maddie's brother would have deliberately caused a car crash in order to grab him. Especially since he worked for the FBI. Surely they didn't allow such unorthodox methods.

He eyed his phone. Maybe Maddie could shed some light. Plus, he really needed to hear her voice.

She picked up on the third ring. "Oh, thank goodness. Colton, what on earth is going on?"

"Not Colton," Jake said. "He's in another room trying to reach Rick. You sound panicked. Are you all right?"

She exhaled. "I'm okay. I think. I just had another operative come to my apartment looking for Rick. He said he's trying to warn Rick that he's being set up."

Though his journalistic instincts were now screaming, Jake kept his voice level. "Popular guy. You know, no one ever told me exactly what covert operation your brother actually works for. I find it kind of odd that they'd concern themselves with a reporter like me. I'm not even famous."

She hesitated, just long enough for him to wonder if she'd tell him the truth.

"That's classified," she finally said. "I'm sorry, I can't tell you more than that."

"Kind of like what Rick does for the FBI?"

She hesitated a tad too long. "Um, yes. As for how you came to be on their radar, Colton received some intel on you and apparently the meeting with Rick and Carmen—and me—was the last straw."

"The last straw?" he repeated, incredulous. "Let's see. Colton broadsided me with a box truck and then tied me up and transported me in the back because he found it *annoying* that I met with you, Rick and Carmen? That's crazy."

"You're right, it is." She sounded genuinely upset. "I'm sorry. Tell me where you are and I'll swing by and pick you up."

"That's just it. I couldn't see where we went, so I have no idea where we are. You'll have to ask him."

The hiss of her sharp intake of breath showed her reaction to that. "Seriously?"

"Yes. Like I said, he transported me here in the back of a box truck. There were no windows. No matter what his reasons, this was really extreme," he continued. "I think my car might be totaled. I'm damn lucky I wasn't hurt." The anger he'd been keeping banked threatened to erupt. Directed at the wrong person. He swallowed hard, hoping he could maintain his equilibrium.

"I'm glad you weren't." The warmth of her tone took the edge off. "And if you don't have insurance on the car, I'll make sure Colton pays to have it repaired."

She'd make sure? "Are you saying you can tell your brother what to do?"

"No, not at all. I'm telling you I'll go to bat for you with my brother. What he did was wrong and he needs to make reparations."

For the first time ever, he finally understood the term *mental anguish and suffering.* This was more than the damage that had been done to his vehicle. He'd been run into—on purpose—and tied up and kidnapped. By her brother. For no good reason at all.

"That's it? The extent of your outrage?" Though he tried, he wasn't able to keep the bitterness from his voice.

"Jake, I'm as appalled as you are. And shocked. But whatever else I might be, I'm not my brother's keeper," she explained. "Like I said, he works for the same outfit Rick does. These guys are used to operating under the radar. Sometimes they go to extraordinary lengths to get what they want."

Something in her voice…

"What are you not telling me?" he demanded. "I can always sniff out when people are trying to hide the truth."

She laughed. "Don't go all reporter on me. It's me. I'm as upfront with you as I can be. But there are some things I can't say. Just like we can't pass on what Rick and Carmen told us. If they want Colton to know, I'm sure they'll fill him in."

"I didn't say anything," he said, relieved. "And I believe your brother is calling Rick now."

"Good. Then it's out of your hands. Look around and see if you can find any clues as to your location."

"Doubtful." He pinched his nose. "Considering that I'm in a windowless room in some kind of bunker."

"Are you talking to my sister?" Colton had come back

into the room. He leaned against the door frame, arms folded.

"Yes," Jake said. "Can you tell me where I am so she can come get me?"

One brow raised, Colton nodded. "Let me tell her myself. I need to ask her something anyway."

"Hold on," Jake told Maddie, and then handed over the phone.

"What's going on?" Colton asked his sister, his tone urgent. "As soon as I started trying to reach Rick Fallin, I was ordered to back off. Wait—don't answer me. Not on an unsecured line. We need to talk in person."

He listened for a moment. When Colton spoke again, a thread of urgency undercut his tone. "Rather than an address, I'm going to give you a clue. Remember when Dad used to take us camping when we were kids? Same place. And make sure you're not followed."

Evidently Maddie understood the reference. Colton punched the off button and handed the phone back to Jake. "She'll be here in a few hours," he said. "Might as well make yourself comfortable. There's a bathroom through there." He pointed. "And a kitchen with a fridge stocked with soft drinks. Or beer, if you'd prefer. I've even got a TV." He shrugged. "You don't have to stay out here in the garage."

"The garage?" Stunned, Jake looked around. "This is a garage?" There were no tools, no machinery, nothing to indicate the usage of this room. "I thought it was a bunker."

"Nope. You were wrong." Colton grinned. "This is my father's hunting cabin. He used to bring Maddie and me up here when we were kids. That's how she knows where to go."

"How far are we from Galveston?"

"A couple of hours. Come on." Motioning Jake to follow, Colton turned and went inside the house.

Curious, Jake followed him. The cozy, rustic retreat was so far opposite of what he'd been expecting that he couldn't help but laugh.

"What?" Colton asked, turning to eye Jake over his shoulder.

"Nice place," Jake said, shaking his head. "Though it's not the sort of place I would have expected an FBI agent to bring a captive."

"Oh, that." Colton tugged at his collar, grimacing. "I was actually acting on my own behalf, not the Bureau."

"Figures." Wandering around the room, Jake realized he could picture a younger Maddie here. Outside, he could see a lot of tall pine trees, as well as live oak and silver leaf maple. A bucolic scene, under ordinary circumstances. However, this situation was far from ordinary.

He didn't see a single other person. Or house. Nothing but forest and sky. Looking out the big picture window, Jake realized they were miles from civilization. East Texas, most likely. Still, none of this made sense.

Jake turned to face the other man. "Mind telling me why?" he asked quietly. "None of this fits. Why'd you go through such extremes to capture me? Wouldn't it have been a hell of a lot easier if you simply asked to have a word with me?"

"Easier, true. But not nearly as much fun." Colton chuckled. "I'm kidding. I did what I did for a reason. Other people are watching you, getting ready to pounce. I wanted to make them believe you'd been abducted so they'd back off."

"Other people are watching me?" Jake asked. "Again, why?"

"Because you represent a threat." Colton's ambiguous response didn't help at all. Obviously, he knew that. He clasped Jake's shoulder and squeezed. "Let's wait until Maddie gets here. Once I speak privately with her, it's entirely possible we can clear this entire thing up."

Head aching, Jake nodded.

Maddie. The one person he'd believed he could trust. Clearly, he'd been wrong.

Chapter 16

Rick caught up with Carmen and grabbed her arm. Her skin felt soft and smooth under his calloused fingers. Though she flashed a quick smile at him, she shot a clearly disgruntled look at Scott's back. The other man sure moved fast, especially considering he hadn't appeared all that eager to get started. His jerky movements reminded Rick of the crabs he sometimes picked up on the beach, trying to run away. This made Rick wonder if Scott might be on drugs.

Naturally, he couldn't ask. He couldn't even give the other man a rudimentary sobriety test. Since Gus and Landers brought up the rear and were only ten feet behind them, Rick didn't speak.

He might not know all of what was going on, but his sixth sense was working overtime. In an already weird situation, something else was definitely off. He hoped they'd find out what before all hell broke loose.

Once inside the barn, little had changed. Dust still coated everything, though their footsteps from before remained. When he spotted the wolf paw prints, she wondered how they'd escaped notice, but no doubt everyone assumed some wild animal had entered and then left when no food had been found.

As soon as they reached the back corner, Scott stopped, swaying slightly on his feet. He eyed Carmen with bleary red eyes. "I've brought the vial here and it's in the cooler. We must use extreme care when handling it."

"Vial?" She stared at him. "Of what?"

"The virus." He stared back. "What else would I have a vial of?"

"Point taken, but I thought we'd work on the infected subject first, not a vial. With an actual body, we can skip several steps right away. It's important to see how this virus mutates in a live body."

His smug grin made him look drunk. Rick revised his thought about drugs to include alcohol. "We can do both. You work on the body and I'll take the vial." Scott puffed out his chest. "I'm sure you know, but I'll say it anyway. It's imperative that we take precautions so we aren't infected." His condescending tone had Rick gritting his teeth.

He wondered what it cost Carmen not to snap at this fool. Cool, calm and collected, she only nodded and stepped away from them both. "Full suits," she said, gesturing to a wall of closed lockers. "I checked them out before. They're old, but I did a cursory examination and found no tears or holes. There are enough for all three of us to have one."

"We'll check them again," Scott interjected. "Not that I don't think you're thorough, but I personally don't have any desire to die because these people skimped on proper precautions."

Now Rick had to curl his hands up into fists to keep from doing anything foolish. Judging by Carmen's narrowed gaze, she felt the same way.

"I second that," she finally said. "I don't want to die, either." Her first lie, at least to Scott, since the virus wouldn't affect her. She was already dead. Again, Rick admired her acting ability. There were many facets to Carmen and her beauty was the least of them. He thought he might really enjoy getting to know her, which surprised him.

"Landers here is going to stand guard," Gus announced. "He'll remain in position outside the lab until someone comes to relieve him."

Landers strutted around, glaring at them. He obviously considered himself a deadly menace. One look summed him up. A bully.

Still, of course it would have to be Landers. Judging from the menacing way he held his rifle, he hoped someone would give him a reason to use it, whether smashing someone with the butt of it or firing off a few shots. Rick entertained a brief fantasy of shifting into a wolf and ripping out the other man's throat.

"I don't think he needs a suit, though," Scott said slyly, pointing at Rick with a shaking finger. "Why waste one when we might need a backup? He's only your assistant. There's no reason for him to come inside the lab."

Inwardly tensing, Rick waited for Carmen's response instead of reacting and telling this fool what he thought of him.

"I want him there," she said smoothly. "That's reason enough."

Though Scott mumbled something under his breath, he didn't challenge Carmen any further.

Once they'd all suited up, Scott and Carmen went through the purifying process to get into the sterile environment. Though wearing the claustrophobic and cumbersome suit, Rick remained outside the chamber, announcing he was ready to bring them whatever they needed.

Carmen nodded, her smile letting him know that this setup pleased her. Him, too, despite his orders. If something went wrong, neither of them wanted Rick to be the test subject for ascertaining whether or not Shape-shifters were immune to the virus.

Something about Scott's movements worried Rick. However, even if the other scientist planned to "accidentally" infect Carmen, the virus wouldn't hurt her. What Rick couldn't figure out was the other man's agenda. Clearly, he had a grudge against the CDC. Yet he seemed intelligent, so he had to realize the fact that he'd successfully stolen a vial of the virus made him a force to be reckoned with.

He could have had all the power to himself. Instead, he'd chosen to align himself with a fringe group of crazies.

Unless… Once again, Rick realized there had to be a lot more to this story than he realized. It was like peeling back layers on an onion.

Right then he decided to join Scott and Carmen inside the lab. In there, he could keep a closer eye on things.

When she'd first begun working with biological diseases, Carmen had found the suits cumbersome and awkward. These days, she actually liked them. They reminded her of the old days, when Vampires had believed it necessary to sleep in coffins.

"The vial is in here," Scott said, his voice muffled due to his headgear. "I waited for your arrival before running any tests."

Something in his voice. She gave him a sharp look. "Are you absolutely certain of what you have?"

Before he could answer, Rick stepped into the cleansing room. A moment later, he joined them inside the lab.

"I'm so glad to have you here," Scott said, rubbing his gloved hands together. "You can be of much more assistance than if you'd stayed out there."

For herself, Carmen felt the opposite. For safety's sake, she'd much rather have had Rick stay where he'd been. Of course, she couldn't vocalize that. She didn't want any of the people to have the slightest inkling how important Rick was to her.

The knowledge slammed into her like a punch to the gut. Despite everything, she loved him. Even though she had no idea how he felt about her.

Scott said something and she shoved the newfound knowledge away. She'd examine it later.

"We need to bring the victim in," Scott said, carefully placing the vial back inside its Styrofoam nest. "After we do blood samples, I want to make sure he has the same virus."

Carmen shrugged. "Sounds good."

Barking out his request to have Ted brought in to Landers, Scott gestured to Rick. "You go and help him. See if there's an extra protective suit he can wear."

To her surprise, Landers instantly obeyed. Since one suit remained, he clumsily put it on while they all watched.

Once Landers finished, Rick went back through the disinfecting area and joined the other man. Together they left the barn.

She and Scott waited silently until they returned with the still sealed carrier that contained the hapless Ted. Each man held one end, though due to the rigid shape of the container, she couldn't tell which was the head and which was the feet.

Poor Ted. She couldn't help but wonder if he'd even be alive once they opened the enclosure. Either way, it wasn't going to be a pretty sight. The virus wasn't just lethal, it was disfiguring, as well.

Landers and Rick stood in the decontamination chamber, holding Ted between them. When the light turned green, they entered the clean room.

"Over here," Scott directed, gesturing at a long stainless steel table. He stood watching, impatiently shifting his weight from one foot to the other. Once the container was settled, he ordered them to step aside.

Landers complied immediately, going so far as to leave the room. Carmen noticed he didn't remove his protective suit, though, even as he made sure to put as much space as possible between himself and the virus.

Just as Scott reached to unfasten the first of the three clips, shots rang out, coming from somewhere outside the barn. Landers attempted to spin, but the heavy protective gear made him clumsy, and he fell. Hard.

Rick grabbed Carmen, attempting to push her to the ground. She twisted away from him, or tried to. Moving in these suits was like trying to swim in quicksand.

"Take cover," he ordered, clearly forgetting momentarily that she was a Vampire and invulnerable to guns and bullets. Just as he was, unless the shooter happened to be savvy enough to have used silver bullets. Humans never did, since they had no idea Shape-shifters even existed.

Another volley of shots. Scott, who'd frozen in place,

cursed loudly. "Those idiots," he said. "How can they not understand the importance of what we're doing in here? They swore they'd keep us safe."

"Yeah, well, I guess they failed," Carmen told him. "And if you want to stay alive, I suggest you drop to the floor and take cover."

"Drop? In this suit?" He shook his head. "Impossible. I notice both of you are still standing."

Carmen and Rick exchanged looks. "True," she admitted.

Through the clear glass, they all watched as Landers struggled to rise to his feet. It would almost have been comedic, if not for the sound of more gunfire, closer this time.

Rick shook his head. "What the hell are they up to?"

"I don't know," Scott answered, as if the question had been posed directly to him. "But we need to protect this virus. We can't let anyone else get their hands on it."

Great. The last thing Carmen would have suspected was some rival group attempting a raid. But then again, why not? This entire situation had been crazy.

A moment later, the barn door crashed open. Five fully armed men stood in the opening. Landers cursed again, fumbling to remove the suit so he could reach his own weapon.

"Freeze," one of the intruders yelled, training his rifle on Landers. Landers froze.

Carmen again glanced at Rick. Unbelievably, he wore a wide grin on his face.

"Friends of yours?" she asked.

"You might say that." Rick waved. "Hey Pete, over here."

What happened next seemed to go in slow motion. Rick unclipped his headgear, pulling it off his head in one easy motion.

Horrified, Carmen shouted at him to put it back on. For a second he only stared at her, clearly having forgotten the danger. Then, realizing, he slammed the headgear back into place, securing the clips with fumbling gloved fingers. "It should be okay," he said. "We haven't opened Ted's container or the vial. Since the virus isn't airborne, I should be all right."

Scott nodded in agreement. "He's correct."

Meanwhile, the team of armed men came closer. "Clean lab?" the one named Pete commented. "Fancy."

"Yeah." Rick grinned. "Give us a second and we'll be right out."

"Wait a moment." Scott stepped in between Rick and the exit. "Do you know these people?" Then, without waiting for an answer, he groaned. "It's an inside job. You two are working with them, aren't you?"

"I have no idea who these people are," Carmen protested. Though Rick clearly did. She wasn't sure how all this factored into his undercover role, or what the men were doing here, so she'd let Rick take the lead.

"Relax," Rick said, glaring at Scott. "They're not here about the virus. They're working with me on something else. Now if you'll excuse me..." Without a backward glance, he went out into the cleansing chamber and finally out into the other room where Landers still stood as still as a statue.

This time, when Rick yanked off his headgear, he took a deep breath and smiled. "Much better," he commented, before relieving Landers of his rifle. Shedding the rest of the bulky suit, he stepped outside with the other men and closed the barn door behind him.

"Do you trust him?" Scott asked, glancing sourly at the closed door. "Or are we about to be killed in the midst of some sort of coup?"

She told the truth. "Honestly, I have no idea what's going on."

"I thought he works for you."

"Rick?" She shrugged, as if she didn't care. "We're partners. But I don't know everything about him, and he doesn't know everything about me."

Scott's scowl told her what he thought of that. "I can assure you that there are powerful people behind this backward group, the Sons of Darkness. How else do you think they got funding to build this lab? There are forces at work here that you—and he—cannot possibly comprehend."

"Ah, but I do," she said quietly. "The future of the world is at stake. Power and powerful people will crumble before the death and destruction that this virus can bring. That's why it's imperative that an antidote be found quickly."

His jaw went slack, as if he found her statement not only shocking, but absurd. "If the combined forces of the best infectious disease biologists working for the CDC can't find an antidote, how can you possibly believe we can?"

"Because I'm just that good," she responded. "Now, while we don't have any idea what's going on outside this barn, how about we get to work? No one is going to be foolish enough to interrupt us while we're working with an infected body."

Considering for a moment, Scott finally agreed. "Who knows," he said, his tone bleak. "Maybe we can come up with an antidote before someone shoots us."

"Maybe we can," she agreed. "Let's get to work."

Seeing Pete not only was a major surprise, but Rick knew immediately that something had to have gone terribly wrong. Otherwise, his team never would have risked unmasking his cover.

But first, they all exchanged greetings, amid much back clapping and arm clasping. "Sorry, man," Pete said. "But we had to take out the others up in the house."

Gus and his crew. "How many were there?" Rick asked. "The number of people at this place seems to fluctuate quite a bit."

"We rounded up five." Pete grimaced. "We were just going to contain them, but one of them—the bald one— decided to try something stupid. As soon as he started shooting, the others went for various weapons. We had no choice."

Which meant Gus and his gang were all dead.

"What about the ones in the barn?" Pete asked. "I know you're working with Carmen, but who are the other two men?"

"One is part of the gang. The other is a former CDC scientist they've brought in. Or so he claims." Rick shook his head. "What the hell are you guys doing here?"

"We heard you were given orders to be the test case for the virus, to see if it affects Shifters." Pete's narrow-eyed gaze told Rick what his friend thought about that.

"True. I was. I don't like it, but I can't fault the logic. One person is acceptable collateral damage, especially if my sacrifice saves others."

"It's a trap." Pete crossed his arms, his expression grim. "They already know the virus kills us. They have documented proof. Several of the dead over in West Latvia were Pack."

Stunned, Rick wasn't sure how to respond. When he did, he could come up with only one question. "But why? Why would they ask me to die if they already know?"

"I don't know. Who have you pissed off lately?" Pete

asked, clearly only half kidding. "Or did you find out something you weren't supposed to?"

"Not that I know of." Genuinely perplexed, Rick thought back. "Olson Ferring's been giving me my orders. Does he know you guys are here?"

"Hell no. As soon as we found out what was going on, we headed out to rescue you. No way we're letting one of our own go down without a fight."

Grateful, Rick nodded. "I appreciate that."

"Good. Let's go. We want to get you out of here before the powers that be find out what we've done."

While that idea held a lot of appeal, Rick wasn't running off and leaving Carmen. "I can't," he said. "This mission is too important."

Pete eyed him. "You're not making sense. I just told you that you're being set up."

"And I appreciate that. I can now take effective precautions. But if there's even the slightest chance that the two biologists in there can come up with an antidote, I've got to make sure it gets into the right hands."

Squinting at him, Pete finally slowly nodded. "It's your funeral."

"It's all of our funerals if we don't find a way to stop this virus," Rick said. "I honestly believe this may be our last hope."

"Seriously?"

"Yeah. Unfortunately. I appreciate you guys having my back, but I can't leave."

Slowly Pete nodded. "Then we're staying with you."

Touched and honored, Rick nodded. "You need to understand you all could die if this goes south."

Pete shrugged. "We will all die anyway if what you say is true and this virus starts running rampant through our population. Better to be on the right side and go down knowing you did whatever you could to prevent it."

Those words were, in a nutshell, the reason why Rick's unit was the best of them all.

"Go on back in there," Pete directed. "Me and the guys will stay outside here and guard the place."

Taking a deep breath, Rick turned to head back into the barn.

Working carefully, Carmen and Scott opened the container that held Ted's body. Once they got it fully opened, inside was another body bag that they had to unzip.

The instant they did that, a horrible odor hit them, so strong it sent Scott reeling away from the table. Even Carmen, who'd smelled many awful things over the centuries, fought to keep from gagging.

Then she caught sight of what had once been Ted. "Will you look at that?" she breathed. "It's not even recognizable as having been a human being."

Her statement brought Scott rushing over to see for himself. Eyes huge, he stared down at the writhing mess of goo inside the body bag. "What the hell is that?"

"What the virus does to its host, if allowed to incubate after death," she replied. "That's why they've been burning the bodies over in West Latvia."

Though he nodded, Scott didn't take his gaze from what Carmen now thought of as virus breeding ground central.

"We should be able to get some good samples from this," she said. "Can you please bring me three new test tubes?"

Moving like a man in a dream, he complied. When he handed the first one to her she saw his hands were shaking. For the first time, she wondered if he'd truly have the balls to handle this type of work.

"What department did you say you worked in at the CDC?" she asked, keeping her voice casual.

"I didn't."

Not a good answer. Since time was of the essence, she decided to cut to the chase. "Do you have any idea what you're doing?"

Instead of his usual bluster and bragging, Scott merely swallowed hard. "I wasn't on the front line in the lab. My job was more data focused."

In other words, he entered the data into a computer.

While that job, too, held some importance, the fact that he'd passed himself off as a top research scientist infuriated her. "Why?" she asked, knowing he'd understand the question.

"Because I wanted to do some good," he responded. "I am a degreed, trained biologist. I took a data entry job as a way to get into working at the CDC with the hopes I could eventually move into the research lab. When I saw my chance, I took it."

"Your chance? You stole a vial of a deadly virus and took it from a controlled environment out among mankind."

He at least had the grace to appear ashamed. "What else could I do? When the Sons of Darkness contacted me, telling me how they had a clean lab and offering me the opportunity to save humankind, how could I refuse? How could anyone refuse?"

She opened and closed her mouth, not sure how to answer.

"Anyway," he continued, apparently taking her silence for agreement, "what's *your* story? You act like you're some super hotshot scientist, but did you ever even work for the CDC?"

"Nope." And that was all she intended to say about that. "If you want to help me analyze these tissue samples, you'd better get busy."

To his credit, he once again stepped up. Looking as if he might vomit at any moment, he watched while she filled the first test tube halfway and placed it in the metal stand. When he handed her the second, his hands weren't shaking as noticeably, though the tremor was still there.

Once all three test tubes had been filled, they carefully zipped up the body bag and also reclosed the container. "We'll need to burn that," Scott commented.

"True," she agreed. "But not yet. Right now, I want to take advantage of all the active tissue samples."

The barn door opened, sending a beam of brilliant sunlight to light up the other part of the barn. Rick stood silhouetted in the door for a moment before he closed it. He hurried back to the lab area, entered the antechamber and quickly suited up. After rushing into the decontamination room, he once again entered the lab.

"Well?" Scott demanded. "Are you going to tell us what's going on?"

"No," he answered, his voice muffled behind the headgear. "That's on a need-to-know basis. And right now, you don't need to know."

Chapter 17

Though it had been years since Maddie had visited her father's old hunting cabin, she knew the way there as if she was still a regular visitor. Once upon a time, she had been. Before she and Colton had been born, their grandparents had gone in with their own siblings and purchased a hundred-acre parcel of land in Southeast Texas. Each family had constructed several small cabins, careful that none of them were in sight of the others. Young Shifters learned how to change here, and how to hunt. They'd had family reunions and group hunts, and celebrated birthdays and anniversaries there. Despite the pall of the occasional divorce and remarriage, the tradition continued strong.

But then Colton and Maddie's father had been killed. This horrific act, a brutal murder with a silver bullet, had forever changed their tight-knit clan. After his death, their stepmother had wanted nothing to do with the rest of the family. She'd sold what she could and moved away.

Since the cabin remained deeded to the still-living grandparents, she'd been unable to get her greedy hands on that.

These days, with all the kids grown and their elders traveling, the cabins weren't used much. But they would be, as soon as the next generation of Shape-shifters was born.

Driving, Maddie's heart quickened at the thought. She'd been too busy establishing her career to even think of having children. And to be honest, she hadn't met anyone she'd even consider mating with. Until now. Until Jake.

Now that she'd had the thought, instead of shutting it down, she allowed herself the luxury of trying to imagine what their babies would look like. She'd hope they had Jake's beautiful skin tone rather than her freckled, pale one. In fact, she'd rather they'd totally resemble him, as he was the most handsome man she'd ever met.

Damn. Gripping the steering wheel, she shook her head. When had she become so far gone? Jake's capture, even if by her own brother, had forced her to face the truth.

She loved him. Truly, madly, deeply. Amazed, she turned up the radio, singing along as she drove. She drove fast in the passing lane, noted what vehicles were around her, and then switched to the far right lane and a much slower rate of speed.

None of the original group of cars stayed back with her. They all passed her.

She did this several times on the trip, with the same results. Then, just before she made the turnoff to take her east, she pulled in to a fast food restaurant. After sitting in her car for a few minutes and checking out all the other vehicles that pulled in after her, she got out and stretched her legs. Inside, after using the restroom, she bought a large coffee and a sandwich. When she returned to her car, she locked the doors and sat there until she'd finished eating.

Again she went through the parking lot, noting vehicles, before pulling out. She kept a close eye behind her, but saw nothing of interest, so she got back on the highway and took the necessary exit.

Once more, in an overabundance of caution, she performed her little test. Fast, then slow. Finally satisfied that no one was trailing her, she continued on to her destination.

Not a single other car in sight, she turned off the main road onto the familiar gravel one. As she drove through a set of open iron gates marked Private, her heart rate sped up. Odd how even with so many years since her last visit, this still felt like returning home.

Finally, the first cabin came into view. Set deep within a copse of trees, the weathered wood blended with the rich colors of earth and forest. A flood of memories rushed back, but Maddie continued on. Her family's cabin was much deeper, near the river.

After passing three other cabins, she finally rounded a curve in the road and got her first glimpse in years of the one belonging to her family. The faded gray color gave it a homey look. She felt a rush of nostalgia as she turned in the horseshoe-shaped drive.

Parking behind the white box truck, she got out of her car and headed toward the back door. Despite the sidewalk, no one ever used the front entrance to the cabin. The back side, with its large wooden deck, had been deliberately made more inviting. As she crossed the walkway and the overgrown flower beds, the back door opened and Colton came out.

"You made great time," he said, enveloping her in a quick hug.

"I did," she agreed, looking past him for Jake. "And I made sure no one followed me."

"Perfect." His gaze followed hers. "Looking for something?"

"Quit." Pulling away, she punched his arm. "Where is he? Please tell me you don't still have him locked in the garage."

"Where else would he be?"

She stared in disbelief. "Judging by your frown, you don't see how awful that is."

"What? He's fine. I didn't want to bring him into the house until you got here."

"Why not?" Turning to face him, hands on her hips, she glared. "Afraid of a human man?"

He actually appeared offended at her words. "That wasn't it. I needed to talk to you first and find out how much he knows. Is he aware that you're Pack?"

"No." She swallowed. "We haven't reached that stage in our relationship yet. It's all too new."

His gaze searched her face. "Yet you seem pretty certain about your feelings."

"I am. When you know, you just know. I can't explain it any more succinctly."

Though she could tell he had no idea what she meant, he slowly nodded. "I haven't had a chance to get to know him very well. Actually, he's really pissed at me. And I can't say I blame him." He shrugged. "Eventually, he'll understand what I did was for his own good."

"Was it?" she asked, crossing her arms.

"Yes. Some of the other Pack Protectors got wind of the fact that he is planning to write an exposé on Broken Chains. I have to tell you, that went over like a ton of bricks."

"Where did they get that info?" she asked. "As far as I know, he's only mentioned it to me."

"Apparently, he approached who he thought was some random guy and offered him money to help him get in."

She groaned. "Yes, he mentioned that. Let me guess. The guy is a Protector."

"Bingo. Orders came down from Headquarters yesterday that he was to be brought in and interrogated. If they learned he knew too much, he was to be...reprogrammed."

A shudder crept up her spine. "He doesn't know anything, I promise. All I've done is misdirect him."

"I believe you. But you know how it is. Once a report is made, it has to be investigated. That's why I staged such an elaborate abduction."

"Because you want them to believe...what, exactly?"

"That a Protector unit has grabbed him. There's still the occasional infighting in the group. Competition is fierce to see who can find the most threats and neutralize them."

"Are there truly that many?" she asked, still skeptical. "I mean, come on. Everyone knows about the consequences of revealing the truth to humans and no one wants to be picked up by the Protectors. I'd think that alone would act as a huge deterrent."

He shrugged. "What can I say? People can be stupid."

Since she had no answer for that, she glanced at the house. "Can we go get Jake now? I imagine this has all been stressful for him."

"Sure." Colton shook his head. "But if you ask me, that guy's plenty capable of dealing with stuff like this.

He's a well-respected journalist who's written articles from all over the world, including dangerous war zones."

"You looked him up?" she asked, incredulous.

"Didn't you?"

Instead of responding, she punched him in the arm and pushed past him to get inside the house. As she hurried toward the garage, Colton stopped her. "I was kidding. He's not in the garage anymore. He wanted a shower, so I let him use the bathroom." He pointed at the closed door. "Unless you intend to go in after him, you might as well wait with me in the kitchen."

"Don't tempt me," she muttered.

Hearing that, her brother made a face. "Gross. Don't even think about it."

The bathroom door opened before she could reply. Maddie's thoughts scattered at the sight of Jake, his close-cropped dark hair damp, button-down shirt open to reveal his muscular chest. Unable to help herself, she let her gaze roam to where his jeans rode low on his hips. To top it all off, he was barefoot. He hadn't yet seen her because he appeared to be preoccupied rubbing at one of his wrists.

"Rein it in, Kinslow," Colton murmured, elbowing her hard. Raising his voice, he invited Jake to join them in the kitchen.

Jake looked up and his gaze locked on Maddie. Swiftly he crossed the room and went to her, took her in his arms and held her. Heart hammering, she snuggled close, relishing the warmth of his skin, the feel of his muscular body, his unique masculine scent. *Mine*, she thought, unbidden. *All mine*.

"Oh, for the love of…" Colton turned away. "Anyone want coffee?"

Raising his gaze, Jake's expression hardened. "Will it be laced with something to knock me out?"

"Ouch." Colton shook his head. "Look, as I told my sister, I had good reasons for doing what I did."

"And they are?"

Maddie swallowed. Now came the tricky part. She wanted to tell Jake the truth, just not all of it. "There's another group that's after you," she said. "Colton did what he did to make them believe you were abducted. That will buy you some additional time."

Judging by his closed off expression, Jake wasn't buying it. "After me? Why?"

Colton took over. "This group believes you might have stumbled on some classified information. They'll do anything to keep you from revealing it to anyone."

"Classified?" Now Jake frowned. "I haven't come across anything like that. Believe me, I'd know. I'm a reporter. We're good about quickly comprehending things like that."

Aware she couldn't glance at her brother, which might make Jake realize they weren't telling him the full story, Maddie kept her gaze trained on Jake. "You know that and we know that, but this group doesn't. They want to bring you in for questioning."

The ever-observant Jake picked up on her use of that particular phrase. "Are they law enforcement?" he asked.

"More like covert ops," Colton interjected. "That's why letting them nab you wouldn't have been safe. They operate outside the constraints of the law."

"Where's your evidence?"

Both Colton and Maddie froze at Jake's question.

"You'd better believe he wants evidence," Maddie said, finally looking directly at her brother. "He's a reporter."

"And as such, I need proof." Jake shook his head.

"Facts, not speculation. What hard evidence do you have that this story you're telling me is true?"

"Because I'm one of them," Colton finally said, anger flashing in his gaze. "And believe me when I tell you that you're a wanted man."

While Colton's story had holes in it large enough to drive a truck though, Jake could also see elements of truth. He understood they—and this included Maddie, which bothered him—were trying to manipulate him. For what reason? That had yet to be revealed.

"All right," Jake finally said. "Let's say I decide to believe you. I'm a wanted man. But I also know top secret government agencies don't go after someone on a hunch. They need proof. Hard data. So tell me, what do these people have on me?"

Neither Colton or Maddie responded. When Maddie reached over to take his hand, he moved away. Though hurt flashed across her mobile features, she didn't say anything. Of course not. What could she say, other than an outright lie?

"I trusted you," he told her. "The one thing I thought I could always count on was you being straight with me."

"I *am* being straight with you," she exclaimed. "There are just certain things I can't tell you."

"Sorry, that doesn't cut it. If you want me to believe any part of what you say, you've got to tell me everything."

When Maddie looked down, Jake felt like she'd just stabbed a knife into his heart.

"I can't," she whispered. "Believe me, if I could, I would. But this is the very information those others are worried you already know. If either Colton or I were to fill you in, it'd be like marking you for dead."

The pain in her voice only compounded his own. Hardening his heart, he looked from the woman he'd thought he might love, to her brother. "Are we finished here? If so, I'd like to go."

Instead of answering, Colton glowered at him. The ferocity of the stare reminded Jake a bit of a wild animal, attempting to prove dominance with only a look.

"Stop it, you two." Maddie's voice seemed to catch in her throat. With a strangled sob, she ran out of the room.

"Great," Colton groused. "Now look what you've done."

Dumbfounded at the comment, Jake strode over to the window, hoping if he stared long enough at the beautiful forest, some of his feelings of betrayal would fade. Of course, that would be wishful thinking. He wasn't sure he'd ever get over the knowledge that Maddie wasn't at all the person he'd believed her to be. That kind of hurt ran deep.

"Do you mind if I ask you a question?" Colton asked. "It's important, so I'd like you to really think about it before you answer."

Both impressed and appalled that Colton seriously believed Jake would do anything he asked, Jake didn't even acknowledge that he'd heard the other man.

However, that didn't seem to faze Colton. "What exactly is your relationship with my sister?"

Jake ignored him.

"Are you friends," Colton continued, "or more than that?" Colton came closer, even going so far as to dare to reach out and grip Jake by the shoulder.

Jake spun, knocking the other man's hand off. He felt like all of his regret, his bottled-up rage, blazed from his eyes. A warning. "None of your business," he said, his voice hard. "Whatever might have been between me and Maddie is dead now anyway."

"Aha! Now you're admitting there was something between the two of you."

"Enough." Jake wandered away from the window and sank back down on the couch. "You and your stupid games are exhausting. I just want to get out of this place and go home, back to my normal life. Back to reality."

"If you do that, I can guarantee those other guys will grab you." Colton sat down on the other end, as far away as the sofa would allow. "And what I'm asking you is important. It speaks to the things Maddie couldn't say. You see, among our kind, there are certain truths one can only admit to someone who is the one who will become our mate."

"Mate?" The change in subject only made Jake's head hurt worse. "As in soul mate?"

"That, too." Colton shrugged. "I think if you and Maddie took the time to talk about how you feel about each other—about your expectations—that might help her know what to do."

"You're not making sense." Jake dragged his hand through his hair. "None of this does."

"I get what you're saying, but I promise you, there's sound logic behind it." Leaning forward, Colton spoke earnestly. "If you care at all—even the slightest bit— for Maddie, go find her and talk to her. She's hurting right now."

Since Jake was hurting, too—though he'd be damned if he'd admit that to Colton—he pushed to his feet. "Any idea where she might have gone?"

"Yes. Out in back there's a trail that goes into the woods. Follow that to the pond. There's a small fishing dock there. When we were kids, it was always her favorite place to go when she needed to think."

Throat tight, Jake nodded. When he turned to go, Colton called after him. "Don't you hurt my sister, understand?"

Ignoring him, Jake left the cabin, and started down the path. He had to admit, the beauty of the apparently remote area surprised him. The pine trees and tall live oaks meant they were in East Texas, a part of his state that he particularly loved.

He spotted her in the distance as soon as he rounded a curve in the path. Like her brother had said, she sat with her back to him at the end of a short wooden pier. Her legs dangled in the water and the breeze lifted strands of her long red hair. Just the sight of her had his chest feeling tight.

Everything about her…her inner and outer beauty, her kindness, her compassion. To him, she was perfect, she was everything that was good and right and true. Of course, this made her apparent betrayal that much more difficult to bear.

Though Colton had hinted there was more to the story. Of course. There always was. Jake could only hope Maddie cared enough about him to reveal her side.

"Hey," he said softly.

When she turned to face him, he saw that she'd been crying. "Hey," she replied, the despair in her voice matching the hopelessness in her eyes.

With every fiber of his being, he wished he could offer her comfort, that he could simply open his arms, pull her close, to tell her everything would be okay.

Instead, he jammed both hands into his pockets so he wouldn't touch her and walked out to the end of the pier. "Mind if I join you?"

"I'm not sure," she answered. "What do you want?"

Fresh hurt stabbed him. "Maddie, when did we become so adversarial?"

"When you started pushing for answers I couldn't give," she cried out. "All I've done is try to protect you. And right now, I'm not even sure why. You've made it clear you value getting a story more than anything else. More than...me." She turned her back to him, her shaking shoulders evidence of her silently crying.

He stood, frozen, while an awful certainty filled him.

"Maddie, whatever you've gotten yourself mixed up in, let me help you. Not for a story, but because I genuinely care about you. I can't protect you if I have no idea what the danger is or where it's coming from."

"You want to *protect* me?" She made a sound, some sort of awful cross between a laugh and a sob. "The best way to protect me would be to let Colton help you stay safe."

Before he could respond, a sound behind him made him turn. Colton came jogging up. He stopped when he reached Jake and he motioned to Maddie to come closer.

To Jake's surprise and annoyance, she pushed to her feet and joined her brother.

"What's up?" she asked.

"I've got news," Colton answered, excitement ringing in his voice. "Rick's unit is already on the move. They're going in and attempting a rescue."

Maddie gaped at him. "But wouldn't that be going against the chain of command?"

"And their own orders?" Jake interjected. "What gives?"

"They stick together, the guy I spoke to said. No man left behind and all that. No way do they plan to let the Protectors make Rick some sort of sacrificial lamb."

"Protectors?" Jake asked. "What do you mean?"

Maddie and Colton exchanged a quick look.

"That's the name of their unit," Colton responded. Jake wasn't sure how, but he knew the other man was lying.

Again.

"What about the virus?" Maddie rubbed her hands together as if she was cold. "Any news on any front on progress in developing an antidote or a preventative vaccine?"

"No. I can only assume they're still working on it."

Still stewing over the way both Maddie and her brother felt compelled to exclude him, Jake cleared his throat. "Hey, if they're Protectors, how about you ask them to protect me?"

Though the question made sense to him, clearly it didn't to the other two. Maddie appeared horrified, while Colton tried hard not to laugh.

"That's the thing," Maddie said. "Unfortunately, the Protectors are actually the ones who want to harm you."

Judging from the sharp look Colton sent her, she'd said too much. Maybe she had, but once again, Jake didn't understand the subtext.

He waited to see if she—or Colton—would elaborate, but of course neither did.

"Whatever," he said. "Since we seem to be at a bit of a stalemate, I'd like to be heading back to Galveston now. If one of you wouldn't mind dropping me off in town at the bus station, I'm sure I can get myself home."

"Bus station?" Colton spoke in a tone of utter disbelief. "There's no bus station within fifty miles of here."

"You can't go back now," Maddie added, her voice slow and measured. "There's no telling what they'll do to you if they bring you in now."

"I'll take my chances." He looked from one to the other. When neither of them spoke again, he sighed.

"Fine. Then point me in the direction of civilization and I'll walk."

"I'm sorry, Jake." Colton stepped in front of him. "Maybe we weren't clear. You're not going anywhere."

"Step away from me," Jake ordered. "I'm not tied up, so if you plan to stop me, it's going to get physical." He moved to go around Colton, but the other man grabbed him.

Jake shoved. Hard. Clearly, Colton wasn't expecting this. Jake wrenched himself free and shouldered the other man, hitting him hard in the gut. Colton staggered backward, trying to regain his balance, but couldn't. Off the edge of the dock he went, hitting the murky water with a huge splash.

Though he wanted to laugh, Jake knew better. Instead, he dusted his hands off on the front of his jeans, and took off at a jog toward the gravel road.

Except he hadn't counted on Maddie. She moved so fast he barely had time to evade her. Launching herself at him, she tried vainly to knock him to the ground.

He spun and the second time, he caught her, pinning her arms to her sides. "Settle down," he ordered.

Eyes spitting green fire, she continued to struggle. Just long enough for Colton to come up behind him and clock him under the chin.

When he came to, his hands and feet were bound. They'd left him lying on the ground, with Maddie—the traitor—watching over him.

"He's awake," she called out, and Colton came into his view.

"Help me help him up," Colton ordered. When they had him standing, Colton informed him they were going to march him back to the house. "Don't try yelling," he said. "There's no one else up here now, so no one will hear you."

Ignoring the other man, Jake looked at Maddie. Despite the pain in his pounding head, his heart hurt more.

"Don't do this, Maddie," he implored. "I've done nothing to warrant being treated this way."

She swallowed. "I know it might not seem like it, but it's for your own good. This is the only way we can keep you safe."

Drawing himself up, he shook his head, which sent bolts of pain through his jaw and head, making him wince. "Let me make this clear. If you don't help me get free, I'm done. I want nothing further to do with you, ever. Understand?"

Eyes dark with emotion, she gave a slow nod. "If that's the price I have to pay to save your life, then yes."

Chapter 18

Though she might have wished for less masculine posturing between the two men, Carmen couldn't help but thrill at Rick's refusal to clue Scott in on whatever had just happened with the intruders. She wasn't sure she still trusted the other biologist, and apparently Rick felt the same way. The fact that Scott had lied about his qualifications still pissed her off. Though no doubt he had his own reasons, the seriousness of this task left no room for anyone to fall short.

Another time, she might have stewed about his ignorant delusions. Not now. She knew she couldn't let anything distract her. Not this time, not when she was so close to obtaining an analysis and identifying the exact biological makeup of the virus.

Excitement thrummed through her. Sure, no doubt the CDC had felt the exact same way, and those biologists were just as qualified as she was. But something—call it gut instinct or woman's intuition—told her she was right on the edge of a major breakthrough. If she could just keep Scott out of her way while she worked. Judging by the bumbling way he fumbled around the lab, it would only be a matter of time until he made a costly error.

No one could afford the luxury of cleaning up a catastrophic mistake. Due to the urgency of the task, they would be working fast, which carried another form of risk. While vaccine development was usually a long and complex process, the world didn't have the luxury of waiting ten to fifteen years.

Later, when all of this was over, she planned to have a long talk with Scott about the importance of being honest about one's credentials. Right now, since she didn't have time, she had to get right to work and see what she could discover. Anticipation raced through her body as she set her tools out and prepared to begin.

Even though she knew the CDC would have followed these same steps, she began her exploratory stage. She needed to go through the hopefully weakened virus particles. By having Ted's corpse, she had already been able to skip a step—the one in which she'd use cultures to identify the cellular response to the virus in humans.

She planned to develop numerous candidate vaccines, since she knew most of them wouldn't produce the needed immune response. Once again, in a noncrisis situation, this process usually took one to two years.

In this part of the experiment, she intended to act in as close to a nonscientific manner as she could. While still following protocol, she planned to develop all kinds of radical combinations and hope one of them worked. More like gambling than true science, but desperate times called for desperate measures. All she could do was work hard and hope the metaphorical lightning would strike.

Not her usual painstaking and methodical way of working, but she knew she'd have to be bold if she wanted results.

At least she trusted Rick to keep them safe.

As if he'd read her thoughts, Rick stepped into the antechamber and once again went through the brief cleansing process. Though Carmen continued working, she remained überconscious of him, almost as if she was tracking his every movement.

Not good. No distractions. As he entered the actual lab, she looked up to tell him exactly that. Before she could, he crumpled to the floor in midstep, his bulky protective gear settling around him in a puff of inflatable padding.

"Rick?" Putting aside the sample she'd been working on, she rushed to him. She rolled him over so she could see him. Stunned, she gasped. What she saw horrified her.

Sores had begun blooming all over Rick's handsome face. Even under the headgear that was supposed to have kept him safe.

Which meant something had happened to his suit. Frantic now, she managed to unclip his headpiece and remove it. When she did, he managed to open his eyes.

"What happened?" he croaked. "I feel like I've been hit by a freight train."

While she tried to formulate an answer, a tear sneaked out of her eye and streamed down her cheek.

Seeing this, he cursed. "The virus?"

Slowly she nodded.

"How?" He licked his cracked lips. "I thought this outfit was supposed to protect against infection."

"It is," she answered, watching as more and more sores appeared on his skin, right before her eyes. Brushing away her pointless and useless tears, she leaned down close, putting her mouth near his ear. "I promise you, I won't let you die. I'm going to continue to work on figuring out an antidote and vaccine. But if I don't find it in time, I'll bite you and kill you that way." And hopefully, that first death would end the virus. When he reawakened as a Vampire, it wasn't illogical to assume that he'd be invulnerable, as well.

But right now, Rick's condition rapidly worsened. He was dying right before her eyes.

"No. Not even as a last resort," he managed, even as blood vessels burst and turned the whites of his eyes red. "I'd rather die than join the undead. Develop the antidote and save me. Save the world." The last word trailed off into a gurgle as he slumped over again, unconscious.

Muttering a string of curses in a language that had been long forgotten, she eased him into what she hoped was a comfortable position and climbed back to her feet.

When she looked over at Scott, she realized the other man had been watching them intently. "What?" she asked, confident he hadn't been able to hear what she'd said to Rick.

"He looks bad," Scott said, shrugging. "I'm thinking it won't be long until he's in as bad shape as the first guy." To her annoyance, he sounded surprisingly comfortable with the turn of events. Of course, why wouldn't he, since clearly his protective suit still did its job?

"I think he's going to die really quickly," Scott continued.

Carmen lurched toward him, as quickly as she could in the bulky suit. "So help me, if I find out you're the one who sliced his protective gear, I'll ram this virus down your throat. Was it you?"

Scott blanched, taking a step back. "Of course not,"

he protested, stumbling over the words. "I'd never do a thing like that. Are you certain it was cut?"

"I didn't take the time to look." She kept her voice cold. "We don't have that luxury. I'm going to get back to work immediately. I'll need you to stay out of my way. Understood?"

"Crystal clear," he replied, nodding. And then he, too went down, hitting the cement floor hard. Hopefully, his suit helped cushion the blow, though judging from the sharp crack she heard, his facemask most likely had been compromised.

Which clearly no longer mattered. Cursing the cumbersome gear, she rolled Scott over. Huge sores had also begun to erupt on his face, which meant someone had sabotaged his suit, too. A spidery web of lines showed she'd been right about the facemask.

If both men's suits had been compromised, most likely hers had been, too. However, she had one advantage here that the saboteur knew nothing about. The virus couldn't touch her. In fact, she saw no need to continue to wear the cumbersome protective suit.

"Screw this," she muttered, removing her own headgear and gloves. She quickly stepped out of the rest of her gear, aware that whoever had messed with them had no idea she would be invulnerable.

She didn't care. None of that was important. What mattered now was the need to save Rick's life. And Scott's, too, after Rick's.

Rick groaned, a tortured sound. Judging by the rapid progression of this virus, she had less than six hours to either come up with an antidote or she'd have to bite him and turn him into a Vampire to keep him from dying on her.

Despite Rick's request that she not do that, she wasn't

about to lose him. She'd do whatever she had to in order to keep him alive, even bite and turn him. Hell, even that possible solution had an uncertain outcome. While Vampires were impervious to the effects of the virus, she wasn't sure that would still apply to someone who had been infected before becoming a Vamp. She hoped she wouldn't have to actually find out.

She had to come up with the antidote. While wanting to save the world was altruistic and noble, saving Rick hit much closer to home.

Working at near Vampiric speed, she examined slides, worked calculations, tested and did it all again. And again and again, refusing to let her rising frustration deter her.

While both Rick and Scott lay on the floor nearby, the virus continuing to destroy their bodies.

One hour passed, or maybe two. Hell, it might just as easily have been three or four, for all she knew. Time flowed in a continuous stream of awareness, and while she knew she was working against a ticking clock, she couldn't allow that knowledge to throw her off her game. Scientific fact had little room for improvisation, but she'd learned long ago to trust her gut and go with her instincts. Sometimes a move that might at first seem illogical turned out to be the exact detour that had needed to be taken.

Testing. Nope. Move on to the next. And again, not the response she'd been hoping for, or needed. Every now and then, she'd leave her work area to check on the two downed men. The virus continued to spread with alarming speed, but they were both still breathing.

Aware they wouldn't be for much longer if she continued to fail, she renewed her efforts, increasing her speed. Though Rick's supposed friends remained outside, ostensibly guarding the lab, she was glad they didn't look in on her. If they did, they'd only see a crazed woman working so fast she appeared as a blur.

Though supremely focused, fear of losing Rick guided her every movement. She couldn't lose him. Not now, not ever. If she could save him, she could save the entire world.

Growing more and more desperate as each test failed, she tried to take an objective step back in her mind. She was missing some common denominator, but what? Though she racked her brain, she couldn't hit it. Again, she tried. Again. And again.

While meanwhile the virus continued to devour the bodies of the two men on the floor. Time was running out.

"Hey!" One of the new men, Rick's friend, entered the antechamber and peered at her through the glass wall. "What's going on in there? Why is Rick on the floor? What did you do to him?"

"Stay back," she ordered. "Someone sabotaged their suits and they were infected with the virus. No one is to come anywhere near this lab. Understand?"

Instead of recoiling in horror, he didn't move. "Why are you not wearing your protective gear? Are you infected, too?"

"Whoever messed with the suits probably ruined all of them," she explained. "I work faster without it, so I went ahead and took it off."

His eyes widened. "That's a huge risk to take."

"Maybe." Letting her impatience show, she returned to her microscope, viewed the next slide and entered the data into a computer program. "I don't have time to chat."

When she looked up again, he'd gone.

After running through all her slides, she returned to poor Ted's decomposed body and extracted another round of samples. As time had passed, what had once been flesh and bone now resembled a soupy sea of organisms. It horrified her to realize if she didn't make some sort of breakthrough soon, Rick and Scott would look like this.

They were running out of time. Once more she ran her tests, hoping, just once, for a change in variables. But she found nothing. Learned nothing. This had become beyond frustrating. She wanted to throw the vial against the wall and watch it shatter.

Of course she didn't. Vexing, true. But she wouldn't consider a total failure. She couldn't. Not yet.

Another glance down at Rick. Neither he nor Scott had moved at all. She hurried over, horrified at how quickly the sores had spread. This thing was brutally quick.

Rick's eyes opened and he gasped for air. She forced herself to turn away and ran one more round of tests, fingers flying as she entered the data into the computer.

The tightness in her own chest made it difficult to breathe. She couldn't lose him. Not after waiting so many centuries to find someone like him. She'd waited so long to find…love.

Love. Of course. If all the poets and singers were correct, the magic of love would prevail. The antidote would be found, the vaccine developed, and the world would be saved.

Carmen, however, knew better. She'd lived through the Black Plague. Seen the death and destruction of religious purges, more disease, and murder and mayhem. There'd been love then, too, for others rather than her, and still they'd died by the thousands.

She would not let Rick die.

Decision made, she left the computer running the last batch of calculations and hurried over to Rick. Dropping to her knees, she found a spot on his neck still untouched by sores. Pressing her mouth against his skin, she felt her fangs elongate. With a quick, savage motion, she pushed them into him, piercing the vein, and began drinking his blood. She hoped she hadn't waited too late.

He went rigid, then let out a slow sigh. As he relaxed into her deadly embrace and the metallic taste of his beloved blood filled her mouth, she nearly swooned.

This was the point where she normally would stop. Right before the heart stopped beating, so the human would wake in the morning slightly weak and confused, with no memory or idea what had happened.

For Rick, she'd take this all the way. Even though she hadn't made another Vampire in well over one hundred years, this wasn't the kind of thing one forgot. This was, however, the first time she'd made a Vampire because of love.

Dimly she heard the computer chime. A moment later, it chimed again. Carmen froze, slowly releasing Rick. That particular sound meant a successful combination had been reached. She'd entered the variables and let the program run the tests. Success? Setting Rick gently on the floor, she hurried over and peered at the screen.

There. Flashing bright red. A possible antidote, which meant a plausible prototype for a vaccine.

She could make a syringe of this in minutes. Did she even have minutes? Glancing at Rick, she let her fangs retract while she tried to decide what to do. Should she risk it, knowing the antidote might fail to save him? Or continue making him a Vampire, even though he'd expressly asked her not to?

Pleasure mingled with pain as he relaxed into a gentle yet fierce embrace. Was he dreaming? Whose arms held him? He tried to find a scent, but couldn't. Carmen? Or was there someone else, a doctor, a nurse? Was he still in the lab or had he been moved? He had no idea. Hell, he didn't even know what day it was.

Then he floated. Straight up off the floor and out of his body. He'd heard of such things happening, right in the hour of death. Was he dying, then? He'd been sick, he remembered. That hellish virus. The last thing he'd seen had been Carmen feverishly working to find a cure. Had she? If anyone could save the world, he'd be betting she could.

If she had, then why had he died? He couldn't see Carmen allowing that to happen. She was a warrior Vampire, that woman. No way would she let him die, not on her watch.

Maybe he wasn't dead. Experimenting, he inhaled. The instant he did, he was no longer floating and he slammed right back into his body. With that came horrible, pulsing hurt. Fever and the awful, horrible knowledge that the virus was busy eating away at his body.

Nope. Definitely not dead.

Then where… Listening, he heard nothing. No sound, not even the steady beat of his heart that he'd always taken for granted. If he didn't have a heartbeat, that would mean Carmen had turned him into a Vampire. Even though he'd expressly asked her not to.

Pain knifed through him. Did Vampires suffer as their human body died and they became undead? He'd never thought to question, hadn't cared enough to wonder. While he knew he should be furious, he couldn't seem to summon up enough strength for even anger.

Some kind of internal struggle seemed to be going on inside his body. Either the virus was dying or he was— and he couldn't be sure which.

"Rick." Carmen's voice. Pleading. "Rick, can you open your eyes?"

He tried, oh he tried, but the lids felt stuck together and he couldn't manage to fight his way through the murk.

"Can't," he managed to say, though most likely the word came out garbled. "What's happening to me?"

Silence. He figured she probably couldn't understand him. He didn't blame her. His tongue wasn't working right. "Help."

That word rang clear as a bell.

"Sit tight," Carmen replied. "I've figured out a potential antidote and made a small test batch. You're going to be my lab rat. I just injected you with it."

Which meant she hadn't made him a Vampire. Relieved, he tried to nod again, failed. Instead, he succeeded only in drifting back to sleep.

The next thing he knew, he snapped open his eyes, squinting at the bright light shining at him.

"There you are," Carmen said, almost chirping. "I've been monitoring your progress and I'm 99 percent sure the antidote worked. I've already put a call in to the CDC. However, no one there would even talk to me, so your friend who's helping guard the place is pulling a few strings. We need to get this stuff processed in huge batches, and for that we need their help."

Confused, he blinked, finally closing his eyes to protect them from the glare.

"Oh, sorry," Carmen said, and moved some sort of lamp she'd had shining at his face. "I used that so I could chart the progress of the sores as they receded."

He turned his head slightly and saw Scott lying prone nearby. Carmen followed the direction of his gaze and nodded. "Yes, I gave him a shot, too. After I was sure yours was working. He hasn't come awake yet. I think yours happened more quickly because I..." She looked down, before resolutely raising her chin and meeting his eyes. "I bit you."

"I thought you did," he managed, still struggling to push out the words. "For a moment there, I felt myself dying."

She grimaced, though she appeared unashamed. "I came really close to changing you so I could save your life. The computer pinging to let me know I'd finally found a successful calculation was the only thing that stopped me."

He tried to smile, but knew it probably appeared more like a grimace.

Apparently, she did, too, judging by the stricken look on her face. "I'm sorry, okay? I know you said not to, but I just couldn't let you die. I...care too much about you to do that."

A wave of warmth flooded him, giving him just enough strength to push up onto his elbows. He tried to search his muddled mind for just the right words, aware he needed to tell her how he felt, but instead exhaustion slipped back over him. He lay back, let his eyes drift closed and went off once again to oblivion.

Time passed. How much time exactly, he wasn't sure. When he next opened his eyes, the third reawakening, he felt as if he'd been reborn. Energy surged through him, enabling him to push to his feet. He turned slowly, stunned to realize he was still in the lab. Scott remained motionless on the floor near him. A quick glance revealed the other man hadn't survived the virus. Evidently, the antidote had been given too late to save him.

"Carmen?" Rick called, puzzling over the realization that she wasn't there. He tried again, louder. "Carmen? Where are you?"

Nothing but silence. Okay. Maybe she'd gone to the CDC with her antidote. That was the only reason she'd leave.

"Pete?" he hollered next, knowing his teammate had to be still standing guard. "Pete, I need some help in here."

Still nothing. It felt…eerie. Unsettling and worrisome. Something was wrong. He knew his team. None of those men would ever willingly abandon their post.

Then where were they?

He rushed to the door, amazed at how good he felt. Strong, alert, capable. As if he hadn't nearly died from a horrible virus. He exited the lab, quickly searching the barn. Other than shadows and dust, he saw nothing.

Outside, the compound appeared deserted. Moving carefully, wishing he had a weapon, he searched the house first, noting that Pete and the team had moved the bodies of the Sons of Darkness. Most likely, they'd been buried. Or burned, if burial wasn't an option.

But where the hell was everyone? When he realized all the vehicles were gone, he swore loudly. He cursed even more when he finally saw the warning signs that had been posted all around the property.

"Warning! Deadly Plague Contaminated area. Stay away. Entrance will result in death."

Who had done this? What had happened to Pete and the rest of the team? Rick knew his guys wouldn't have left willingly, even with the threat of a virus.

He thought back. The last he'd heard, Carmen had been trying desperately to reach the CDC. Had she succeeded and if so, had her phone call triggered some sort of crazy reaction? As in, a small army had been dispatched to bring everyone in?

Or had the situation been even worse? Had Carmen's call actually alerted the real terrorists, the ones who'd pushed so hard for a war in West Latvia, finally unleashing a deadly virus that nearly decimated the population?

Since Carmen had developed an antidote and a vaccine, that made her existence extremely problematic for anyone who didn't want the virus stopped. The fact that her findings were priceless would be their sole reason for keeping her alive. Of course, they had no way to know there were only one way to kill her—a stake through the heart. He knew Carmen would be careful not to turn over her findings to anyone but the CDC.

With no vehicle, he had no way to go looking for her. So he did what he had to do. He put in a call to the only other Protector besides his team that he trusted. Colton Kinslow, Maddie's brother.

When he learned Jake and Maddie were with Colton, Rick felt relieved. If anyone could successfully locate Carmen and the precious antibodies, those three could. Especially—and surprisingly—Jake. Rick had spent some time looking up the journalist and he'd come to realize the other man had great instincts. He couldn't have been as successful as he was without them.

Together, they all made a great team. And together, they'd find their missing fifth, plus Pete and the guys. Rick was betting on it.

Chapter 19

The hard fury in Jake's eyes as he gazed at her damn near broke Maddie's heart. "It's for the best," she whispered, almost under her breath. So low, she couldn't be sure Jake heard.

But her brother did. Colton grimaced and shook his head. "You're right. It is all for the best," he said. "You know that, even if he doesn't. Better to keep him alive, even if he hates you for it."

Though *hate* was a pretty strong word, she considered it an accurate depiction of Jake's feelings toward her right now. Ignoring her brother, she crouched down near the man she loved. "I'm sorry," she told him. "If there was any other way to keep you safe, I'd take it."

"You're full of it," he responded, glaring at her. "You and him. I don't know what you're up to, but now I'm positive it isn't good. And I'm willing to bet whatever it is ties in to the door in the alleyway back in Galveston.

Whatever illegal activity you're involved in, you should be aware that it will eventually come to light. No matter if I'm the one to expose it or someone else."

"Illegal activity?" Colton interjected, incredulous. "What makes you think that?"

"Ha." Jake spat the word. "Think about what you just said, man. Really think about it."

"Jake," Maddie began.

"No." Now he wouldn't even look at her. "I have nothing left to speak to you about. You or your crazy brother, with your secrets and lies. Everything bad that's happened to me since I found that damn door that won't open, is tied to you. Don't bother to deny it." He lifted his chin. "I'm a great journalist and I trust my gut. Every instinct I possess is screaming that you're lying."

"Lying?" Colton snorted. "More like omitting what you don't need to know."

"Same thing." Jake's hard tone matched his unyielding expression. "Just cut the BS. I know I'm right. All of this is related somehow. And once I get away from you two, I'm warning you, I'm not giving up until I find out what it is."

Colton shot Maddie a meaningful look. She ignored him, focusing all her attention on Jake. When Jake met her gaze, he didn't look away, and she swore she could see the tiniest bit of softening in his eyes.

Or perhaps that was wishful thinking.

"Well, Maddie?" he demanded. "Tell me I'm wrong."

"You're not wrong," she replied, her voice soft. "It does all tie together. Everything."

At her words, he swallowed. His jaw hardened. "Is there really a deadly virus? Or was that a cover for more unlawful activity by Carmen and Rick?"

Before Maddie could even respond, Colton laughed.

"Come on. You watched the news. You saw what's happening over in West Latvia. I know you think we're trying to pull the wool over your eyes—for whatever reason—but come on."

Still focused on Maddie, Jake ignored him.

She dragged her gaze away from him to look at her brother. "Colton, Jake and I need some privacy. Will you give it to us, please?"

Her brother started to protest, but she silenced him with a quick glance. Grumbling under his breath, Colton left the room, slamming the door behind him.

"It's time I tell you something," she said. "No, not just something. Everything. Beginning with this. I love you."

Though his gaze softened, Jake didn't reply in kind. She squashed her disappointment, reminding herself that she couldn't blame him right now. He didn't even know if he could trust her.

Nothing ventured, nothing gained. She had no choice but to go all or nothing. If he didn't feel the same way, she'd have to walk away.

Except she knew, deep down inside her, that Jake cared for her as much as she did him.

"Jake?" she prompted. "I know this is pushy, and I'm aware you're mad, but I need to know how you feel about me?"

"Why?" he shot back. "So you can use my feelings against me? No thanks."

"Do you really think I would do that?" She didn't bother to hide her hurt.

"I have no idea, Maddie. The way you've been acting since your brother ran into me and kidnapped me makes me wonder if I really know you at all. You tell me."

She pushed to her feet and paced, trying to find just

the right words. When she turned to face him, she hoped she could somehow make him understand.

"I know there's been a lot of craziness going on," she said. "And that's an understatement. But we have laws. I can't tell you everything without knowing how you feel about me." Actually, Pack law forbade her revealing her true nature without being in a committed relationship—engaged or married—though she was willing to stretch the boundaries just a little. After all he'd been through, Jake deserved at least that.

"We?" His harsh voice matched his rigid profile. "Who is we, exactly?"

"My kind," she answered. "We're not like everyone else." Her heart began to race. She was too close to dangerous territory. *Forbidden* territory. Unless they were a committed couple, she could face serious consequences if she said any more.

As if he sensed this, Jake raised his face to hers. Their gazes locked. Maddie's heart skipped a beat as anticipation zinged in her veins.

"We've got a situation," Colton yelled, slamming back into the room. "I just talked to Rick. Carmen developed an antidote and a vaccine for the virus, but she's disappeared. Along with Rick's entire team of Protectors."

Maddie's nervous euphoria vanished. "Where is he?"

"At the compound of that fringe group that initially tried to barter the virus."

"Do we need to go pick him up?" she asked. "And does he have any idea where Carmen might be?"

"Yes and no." Colton grimaced. "He says all the vehicles are either missing or disabled. Short of hitchhiking, he has no method of transportation. We need to head that way now."

"Okay." Maddie jumped to her feet. "Let's get going."

"Take me with you," Jake ordered. "There's no way you're leaving me out of something like this."

Colton eyed him. Then he slowly nodded. "He's right," he told Maddie. "Did the two of you have time to have your little talk?"

"No." She didn't bother to hide her disappointment. "We didn't. But there's plenty of time on the drive south, if I can get you to put your earbuds in and listen to music. We'll use my car. I have satellite radio and Bluetooth."

Colton gave a slow nod, looking from her to Jake and back again. "I was going to congratulate you, but I think I'll just wish you good luck instead."

Since the closed-off expression had returned to Jake's handsome face, she understood exactly what he meant. "I'll take it," she said. "And thanks."

"Ahem." Jake cleared his throat as he held up his bound hands. "Are you going to untie me?"

"Not until we have your word you won't try to escape," Colton replied.

"My word?" Now Jake mocked him. "How do you know whether or not my word's worth anything?"

Colton's response came quickly, direct and to the point. "Because I know my sister. She wouldn't have fallen in love with a man who didn't have integrity."

Touched, Maddie patted her brother on the shoulder. "Thank, Colt."

He smiled down at her. "You're welcome, sis."

"If you two are done heaping praise on each other, I'd like to get going," Jake interjected. "And cut the crap about being in love with me," he told Maddie. "I know better."

His words made Colton's smile vanish. "Get in the car," he ordered. "Before I say something I might regret."

"Go ahead." Jake didn't back down. "The two of you

are nuts. This all is beginning to feel like a very bad dream."

Despite everything, hurt stabbed Maddie. Deep. Somehow, she managed to lift her chin and meet Jake's eyes. "Are you going to give us your word or not?"

Though he swallowed, he finally nodded. "You have my word. I won't try to escape."

Immediately, Colton cut Jake's bonds. "Perfect. Let's get on the road."

Without another word, Jake marched to the car and got into the back seat. Maddie sighed. "This is going to be more difficult than I thought."

"Yeah, I'd say so." Grimacing, Colton shook his head. "Injured male pride is hard to work around. But I have faith in you, baby sister. If anyone can do it, you can."

"Thanks." After several deep, calming breaths, she walked over to the car and got in on the opposite side from where Jake sat. Colton climbed in the front seat and she handed him her keys. He started the engine, put in some earbuds and synced them with the radio, put the car in Drive, and they were off.

Next to her, Jake sat in stony silence. Mentally, she rehearsed and discarded several different ways to get him to open up. Finally, she realized she'd need to go with her gut instinct and speak from her heart.

"Jake," she began. "You know me."

He didn't respond at first. When he finally swung his head around to look at her, the mingled anger and pain in his chocolate eyes made her entire chest ache.

"Do I?" he asked. "I'm beginning to wonder about that. Ever since the day we first met, you've done nothing but hide the truth from me. The door in the alley, the secret club, the virus, this group of people you called the Protectors. I have no idea what's actually going on, though clearly you and your crazy brother do. You say you want to tell me, but then it's like you need a declaration of love from me first. Have I gotten this right?"

Slowly she nodded.

"That's what I thought. No way, Maddie. I refuse to allow you to use my feelings like that. I'm not bargaining with you, telling you that I love you, just to finally get the truth. That's wrong. All kinds of wrong."

Though she hated her desperation, she seized on his words. "What exactly are your feelings toward me, Jake? Can you at least tell me that?"

His jaw tightened. "Why does that even matter now, Maddie? Can you tell me that?"

When she didn't immediately answer, he nodded. "That's what I thought. I don't appreciate being used and treated like a prisoner. That's all you and your brother have done since he rammed me with his truck. It doesn't matter how I feel about you or you about me. Love can never flourish in an atmosphere of distrust and lies. Surely you can see that."

As his words sank in, she realized he was right. Had the situation been reversed, she would have felt exactly the same way he did. Quite possibly worse.

Now she owed him the truth. Even if it meant breaking Pack law, even if that meant she could face the ultimate punishment—reprogramming or…death.

Of course, if Colton knew, he'd try to stop her. She glanced his way. Earbuds in, he appeared to be intent on the road.

"Jake," she said quietly, leaning toward him. "Say something awful about my brother. I need to see if he responds, so I can make sure he's not secretly listening. I'm going to tell you the truth about everything."

Though Jake narrowed his eyes, clearly skeptical, he

finally lifted his chin and looked directly at Colton. "Your brother is a fool," he said. "A weak and ineffective liar. The only way he can accomplish anything is with tricks and unnecessary violence." His voice carried the ring of someone who believed he spoke the truth.

Colton didn't even turn around.

"Perfect," she murmured. "I'm going to start with what's behind that door at the end of the alleyway. It's a bar called Broken Chains, and the only ones allowed admittance are nonhumans."

"Nonhumans?" he repeated, frowning. "What are you going to tell me next, that you people are aliens or something?"

His comment made her smile, just the tiniest bit. "No. Actually, it's a bit more incredible than that. By Nonhumans, I mean beings like me and my brother. Broken Chains is a bar for Shape-shifters, Vampires and Merfolk."

Judging from the way he eyed her, he wasn't sure if she'd lost her mind or was seriously trying to pull his leg. Either way, she could tell he didn't believe her.

"Okay, I'll play along," he said, his tone sharp and cutting. "Which are you, then? Because you sure look like a human woman to me."

"I'm a Shape-shifter," she told him. "In the old days, people called us werewolves. I can change and become a wolf, and later change back to human. If we weren't in the car, I'd show you. Oh, and telling a human this without a promise of lifelong commitment is forbidden. In some cases, the punishment is death."

Though part of him privately considered the likely possibility Maddie had lost her mind, Jake also wanted to see how far she'd go with this. And—truth be told—

werewolves would explain the man he'd seen become a huge wolf that night outside the alley. Improbable, true. But technically not impossible.

"That's why those men attacked you," Maddie continued. "Humans aren't allowed anywhere near Broken Chains. It's our refuge, our recreational safe haven."

Not sure how to respond, he settled for simply nodding. One thing he'd learned in gathering information over the years was not to discount people with the most improbable tales. Sometimes the stories they told contained more than a nugget of truth.

But when Maddie proceeded to say Carmen was a Vampire while Rick was another Shape-shifter, he had to wonder if this time would be the exception to the rule.

Over the next several minutes, the things she said got even wilder. She spoke of a large governing body of Shape-shifters called the Pack. They were set up in councils, ranging from regional, to state, to country. And they were all over the world, in every country. Which would mean, if her statements were true, that there were a lot of freaking Shape-shifters in existence.

Though he had no choice but to take everything she said with a grain of salt, he continued to listen carefully. After all, until all this craziness had happened, he'd believed he loved her. Deep down, underneath the hurt and the incredulous realization that she truly believed every word she said, he still did.

More the fool, he. What he didn't understand was the *why*. People always had a reason for their actions, and while perhaps hers might be based on this fantastical world of hers she'd created, surely her brother didn't share in her delusions? That must have been why she didn't want him listening in to this conversation.

Except Colton had made a few comments earlier that

might be construed to indicate he knew exactly what Maddie was going to say. Jake filed that away to examine later. In the meantime, he continued to listen intently.

"Hey, you two," Colton said, removing one of his earbuds. "ETA is in about half an hour. The compound is a lot closer to the old cabin than I'd originally realized."

Wearing a distracted expression, Maddie nodded. "Okay. We're still not done back here."

Though he grimaced, Colton replaced his earbud and returned to listening to music.

Next, Maddie turned to face Jake. "You don't believe me, do you?"

While he hesitated to call her an outright liar, the fact that she even had to ask the question meant she understood on some level how bizarre her story sounded. "It's a lot to take in," he finally said. "But you haven't told me yet about these Protectors you and Colton are trying to keep me safe from."

"They're Pack Protectors, who carry the sacred duty of keeping the Pack safe. They were formed during the Dark Ages, when several of our people reached out to humans, hoping to form an alliance. Instead, they were hunted down like feral animals. The Pack had to do something to keep humans from eradicating our existence. Those first Pack Protectors were the ones who made sure humans believed anything they heard about people becoming wolves was a myth."

He nodded. "That makes sense." Assuming, of course, that he treated everything she said as if it was the truth. For now, he'd simply continue to try to keep an open mind.

"Over the years," she continued, "the Pack Protector organization evolved. Laws were created—and revealing ourselves to humans was forbidden. Telling the wrong person could endanger our entire species. Anything and anyone who was perceived as a threat was taken into custody. They are either eradicated or…" she shuddered "…reprogrammed."

Now he understood where she was going with this. "And they think I'm a threat."

"Exactly." She appeared relieved. "Colton knew I cared about you, so he stepped in and grabbed you before they could."

"I see." For such an illogical premise, it all made a weird kind of sense.

"And since he's a Protector, too," she continued, "he's put his own life at risk by helping us."

Us. A chill skittered up his spine. If what she said was true, she'd definitely broken her own laws, which she'd said were punishable by death.

"You shouldn't have told me any of this," he said. "I couldn't live with myself if anything happened to you because of me."

Her eyes widened. "Does that mean you believe me?"

Because he still couldn't bring himself to flat-out discredit her fantasy—and also because no matter what logic told him, part of it resonated with truth—he shrugged. "I'm still withholding judgment. But if it does turn out to be true, according to what you've said, you have put yourself in danger by telling me any of this."

She searched his face. "I know," she said simply. "That's why I asked you how you felt about me. Because there's that exception to the law. Those in a committed relationship are allowed to reveal the truth."

"But what happens if the human part of the equation changes his or her mind?" he asked, genuinely curious despite his skepticism. "I mean, say a man asks a woman to marry him and she accepts, but once she reveals that she's a werewolf, he backs out. What happens then?"

Maddie froze, her eyes wide. "Are you asking because that's what you want to do? Run away now that you know what I am?"

He could only give her the truth. She deserved that.

"Maddie, I care for you. But all of this—what's happened, what you're telling me—is making it difficult. Can you see that?"

Her eyes mirrored the moment when she realized what his gentle words meant. "You don't believe me," she said, her tone flat. Then, without waiting for an answer, she shook her head. "I guess I'll just have to show you. Not right this instant, but soon."

She didn't speak again for the rest of the drive.

Finally, they left the highway and turned down a paved two-lane road. After a series of turns, they ended up on a gravel road flanked by tall pine trees.

"We're almost there," Colton said, removing his ear buds and glancing curiously at them in the rearview mirror. "Did you two work everything out?"

"Not even close." The trace of bitterness in Maddie's soft voice surprised Jake.

"Bummer." Colton didn't sound too concerned.

"But we'll have it straightened out soon," Maddie continued, still refusing to look at Jake.

One more turn, this time onto a drive marked Private.

"There he is." Colton pointed. Rick stood on the porch of a long, narrow farmhouse, waving. Colton pulled the car up and Rick got in the front.

"Thanks for coming out here," he said, turning to eye Jake and Maddie in the back seat. "Judging from your expressions, you think someone died. What's going on?"

"Nothing," Colton said, at the exact same time as Maddie chimed in with, "I'm telling Jake the truth."

"Maddie," her brother hissed. "You know Rick's a Protector."

"So are you," she shot back. "So what?"

Colton groaned.

Rick looked from one to the other, his brow furrowed. "Jake, are you and Maddie in a committed relationship?"

Taking a deep breath, Jake ignored the stricken expression Maddie wore and the worry in Colton's eyes. He thought about all Maddie had told him, the risk she claimed to have taken, and how empty his life would be without her. Even if she had some sort of mental health issues, he knew he'd help her work through them. Because she was worth it.

"Yes," he said clearly. "We are."

Though tears brimmed in Maddie's beautiful eyes, she held herself together.

"Then I fail to see the problem," Rick concluded, glancing curiously at Colton. "Don't you agree?"

Slowly Colton nodded. He eyed Jake, his expression considering, before returning his attention to Rick.

"What now? Do you have any idea where they might have gone?"

"No. That's the problem," Rick began. Before he could finish, Maddie's cell phone rang.

"Caller ID says Unknown Caller," she reported before answering. "Hello?"

She listened for a moment, her mobile expression going from puzzlement to relief, then joy, and finally worry. "Got it," she said. "Watch for us."

Once she'd ended the call, she practically vibrated with excitement. "That was Carmen. She stole someone's phone and called me. Right now, she's playing along and pretending to be human. She says she wants to find out who is actually behind all this."

Again, Jake noticed that no one reacted at all to the strange part of Maddie's statement—about Carmen pretending to be human.

"Did she give you a location?" Rick asked.

"Yes. She's back in Galveston. In one of those abandoned warehouses near Broken Chains."

Colton cursed. "That's an hour south of here."

"Only if you drive the speed limit," Rick interjected.

They made it in fifty minutes.

"Now what?" Jake asked. "Is there some sort of plan once we get to the warehouse?"

Both men stared at him as if he'd spoken a foreign language.

"No," Rick finally admitted. "We're playing it by ear."

As he pulled up to the curb and parked, shots rang out. Rick swore. "Get out. Everyone, out. Stay on this side of the vehicle."

Using the car as a shield, all four of them crouched behind it. Judging by the *rat-tat-tat* of the gunfire, they were either outnumbered or someone had a fully automatic weapon, or both. Colton cursed. Maddie winced each time a she heard a gunshot. And Rick, with his clenched jaw and a muscle working in his throat, appeared furious.

"You know what we have to do," Colton said. "That's the only way we can move fast enough to take the shooter down."

"I agree." Rick spoke without looking at anyone, all of his attention focused on the warehouse entrance. "And we need to go quickly. Not that Carmen is in any real danger, but we don't need that virus to be spread. Clearly, no one has thought about that or they wouldn't be shooting up the place." He swallowed. "I need to make sure you understand. This virus affects Shifters. If it's been released, you'll be putting your lives at risk."

There it was again. Jake kept silent, fascinated. The word *Shifters*, bandied about so casually. Either all three shared the same delusion, or Maddie had spoken the truth. But how was such a thing possible?

"True," Colton chimed in. "Except didn't you say Carmen developed an antidote?"

"I did." Rick still appeared grim.

"You're right. We have to go in." Slowly, Maddie nodded. "Sorry, Jake," she murmured. "I wanted to show you my true self, but not like this. The timing is bad, but this is necessary."

He tensed up. "What are you going to do? How can I help?"

Instead of answering, she cast one final long look at him before nodding at her brother and Rick. In unison, all three began shedding their clothes, right in front of each other and Jake, as if he wasn't even there. They didn't look at one another, either. Each appeared focused only on their own movements.

Jake had just come to the realization that their insanity had reached another level when shimmering pinpricks of light appeared, surrounding Maddie, Rick and Colton.

Jake froze. What the... Intrigued and alarmed, he watched as the light show swirled and danced, completely obscuring what had to be their by now naked forms.

When the lights finally winked out, three massive wolves stood where Maddie, Rick and Colton had been. The largest of the three had to be Rick. His shaggy gray fur looked as if it had been dipped in black.

The next wolf, just a small bit shorter than the first, must be Colton.

And as for Maddie—her coat shimmered, a pearly sort of gray color that mirrored her human beauty.

Jake stared, struggling to process what he'd just seen. Then the three wolves took off, running directly toward the gunfire, crouched low to the ground.

They moved so fast they were a blur. Jake braced himself, wondering how to react if one of them were hit. But somehow, miraculously, they disappeared inside the warehouse, unharmed.

Despite the shock and tension of the moment, one thing stood out in his mind, like a blazing sign against a pitch-black sky.

Maddie had been telling the truth.

And if this—the existence of werewolves or Shapeshifters—was real, did that mean the rest of it was, as well? He didn't have more than a few seconds to ponder this, because a moment later, the gunfire abruptly stopped.

Maddie.

Heart in his throat, Jake didn't hesitate. Crouching low, he ran for the building, intent on reaching the woman he loved.

Chapter 20

If ever there'd existed a more disorganized bunch of criminals, Carmen hadn't met them. Infighting, power grabbing and a definite lack of respect for the power of the virus that so far remained inside the unbroken test tubes.

So far.

As far as she could tell, there appeared to be two separate factions. If they were connected in any way, she couldn't tell how. They were quite vocal, especially about what they wanted. Each group wanted different things.

But in the end, she figured they were the same. Money and power.

Though West Latvia had been mentioned a couple of times, she still didn't understand what the small European nation had done to deserve such a horrible fate.

The first group, a small, extremely loud trio of short, round men, wanted to destroy the antidote. Though Carmen couldn't fathom how anyone could be so stupid, she carefully kept her face expressionless. She'd kill them before she'd allow them to do that.

The second faction was comprised of seven people— six men and one woman. They appeared more intellectual than the others, and in fact she'd heard snippets of their conversation that seemed to indicate they all had once worked at the CDC. They wanted to coldheartedly release the virus into six major US cities, in a timed and calculated manner. As people sickened and died, they wanted to hold an auction, for the purpose of selling off the antidote to the highest bidder. They then claimed they'd split the proceeds among all of them, including the other group. Carmen knew she didn't believe them.

When the men had come storming her lab, they easily captured the team of Rick's friends, led by a man called Pete. No one seemed to notice that the battle went too quickly, and that the rough and battle-scarred men gave up too easily. No one besides Carmen, that is. She figured they, like her, had allowed themselves to be captured in order to learn about what the terrorists wanted. And make no mistake, Carmen considered them to be terrorists. Anyone who harmed people and wanted to harm more, for the sake of ideology or wealth, should have been considered such.

When the right time came, she'd take them down. She'd even considered killing them all, but decided she wanted them to answer for their crimes.

However, right now she took care so that no one was the slightest bit aware of her power.

As time passed, the arguments became more strident, erupting into small bouts of violence. She, along with Pete and the rest of his team, watched silently, waiting for the fools to turn on each other.

Finally, one of the short, round humans pulled out

a semiautomatic rifle and began shooting. He took out his entire group in the space of seconds before swiveling around to aim at the others, all of whom stood frozen in utter shock.

"Enough," Carmen roared. He laughed, bringing up his weapon to fire on her.

Except she was already on top of him. One of the advantages of Vampiric speed. She knocked him to the floor and snatched his gun away from him.

"Don't move," she ordered.

"How did you do that?" one of the former CDC group wanted to know. "One second you were there—" he pointed "—and the next…"

"Never mind that," Pete chimed in. "Carmen, when you have a minute, please cut us loose."

Just then, three large wolves streaked into the room. They'd obviously run straight into the sound of gunfire, probably aware that there were no silver bullets.

The humans, predictably, stared and gasped, nervously moving closer together. Since Pete and his crew were also Pack, they grinned.

"About time you got here," Pete said, eyeing the largest of the three beasts. "I don't know how much longer we could have kept up this charade."

"Gentlemen, let me remind you we still have a dangerous virus," Carmen pointed out. Keeping the rifle ready, she moved over to Pete and used one of her superstrong fingernails to sever his bonds. "You can free the others," she said.

Jake, the human reporter, appeared. Though wild-eyed, he took in the situation with a long look. "What do you need me to do?" he asked Carmen. She smiled to show him her appreciation. Then she directed him to tie up the remaining terrorists. When one of them began to complain loudly, she squeezed off a round of shots, deliberately missing him, but effectively silencing him. "Anyone else?" she demanded. "Next time, I promise you I won't miss."

No one spoke.

Staying close together, the wolves moved over to the group of captives. Baring their teeth, they gave growls of warning low in their throat. Wide-eyed, they struggled against their bonds, with no success.

"Jake," Carmen said loudly. "Why don't you take your wolf friends outside and bring back Maddie and Rick and their friend? I need to have a discussion with them." That way they could figure out what to do next.

"Okay." Jake turned to gesture to the wolves, but they'd already turned and begun to make their way toward the door.

As Maddie went past, she stopped and looked up at Carmen, grinning. Carmen reached out and tangled one hand in the soft fur. "Good to see you, girl," she said, before letting go.

At the door, Jake stopped. She noticed he didn't follow the wolves outside. She realized this might have been the moment he first realized Maddie's true nature. If she remembered correctly, the gift of that knowledge carried some heavy significance. She hoped Jake understood how difficult it must have been for Maddie to put herself in that position. And how much he meant to Maddie. That, too. Though Carmen had spent most of her long life staying out of other peoples' personal business, she felt sorely tempted to say something to Jake. Just this once.

"Hey," she called out. "Jake, come here for a second."

He glanced at the door before looking at her, as if torn. "I…"

"She'll be back in a minute," Carmen said. "I just have one quick question for you."

Expression wary, he crossed the distance between them. "Okay. What is it?"

"Do you love her?"

Clearly, whatever he'd been expecting, it hadn't been this. "It's complicated," he began.

"No. It's not. There's nothing complicated about it. Either you do or you don't."

He swallowed. Before he could answer, Maddie, Rick and another man rushed inside. With their heightened color and disheveled appearance, Carmen could tell they'd rushed through dressing immediately after shape-shifting back to human. From what she'd heard, they really would have had to hurry, as the act of changing brought often unwelcome consequences, unless one was with their significant other. Judging from the way none of the three made eye contact with the other, they were working on getting that under control.

"Carmen." Rick hurried over, wrapping his arms around her and pulling her close. She felt the force of his arousal and smiled.

"I'm glad you saved that for me," she purred.

"Always." He kissed her cheek. "Believe me, we're all so used to that happening when we change, we're able to control it easily. But when I saw you…"

His flattery made her laugh.

"Hello there." The strange man who'd accompanied Rick, Maddie and Jake walked over and stuck out his hand. "I'm Colton."

"Carmen." After they shook, she studied him. "You look familiar, but I can't say why. I'm usually pretty good at remembering faces, but I swear I haven't met you before today."

"I'm Maddie's brother."

That explained it. "Ah. And you two do resemble each other."

Maddie walked up, carefully avoiding glancing at Jake, though he tracked her with his gaze. "What's going on here, Carmen?" she asked.

"That's my Maddie. Straight to business." Carmen stepped away from Rick to hug her friend close. Again, she considered asking Maddie what was going on with her and Jake, but figured now was not the time. Maddie would tell her later, probably over a drink at Broken Chains.

"Jake," Carmen called, ignoring Maddie's almost imperceptible wince. "Come here. Everyone gather around and I'll tell you what I know. We've got to figure out what to do with these people."

When Jake joined their group, he stood as far from Maddie as possible. Not good, but she had other things to worry about beside the two lovebirds.

"There were two groups here," she said. "I'm not sure how they managed to work together long enough to capture me, but they did."

"What about my team?" Rick asked. "Pete and the guys were there to protect you."

"From what I could tell, Pete and his men allowed themselves to be defeated, so they could be captured."

"Right," Pete agreed. "Rick, sorry to leave you like that, but we knew you'd understand. Headquarters got intel that these people were about to make a huge move with the virus. We needed to stop them any way we could. Turns out, the infighting got so bad that one group took out the other."

"Saved you all some work," Rick said, his voice grim.

"Yes." Carmen felt that familiar tug of desire when

Rick turned his blue eyes her way. "But the group that's dead was the one that wanted to destroy West Latvia. Now we may never know why."

"Oh, I'm sure there are more of them," Rick replied. "The head honcho always sends his flunkies to do the dirty work." He glanced at the now surly group, still tied up and clearly not happy about it. "What about those guys? Where do they come in?"

"From what I can tell, they used to work for the CDC in Atlanta," Carmen said. She'd been watching Jake from the corner of her eye, and that remark seemed to jolt him out of his shock. "They appear to be in it for the money."

"Of course we're in this for money," a tall, thin man with a hooked nose interjected. "The CDC didn't pay us enough, considering what we did. We came close to identifying the biological components of the virus, but then we heard some outsider had actually gotten much closer."

"How'd you hear that?" Carmen asked.

"Scott worked with us. We sent him in to talk to that fringe group of idiots. They were tied in with them." He jerked his head toward the dead guys. "We were understandably upset to learn he'd died after being infected with the virus." His cold gaze locked on Carmen. "Why didn't you give him the antidote like you did your boyfriend there? You let him die. That makes you guilty of murder."

Carmen laughed. She couldn't help it. And not the toned-down form of laughter she'd learned to adopt when around humans. No, this time she let loose with her real laugh, the Vampiric one, with all its glorious undertones of menace and fury. The one that had once sent people scurrying for churches and homes with doors they could lock, because that sound contained a warning that something awful was about to happen.

Immediately, the human man went silent, eyes wide. Head back, Carmen bared her teeth, allowing just the slightest portion of her fangs to show. As predicted, the entire group collectively recoiled. This filled her with a burst of savage joy.

Right then, Rick kissed her. A possessive crush of his mouth on hers, as if he, too experienced similar emotions. Surprised, she kissed him back, pouring all of her energy into the movement of her lips. Since she hadn't had time to retract her fangs, she accidentally drew blood on his bottom lip. The coppery taste only enhanced her enjoyment. In fact, she had to fight to keep from going wild.

When he finally drew back, they were both breathing hard. Grinning, Jake shook his head. "You two need to get a room."

"Maybe we will, once all of this is settled." Carmen turned, loving the way Rick kept his arm around her and his body close. "What I want to know is what we should do now. Has the virus been released anywhere else?"

"Not that we know of," Colton responded. "They've made threats. Do you have any idea who else has the virus besides these guys?"

Carmen shook her head. She glanced back over her shoulder at the man who'd spoken up before. "Answer the question."

"I...no." He swallowed nervously. "I can't do that. If I do I'll be a dead man."

"If you don't answer, your death will come a lot sooner." This time, she let her eyes turn red as she allowed a lot more fang to show. "Because I'll kill you. At least it will be a quick death."

She focused on the pulse beating rapid fire at the base of his throat. On the surface, he might not yet understand she was a Vampire, but somewhere deep in his psyche, he knew. And he understood exactly what her fangs would do to him.

"The CDC is the only other place that has the virus," he finally blurted. "Other than anyone who might have gathered their own samples in West Latvia."

She gave a slow nod. "Good."

"Not that it matters, since we now have an antidote," Rick interjected. "Thanks to you. Now all we have to do is contact the proper authorities and have large quantities manufactured."

Carmen closed her eyes, taking a moment to gather her composure. "Easier said than done. Finding facilities capable of that kind of mass production quickly will be a challenge, to say the least."

"Maybe so, but if they want to save the world, they'll have to figure out a way to do it." Rick sounded so certain, so confident that this would happen, she wanted to kiss him again.

Once, she had been like him. Before centuries of watching humans battle over all the wrong things. She'd witnessed plagues and battle and carnage, and seen firsthand the unspeakable things men did to each other in the name of love and religion. She could imagine the jockeying for power among those in charge, while people died. Seeing the hope shining in Rick's eyes, the honest conviction of his chiseled features, made her feel lighter than she had in ages.

"Have you contacted the CDC?" Jake asked, his own inquisitive expression mirroring the same hope as Rick's.

"Not yet." She looked at Maddie. "I wasn't sure who I can trust. Especially after learning those yahoos over there were all former CDC workers."

"You're right," Maddie said slowly. "We need to go higher up. Someone above the CDC."

At that, Rick and Colton exchanged a glance. "I think we know exactly the right person," Colton said. "Trent Paxton. He's head of the Protectors, but he also is in charge of the US Department of Health and Human Services."

Their confident hope felt infectious. "Perfect," Carmen said. "Does one of you want to make the call?"

"I'll do it," Colton said. "Trent and I used to golf sometimes, back when he worked here in Texas. He'll take my call."

While Colton walked away to take care of that, Carmen noticed Maddie appeared to be on the verge of tears. About to ask what was wrong, Carmen swallowed back the question when Jake took Maddie's arm.

"I was wrong," he told her, looking deep into her eyes. Though his words were meant only for her, he spoke loud enough so everyone could hear.

Since Carmen suspected he did this on purpose, she didn't move. Evidently, Rick had reached the same conclusion, as he stayed, too.

"I'm sorry," Jake continued. "Now everything makes sense. If I hadn't seen it with my own two eyes…" He looked down. "Thank you for trusting me enough to tell me the truth."

Though his words were kind, they clearly weren't what Maddie wanted to hear. She gave a stiff nod and crossed her arms.

Then Jake leaned in and kissed her. A rough kiss, possessive and decisive. The kiss of a man who knew what he wanted.

Seeing this, Carmen and Rick exchanged smiles.

"I love you," Jake declared, pulling Maddie close. Once he had her nestled into the crook of his arm, he turned to face Carmen. "I love this woman," he said. A second later, he told Rick the same thing. "When Colton gets back, I'll tell him the same thing."

Like the sun bursting out from behind heavy storm clouds, a brilliant smile appeared on Maddie's face.

But Jake wasn't finished. Before Maddie could speak, he kissed her again. "You're beautiful. Not just now, but *then*." He glanced over at their captives, clearly aware he couldn't say much.

Eyes huge, Maddie clearly hung on his every word.

"I'd like a committed relationship," Jake continued. "In every sense of the word. In fact, if you're willing, I think we should look for our own place. Once all of this settles down. For sure I'm going to need your help figuring out how to frame my story. There's so much and I'm not sure…"

Though he let his words trail off, his meaning rang clear. He wouldn't do anything to endanger Maddie and her people. The Pack Protectors would have no reason for concern with him.

With a glad cry, Maddie leaned in for yet another kiss. This one was the kind of kiss that should have been shared in private.

Marveling at all this, and overjoyed for her friend, Carmen turned away and took Rick's arm. About to suggest they leave the two lovebirds alone, she winced when one of the captors yelled out in a mocking voice, "You two should definitely get a room."

Maddie broke away from Jake, blushing. They touched foreheads and then, arm and arm, walked outside. Hopefully in the opposite direction from Colton, who still hadn't returned.

Careful to hide his annoyance at the interruption, Rick turned to Carmen. "Can't you do something about those fools?" he asked, gesturing toward their captives. "Like knock them out until someone from the government shows up to collect them?"

His question made Carmen laugh. "I wish. Unfortunately, I'm not a witch. There's not one stitch of magical ability in me."

"Lucky for them." Glowering, Rick took Carmen's elbow and led her as far from the others as they could get without leaving the warehouse. "What do you think about Maddie and Jake?" he asked.

Grinning up at him, she shrugged. "If Maddie's happy, I'm happy. He seems like a good guy. I don't think you Pack Protectors have any cause for concern, if that's what you're asking."

"It's not." He pushed away a sudden rush of nervousness, determined to say what he needed to say. "We make a great partnership, too, you know."

Carmen went very still. "I agree." She watched him, expressionless, as if bracing herself for whatever he might say next.

He refused to be nervous. "You know how I feel about you," he said.

One perfectly arched brow rose. "Do I?" Deadpan, until one corner of her sensual lips curled upward. "Maybe you need to show me again."

Though tempted, he shook his head. "I'm serious, Carmen. How do you feel about making our partnership a little more permanent?"

"You do realize I'm a Vampire, right?"

"Of course. Just like you know what I am. You've already seen my other self." They both kept their voices low.

"Is that what this is about? You're worried because I've seen your beast?"

He wasn't sure how to take that. "Of course not. I've fallen in love with you." He waited for her to say something, anything, but she continued to stand still as a statue, looking down at the floor.

"Carmen, can you at least react? This has never happened to me before, so forgive me if I'm handling it the wrong way."

Finally, she raised her head. To his shock, her beautiful eyes were full of tears. "This has never happened to me before, either," she said, her voice husky with emotion. "Are you sure, Rick Fallin? Are you absolutely positive you want to be with someone like me?"

"Someone smart and beautiful and kind?" he countered. "Not to mention sexy as hell? Why wouldn't I?"

Though a smile tugged at one corner of her mouth, she shook her head. "You know what I mean."

Vampire. She meant Vampire.

He pretended to consider for a moment, before losing the battle and pulling her into his arms. She nestled in, the fit of her sleek body to his exactly right. "Without a doubt," he said. "What about you? Are you okay with having someone like me as your man?"

Instead of responding, she growled low in her throat, then spoiled it all by laughing. "Now that we've gotten that out of the way, I wonder what's taking Colton so long?"

As if her words summoned him, Colton appeared in the warehouse doorway. "We're all good," he said. "Not only did I notify Trent Paxton, but I let various other high-ranking people know. Just to cover our butts. The CDC is sending a team this way now, via private jet. They'll be here by nightfall. Trent's also going to work on getting some of the larger manufacturing companies geared up to start producing the vaccine and the antidote on a rush basis." He glanced back at their captives, who continued to watch with interest. "They're sending the FBI to get those guys, since they're being classified as terrorists."

Impressed, Rick nodded. "Perfect."

Jake walked over, making notes in a notebook he'd gotten from somewhere. "Thanks, Colton, for letting me talk to Trent Paxton. This will be the story of the year once I get it written up. I've already contacted people I know at all the major networks. I'm thrilled that I got an exclusive."

Colton grinned. "I owed you."

"Plus, we're only keeping our end of the bargain," Rick chimed in. Carmen bumped his hip with hers and he put his arm around her to keep her close.

The next several hours were a blur of activity. The FBI arrived first, taking the still bound group into custody.

Carmen stayed busy making copious notes in triplicate. She also took the precaution of taking pics of her findings with her cell phone and emailing them to herself. "One can't be too careful," she said. Rick agreed wholeheartedly.

When the CDC people finally arrived, looking frazzled despite their forced attitude of importance, Carmen handed them all her notes first, including the computer printouts she'd run. Next, she carefully gave them the padded case containing her tissue and blood samples. They took everything, thanked her for helping, turned on their heels and left. Carmen stared after them, her expression inscrutable.

Rick went to her and pulled her close. "Are you all right?"

"I expected more," she confessed. "Foolish, I know. But I single-handedly came up with a solution to save mankind. I thought at least I'd get a letter of commendation or a medal or something." She shrugged. "Shows even someone as old as I am can still be naive."

He hugged her and then nuzzled the top of her head. "Are you ready to go?"

"Yes." She didn't even hesitate. "Your place or mine?"

His breath caught. "I'd sure love to see where you live," he said. "My place is a pretty basic apartment."

"I live in a tomb," she replied. Then, as he stared at her, she laughed. "Just kidding. I own a condo overlooking the yacht basis. Lots of windows and natural light." She kissed him, a quick brush of her lips on his, and then once again, with the promise of more.

"Hey you two," Maddie called out. Hand in hand with Jake, she glowed with happiness. "Jake and I are heading to his house to finish working on the story. I'm planning to spend the weekend there. You've got my number if you need anything."

Carmen nodded. "I promise not to call unless it's urgent. Where's Colton?"

"He said he was meeting a friend for dinner, then planned on going over to Broken Chains for drinks."

"Broken Chains," Jake repeated. "Too bad I'll never get to see inside."

"It's just a bar," Rick and Carmen said at once. They exchanged quick glances, avoiding looking at Maddie lest they give away the truth. Broken Chains was much more than just a bar, more than just an anything. They'd gone there as singles, and as friends. None of that would change, even if they paired off into couples.

"Another successful case completed by The Shadow Agency," Maddie crowed, waving. "See you all later."

After she and Jake had gone, Rick took Carmen's hand

and they walked outside. "We'll have to catch a cab," he said. "I rode here with Maddie, so I don't have a vehicle."

"Let's just walk." She smiled up at him, her white teeth gleaming. "We might even stop at Broken Chains for a quick celebratory drink."

And that's what they did.

* * * * *

COMING SOON!

We really hope you enjoyed reading this book. If you're looking for more romance, be sure to head to the shops when new books are available on

Thursday
14th June

To see which titles are coming soon, please visit
millsandboon.co.uk

MILLS & BOON

LET'S TALK
Romance

For exclusive extracts, competitions
and special offers, find us online:

f facebook.com/millsandboon

⬛ @millsandboonuk

🐦 @millsandboon

Or get in touch on 0844 844 1351*

For all the latest titles coming soon, visit
millsandboon.co.uk/nextmonth

Want even more
ROMANCE?

Join our bookclub today!

'Mills & Boon books, the perfect way to escape for an hour or so.'

Miss W. Dyer

'Excellent service, promptly delivered and very good subscription choices.'

Miss A. Pearson

'You get fantastic special offers and the chance to get books before they hit the shops'

Mrs V. Hall

**Visit millsandbook.co.uk/Bookclub
and save on brand new books.**

MILLS & BOON